THE VIOGNIER VENDETTA

A Wine Country Mystery

ELLEN CROSBY

SCRIBNER

New York London Toronto Sydney

SCRIBNER
A Division of Simon & Schuster, Inc.
1230 Avenue of the Americas
New York, NY 10020

First Scribner hardcover edition August 2010

SCRIBNER and design are registered trademarks of The Gale Group, Inc., used
under license by Simon & Schuster, Inc., the publisher of this work.

For information about special discounts for bulk purchases, please contact
Simon & Schuster Special Sales at 1-866-506-1949 or
business@simonandschuster.com.

The Simon & Schuster Speakers Bureau can bring authors to your live event.
For more information or to book an event, contact the Simon & Schuster
Speakers Bureau at 1-866-248-3049 or visit our website at
www.simonspeakers.com.

Manufactured in the United States of America

1   3   5   7   9   10   8   6   4   2

Library of Congress Control Number: 2010007846

ISBN 978-1-4391-6387-0
ISBN 978-1-4391-8292-5 (ebook)

For Dominick Abel

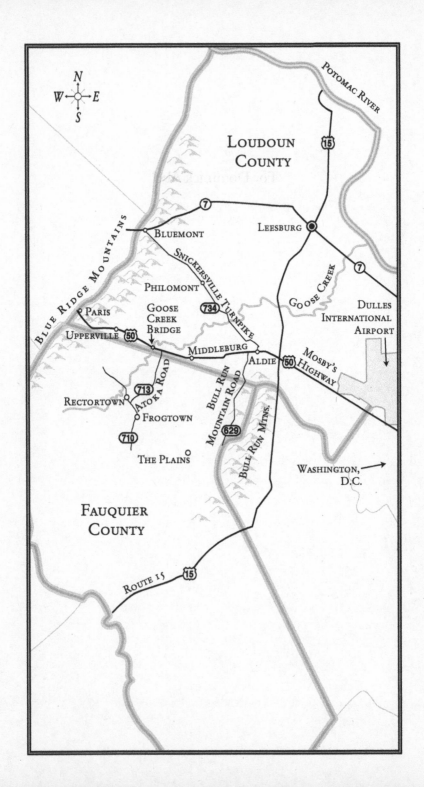

MONTGOMERY ESTATE VINEYARD

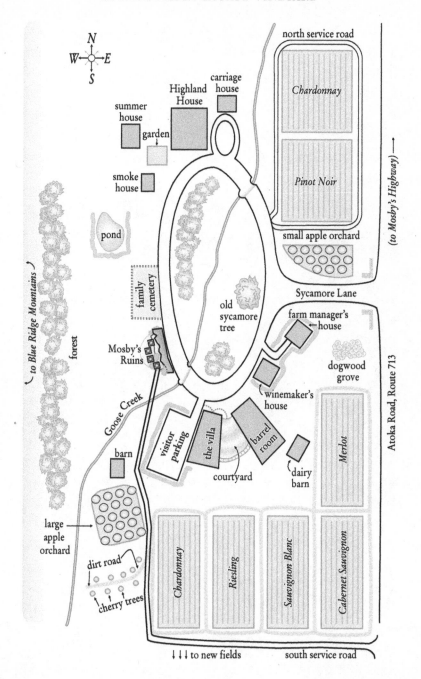

THE VIOGNIER VENDETTA

And wine can of their wits the wise beguile,
Make the sage frolic, and the serious smile.
—Homer, *Odyssey,* translated by Alexander Pope

When they ask me to become president of the United States,
I'm going to say, "Except for Washington, D.C."
—Bernard Samson, character in *Spy Hook*
by Len Deighton

CHAPTER 1

Ernest Hemingway once said you should always do sober what you said you'd do drunk because it would teach you to keep your mouth shut. It's advice you remember the morning after when it's too late and you've already given your word.

Sometimes it's a big deal, like the wine-fueled discussion between Thomas Jefferson and Alexander Hamilton over where to locate the capital city of the United States. In 1790, Jefferson dined with his nemesis Hamilton, plying him with so much Madeira that Hamilton fuzzily agreed to deliver enough Northern votes to pass a bill approving the Southern site President Washington had chosen along the Potomac River. In return, Jefferson promised that the federal government would assume all debts belonging to the thirteen states. If only it were that easy today.

Sometimes it's less significant, like my promise after drinking one too many glasses of my Virginia vineyard's Viognier to get together with an old college friend in that same capital city. What I didn't know at the time was that my decision to meet Rebecca Natale would be as life changing for me as the wine-soaked commitment to carve Washington, D.C., out of Maryland and Virginia was for the country.

The New York City area code popped up on my phone while I was reading in front of a dying fire one late March evening. The number wasn't familiar, but my kid sister, the family gypsy, lived in

Manhattan, where she flitted from a lover's apartment to a friend's couch to someone's house-sitting arrangement. I never knew whose phone she'd borrow to call next. But this time it wasn't Mia on the other end of the line. It was Rebecca. The last time I'd spoken to her was twelve years ago at her college graduation. After that she left her old life—and her old school friends—behind.

All she said was, "Hi, Lucie, it's me."

Just like that. Not a word about all those years with no phone call, no e-mail, no nothing. I never understood why she had cut me off. For a while it hurt. Finally I moved on—or thought I had.

I leaned back against the sofa and closed my eyes. Dammit, why now?

In retrospect, that should have been my first question. Instead I decided to match her sangfroid. "So it is. Long time no see, Rebecca."

"I know, hasn't it been? That's why I'm calling. I'll be in Washington the first weekend in April. I thought we could get together. Maybe you could come into town and stay with me?"

If she could be blasé about the gaping hole in the time line of our friendship, then so could I.

"A sightseeing trip for the cherry blossoms?"

"Oh, gosh no." Her nervous laughter trilled like a scale. Maybe she wasn't so blasé after all. "I work for Tommy Asher now. You might have seen the stories in *Vanity Fair* and *Vogue*. You do know about the Asher Collection being donated to the Library of Congress, don't you?"

Actually I'd seen both articles—the fashion shoot in *Vogue* and the *VF* piece, "The Rise of Wall Street's Recovery Whiz Kids." Rebecca was the glamorous protégée of billionaire investor guru Sir Thomas Asher. Philanthropist, adventurer, and owner of a highly successful—and exclusive—New York investment firm, the eponymous Thomas Asher Investments. As for the library donation, you'd have to be living in a cave for the past few months not to know that he and Lady Asher were making one of the most significant gifts to the institution since Thomas Jefferson sold his personal library to replace what the British burned during the War of 1812. A collection of rare architectural drawings, maps, paintings, newspapers, and correspondence relating to the design and planning of Washington, D.C.

Curiosity outweighed anger and wine washed away some of the old hurt, so I told Rebecca I'd meet her. I even agreed to be her guest Saturday evening at a black-tie gala honoring her boss's philanthropy and patronage of the arts. When she said it was rumored the president would attend, I nearly asked "president of what?" until I realized whom she meant.

The next morning I thought about calling back and explaining that something had come up.

But I didn't.

Washington, D.C., shares a common bond with Brasília and Canberra, since all were invented to be the capital of a country. A peninsula formed by the Potomac and Anacostia rivers, and originally intended to be no more than a seasonal meeting place to conduct the nation's business, it was referred to by Thomas Jefferson as "that Indian swamp in the wilderness." Charles Dickens called the graceless, dirty backwater born of controversy, greed, and deceit the "City of Magnificent Intentions." My late father, Leland Montgomery, said Washington was the place everyone who didn't want to live in the United States went to live.

My French mother didn't agree with any of them. She was captivated by the classic elegance of a city designed by Pierre L'Enfant, a fellow countryman who envisioned broad Versailles-like diagonal avenues overlapping a grid of streets resembling spiderwebs and graced by wedding cake public buildings of columns, domes, pediments, and porticoes in homage to the architecture of ancient Greece and Rome. When my brother, sister, and I were kids, she often made the one-hour drive into town so we could explore the museums, monuments, art galleries, parks, and theaters. After she died, I realized I'd become as seduced by Washington as she had been, but I also knew its dark, violent side away from the federal city, where drugs, crime, and poverty gave the place its other name: "Murder Capital of the United States."

Rebecca had booked a suite for us at the Willard hotel, two blocks from the White House and a stone's throw from the National

Mall. The Willard is an iconic landmark, a place of Old World elegance and luxury with its lobby of elaborate mosaic floors, coffered ceilings, marbled columns, and Federal-style furniture grouped in discreet seating areas throughout the room.

Its nickname is "the residence of presidents" because every U.S. president since the hotel opened in 1850 has either visited or stayed there. Other luminaries on the guest list include Mark Twain, Houdini, Walt Whitman, Jenny Lind, and Mae West. Julia Ward Howe wrote "The Battle Hymn of the Republic" while staying there. Martin Luther King Jr. wrote his "I Have a Dream" speech at the Willard.

A valet held the door as I walked into the splendid lobby past an enormous vase of hyacinths that graced a table of inlaid wood and mother-of-pearl. The old-fashioned clock above the mahogany and marble front desk said quarter to one. I gave my name to the clerk behind the desk and pulled out my credit card. He waved it away.

"It's taken care of." He reached for something from a bank of pigeonhole mailboxes that lined the wall behind him. An envelope. He handed it to me along with the small folder containing my room key card.

"Ms. Natale asked me to give you this when you arrived, Ms. Montgomery," he said. "Welcome to the Willard."

I slid my finger under the heavy vellum flap and pulled out a sheet of paper embossed with the hotel's logo.

In a meeting with Tommy and Mandy all morning. Will be finished by 1. Meet me at the bottom of the steps to the Lincoln Memorial.

I slipped some money to the bellhop who whisked away my overnight case and garment bag and gave a few more dollars to the valet who put me in a taxi a moment later. The cab zipped down Fourteenth Street to Constitution Avenue, where tour buses lined up near the Washington Monument and the south lawn of the White House. Across the scrubby expanse of the Mall, a ring of American flags surrounding the monument snapped in the wind.

At home in Atoka, Virginia, some fifty miles west, the landscape was still painted in winter colors of straw and washed-out yellow green. The Blue Ridge Mountains, which for most of the year lived up to their name, were drab and dun colored. Here, though, the promise of spring already hung in the air. On my drive into town, white dogwood bloomed along the roadside, and the banks of Rock Creek Parkway were massed with daffodils and clumps of crocus. Pale pink buds covered the cherry trees near the Washington Monument like a lace curtain.

The cab dropped me on the Ohio Drive side of the Lincoln Memorial at the far end of the Mall where more blooming trees graced the embankment by the Potomac River. I waited for the light on Independence and wondered why Rebecca had decided we should meet here rather than the hotel.

I understood as soon as I saw her standing on the marble steps of the memorial regarding me like a Greek goddess at the entrance to her temple, a bouquet of yellow roses in her arms. I'd nearly forgotten how her sloe-eyed dusky beauty, inherited from a Vietnamese mother and Italian father, turned men's—and women's—heads. Even now she earned appreciative stares from passersby.

She descended the stairs with the fluid grace I remembered from our days as running partners at school, but everything else about her had changed. Movie-star sunglasses held back her shoulder-length dark hair to reveal large teardrop diamond-and-sapphire earrings. A matching pendant hung around her neck. Somehow I knew the stones were real. She wore a well-cut persimmon wool blazer, cream silk blouse, and slim jeans that looked tailored. The fringe of an off-white silk shawl flung around her shoulders fluttered in the breeze. It didn't look like she was buying her clothes in secondhand shops anymore.

Rebecca knew about my accident, but she'd never seen me with the cane I now use. When her eyes fell on it, I caught the brief flicker of consternation and something else—I think it was shock. She recovered at once, though her laugh was too hearty, too forced, and her hug a little too fierce.

"Oh, my God! I can't believe it! Look at you, Lucie, you look fabulous."

I patted her on the back with one hand, leaning on my cane with the other. This was going to be harder than I expected.

Seven years ago the hospital nurses had been sure the extravagant bouquet of peonies, calla lilies, and hydrangea had been sent by my boyfriend who'd been driving the car that smashed into a stone wall with me in the passenger seat. But I'd recognized Rebecca's distinctive bold scrawl the moment I saw the card.

Who shall decide when doctors disagree, and soundest casuists doubt, like you and me? Don't listen to the docs and don't doubt yourself. Chin up—you'll pull through. R.

So she'd also heard that my doctors didn't think I'd walk again. Later I looked up the quote. Alexander Pope—I should have guessed. Rebecca had a fine mathematical mind, but she possessed a poet's soul. She especially loved the Restoration poets for their interest in reason and logic and their desire to bring order to the natural world. As for the casuists, she shared their practical view of life: Deciding right or wrong on moral issues depended on the circumstances. No absolutes, a kind of shifting value system. Deceiving someone or lying was wrong—unless the consequences were worse if you didn't.

I wondered if she'd changed.

"You're mad at me, aren't you?" The exotic tilt to her eyes always made her look as though she'd just woken up to something that pleased her. Now a new shrewdness glittered in them.

At least we were going to get right to it. Good. No more games.

"Yes," I said.

"Why'd you come?"

"Curiosity. Why'd you ask me?"

The question seemed to surprise her. "It's been too long. I wanted to see you."

Sure she did. "What do you want, Rebecca?"

"Wow, you didn't use to be so blunt." She brushed back a strand of wind-whipped hair from her eyes and laughed uneasily. "I mean it. I wanted to see you. You stuck by me through tough times, Little. I haven't forgotten."

In my freshman year of college, the bewitching and brainy Rebecca Natale had been assigned to be my "big sister" when I'd joined the cross-country team. Back then I called her "Big" since she was also a senior; she reciprocated with "Little."

Running was the only thing the two of us had in common. Rebecca grew up in the hardscrabble Dorchester section of Boston, the daughter of immigrants. She worked a couple of jobs to pay for what loans and a scholarship didn't cover and lived on vending machine food because it was cheap. I grew up in the affluent heart of Virginia horse-and-hunt country, a picturesque region of rolling hills, charming villages, and fence-lined country lanes. My tuition was paid from a trust fund set up by my grandparents.

Two things cemented our friendship—both tragedies in their own way. Rebecca's affair that autumn with a married professor whose wife also taught at the university and the death of my mother in the spring. The sordid gossip that went around school about Rebecca and the handsome, straight-as-an-arrow chairman of the English department, their motel trysts and rough sex on his office desk, shocked everyone. I never asked her about it and she never discussed it—not one single time during the hours and hours we trained together. And when I returned to school, numb with grief after my mother's funeral, it was Rebecca who came to my dorm room and wouldn't leave until I laced up my running shoes and went out with her, day in and day out. Wouldn't let me quit the team. Made sure I showed up for meets.

I stared at her now and knew she was remembering those days, just as I was.

"Are you in trouble?" I asked. "Is that what this is all about?"

"Of course I'm not." I might have believed her too-quick protest if she looked me in the eye, but she didn't. "I've been doing some thinking, and I know I didn't do right by our friendship after I left school. I wanted to see you . . ." She hesitated. "To ask if you'll forgive me."

I hadn't seen that one coming. And she'd phrased it like a yes-or-no question when it was so much more complicated.

"Rebecca—"

She cut me off. "I know what you're going to say. Look, I didn't plan to lay this on you thirty seconds after we see each other for the first time in, well . . . a long time." She gestured to the top of the stairs where Lincoln sat in his splendid chamber. "I've got to buy a couple of postcards. You mind waiting while I dash up to the gift shop? Then maybe we could rewind, start over again."

Or maybe we could slow this oncoming freight train down a little.

"I can climb stairs, Big."

"That's not what I meant—"

"Then stop acting like I'm not up to this, not strong enough mentally or physically."

She could figure out for herself whether I was talking about stair climbing or seeing each other again.

"Oh, God, Lucie, that's the last thing I'd ever do. You're stronger than anyone I know." She placed her hand on my arm. "I mean it."

I turned toward the stairs and wondered what this reunion was all about.

"It's been years since I visited this place," I said. "Let's go."

"Sure." She withdrew her hand. "After you."

Halfway up she said, "I guess 'how've you been?' is kind of a stupid question."

I looked up at the enormous contemplative statue of Lincoln, which had gradually come into view.

"Why'd you wait so long to get in touch? Twelve years since you graduated, Big."

"I'm sorry. It's just that I had a lot of things to work out about myself and my life after everything with Connor . . ."

I waited, but she didn't finish the sentence.

"You ever see him again?"

"Nope. I heard he left teaching altogether. Moved to Wyoming and bought a ranch. His wife's teaching at Georgetown now." She added, "Ex-wife."

I nodded. Somehow I knew there would be more if I waited. There was. She seemed to be struggling with her emotions.

"You never asked me about Connor, never said a word about what happened. Never judged me. I don't know if you realized how much that meant to me, Lucie. Everyone else said I ruined his marriage, broke up his beautiful family."

"I had no right to judge you." We reached the main chamber,

clogged with tourists visiting for the cherry blossoms. "I had no idea what the circumstances were."

"The circumstances were so frickin' complicated," she said with heat. "I never told anyone the truth. Everyone was so concerned about Connor: his life, his career, his wife and kids. No one gave a *damn* about me."

After all these years she still carried that much anger and bitterness in her heart? Somehow I thought she would have moved on, put it behind her.

She took a deep breath, steadying herself. "Whew, sorry. I still get worked up about it."

"It's okay."

Her smile twisted. "Could you hold these flowers while I get my postcards? Then we can go."

"Get them where?"

"Gift shop."

She hooked a thumb at a nearly invisible doorway tucked into an interior wall facing the Mall. I took the roses as she disappeared through the door like Alice down the rabbit hole.

The translucent marble ceiling with its bronzed crossbeams and a few dim spotlights gave the light inside the cavernous memorial a viscous timeworn patina. Laughter and the chatter of tourists and visitors reverberated off the walls, an unintelligible din of white noise. I went and stood in front of Lincoln, reading the words carved above his head.

> IN THIS TEMPLE
> AS IN THE HEARTS OF THE PEOPLE
> FOR WHOM HE SAVED THE UNION
> THE MEMORY OF ABRAHAM LINCOLN
> IS ENSHRINED FOREVER

Somber faced with one fist clenched and hair slightly disheveled, Lincoln stared into the distance as though he'd just come back from a walk and needed to put his thoughts in order. A group of teenagers wearing red sweatshirts stenciled with the logo of their Kansas high school band swarmed around me, shrill and excited. I moved away and shifted Rebecca's roses in my arms. The card, attached with ribbon-covered florist's wire, poked me. I turned it over and read the message.

For Richard Boyle IV: Never find fault with the absent.

How funny. Hadn't she just asked me to do the same for her? I wondered who Richard Boyle IV was and whether I was going to meet him.

"Okay, all set."

She reappeared holding an identical set of postcards of the memorial at night, glowing like a lit jewel.

"Did you know the Lincoln Memorial was modeled after the Temple of Zeus at Olympia?" she asked.

"Does it say that on the back of those postcards?"

She grinned. "Nope. I learned it from the Asher Collection. Tommy hired a curator from the historical society to put together a display in the lobby of our building in Manhattan. Usually featuring his latest treasure—a map or painting or some architectural drawing. That collection is his pride and joy. I'm going to miss seeing it now that it will be in D.C." She shrugged. "Though it's probably the end of the lectures and quizzes."

"What do you mean?"

"Oh, he'd bring some scholar by the office to discuss history or cartography or something to do with whatever he'd just acquired. Gave him a chance to prove he could hold his own with the experts in front of his employees." She rolled her eyes. "Especially when he gave his little quizzes afterward to see who'd been paying attention."

"He tested you on this stuff?"

She nodded.

"I read what a control freak he is. And about his ego," I said. "How do you put up with it?"

Rebecca pursed her lips. "Tommy is . . . complex. He's used to getting what he wants, so it can come off as arrogance. He can also be incredibly charming . . . you have no idea. I guess you have to know him to understand him, why he does what he does."

"It doesn't bother you?"

"Like I said, he's complex."

"Including treating his employees like a bunch of schoolkids."

"That's different. He's appalled at how little Americans know about their own history and that there are people who think 'When was the War of 1812 fought?' is a trick question."

"I think you're exaggerating."

"Okay, how much do you know about it?"

"I minored in European history, remember? It was a trade war between the Americans and the British. They were impressing our sailors and we were mad that they still controlled Canada, plus they helped arm the Indians against us in the West."

"Oh, all right, so you're the exception to the rule. Most people don't have a clue what it was about," she said. "Or that the British burned Washington nearly to the ground. That's what got Tommy interested in putting together the collection to begin with—he was fascinated by the plans and backroom politics that went on to rebuild the city after the fire. He just kept expanding and acquiring items until he owned almost everything out there that the Library of Congress didn't already have."

"Kind of an unusual avocation for someone who's British."

Rebecca gave me an odd look. "Tommy's not British anymore. He's a U.S. citizen. To be honest, I think he did it more to get even. For years it's bugged him that an American rebuilt Shakespeare's old Globe theater in London. He thought it should have been a hundred-percent British project."

"So it's payback?"

"I guess you could say that. I want you to meet him. The gala tonight is going to be a mob scene, but I've put you on the guest list for the opening of the collection next week at the library. There's a dinner afterward in one of the private rooms that are never open to the public. Only about a hundred people are invited. You'll get to know him then. Promise me you'll go."

"I can't remember if we have something going on at the vine-yard—"

"This is important. Promise me."

Why was she pushing so hard?

"Okay, okay. I promise."

"Good." She shoved the postcards in her oversized Coach hand-bag. "Next stop the Wall. You mind?"

The Wall. That explained the flowers. I gave them back to her. She meant the Vietnam Veterans Memorial just across the plaza, hidden by a scrim of shrubbery.

Vietnam belonged to our parents' generation. Maybe Rebecca was paying tribute to a family friend, someone her mother, who'd grown up in Saigon during the war, or her father, who'd fought there, had known.

"No," I said. "I don't mind at all."

Gusts of wind rippled the blue gray Reflecting Pool, distorting the mirrored image of the Washington Monument and rustling the bare branches of the elms that lined the paths like sentries. As we made our way down the steps of the Lincoln Memorial, the Capitol dome, which had been obscured by the Washington Monument, now appeared toy-sized on the horizon. We crossed the open plaza. The traffic on Constitution Avenue sounded muffled, the noise deadened by the seventy black granite tablets that formed a gentle V along the downsloping path.

"Who was Richard Boyle the Fourth?" I asked.

She gave me a knowing smile as though she'd expected me to peek at the card attached to the bouquet.

"My father."

I stopped walking. "Johnny Natale's your father."

I'd met her parents at her graduation. That year it fell on Mother's Day weekend, rough for me. Her parents had been wonderful, especially her beautiful, vibrant mother, Linh, who treated me like another daughter, inviting me to their dinners and celebrations, including me in everything.

"Johnny Natale is my real father as far as I'm concerned. Richard Boyle died before I was born."

"How come you never mentioned him?"

"Because I just found out about him."

Rebecca did not sound like a daughter anguished by the loss of a father she never knew. Instead she sounded calm and matter-of-fact.

We resumed walking, pausing in front of mementos left as tributes. A combat boot, American flags, more flowers, photos encased in plastic, letters commemorating birthdays and events that would never be celebrated with a loved one, handmade cards tucked into the cracks between tablets.

"Why did you write, 'Never find fault with the absent'?" I asked.

Again that fleeting glance and an apologetic smile. "He and my mom never got married. Don't ever mention this to anyone, okay?"

I wondered whom she thought I'd tell.

"Sure," I said again. "I promise."

We reached the apex of the memorial commemorating the first and last American deaths in 1959 and 1975 where two tablets intersected like an open book. Next to me a woman laid a piece of notebook paper on the black stone and began rubbing the paper with the lead side of a pencil. I watched names appear on the page like ghost images. A packet of letters tied with a yellow ribbon lay at her feet.

"I'm glad you came," Rebecca was saying. "I knew you'd understand."

"Pardon?" I dragged my attention from the woman. "Understand what?"

"Why I'm doing this." She knelt and leaned the roses against the wall.

"Richard Boyle died at the end of the war?" I asked.

"Yes." For a second she looked flustered. "I'm not quite sure of the exact date."

"We should find his name," I said.

It was the one thing she hadn't done.

She pulled her oversized sunglasses down and I could no longer see her eyes, only my own reflection in the dark glass. "I can't. I'm late. All I wanted to do was leave the flowers. Can I get you a cab back to the hotel?"

Suddenly she was brisk and businesslike and I got a glimpse of the person she'd become.

"Aren't you going to the hotel, too?" I asked.

"I've got to go to Georgetown to pick up something for Tommy."

"I haven't got any plans. Why don't I come with you?"

"Uh . . . no. You can't."

My face felt hot. "Sorry. I should have realized it's business."

"It's just that it's sort of delicate . . . I mean, Tommy trusted me with this errand. I shouldn't even have mentioned it."

"Sure. I didn't mean to pry." I knew the sound of a door slamming shut, especially coming from her.

"Oh, what the hell." Rebecca fished in her purse and took out her cell phone, tapping the screen a few times. "Take a look at this."

I squinted at the display. "It's a silver wine cooler. Looks like an antique."

"Right, but not just any silver wine cooler. It belonged to James Madison. One of Tommy's ancestors stole it."

"Are you serious?"

She nodded. "He was a soldier who fought the Americans during the War of 1812. Apparently he took it when his regiment looted the White House just before the Brits burned it. Madison had left the city to join his troops, and Dolley Madison ended up fleeing by herself with whatever she could take just before the soldiers arrived," Rebecca said. "That wine cooler has been in the Asher family all this time and Tommy had no idea until recently. He and Mandy are going to return it to the president and first lady."

"Tonight at the gala?"

"God, no." She looked aghast. "He'd never do that. Besides, the Japanese prime minister is in town. There's a reception this evening, so the White House called and sent regrets. Tommy and Mandy are handing it over at a private meeting in the Oval Office on Monday. He doesn't want to admit in public that a family member was a thief and a plunderer, even if it did happen nearly two centuries ago during a war."

"So where's this wine cooler now?"

"Being cleaned by some professor at Georgetown. Ed Shelby. A colleague of the historian who helped put together the Asher Collection."

"Dr. Alison Jennings."

"You know her?" Rebecca seemed surprised.

"Of course I do. She's married to Harlan Jennings. He grew up in Middleburg, a few miles from where I live. I've known him since we were kids," I said, "although I was still in elementary school when he went off to Harvard. I had such a puppy-love crush on him. Worked for his campaign when he ran for the Senate."

Rebecca smiled an enigmatic smile. "What a funny coincidence. I know Harlan, too. He does business with Tommy."

"So I guess we'll meet back at the hotel later? What time are we leaving?"

"The gala starts at seven. Cocktails for an hour, then dinner and dancing after that." She rearranged her windblown shawl. "What are you going to do now?"

"Walk around for a while, I guess."

"Thanks for coming, Little. You have no idea how much I appreciate it."

She hugged me, another swift embrace. Before I could reply, she turned and ran toward the Lincoln Memorial, long legged and graceful as a gazelle, head held high, the wind still tugging at her shawl.

It was the last time I would ever see her.

CHAPTER 2

I spent an hour walking the paths of the Reflecting Pool before I went back to the Vietnam Veterans Memorial. The reunion with Rebecca had been odd, almost as though she had staged it with me as her spectator. She'd changed since I knew her at school; there was a harder edge to her now.

A flock of geese honked noisily overhead as they flew in an untidy V. I stopped in front of Rebecca's roses and did some math. Richard Boyle would have been among the last to die—in 1975—based on Rebecca's age. I put my hand on the Wall and stared at my reflection in the polished stone, letting the heat from the hot granite warm me. Why didn't she want to find him? Being late to pick up a package in Georgetown sounded like a made-up excuse.

I scanned the names of the dead and missing from 1975 and 1974. Any earlier and the numbers really didn't add up. More than fifty-eight thousand names were engraved here, commemorating decades of sorrow and loss for an unpopular war. Wherever Richard Boyle IV was, I didn't find him. Maybe Rebecca knew more than she told me and that's why she asked me to say nothing about our visit here.

The sun slipped behind a wall of clouds and the breeze grew sharper. I turned up my jacket collar and decided to return to the Willard. On my way back to Ohio Drive, I passed others who, like me, knew Vietnam from history books. For us, this place was a tourist attraction the same as the eternal flame at Arlington or the other monuments scattered throughout the city honoring dead heroes. But for some, like the woman who'd left the letters, it had to be like visiting a grave at a cemetery.

On the cab ride to the hotel, I couldn't get Rebecca's face or the face of that woman out of my mind. Both left me unaccountably melancholy.

They were still serving lunch at the Occidental Grill when I got back from my trip downtown. Another Washington landmark, it was located next door to the Willard. A man in a dark suit seated me in a booth where I could study the rows of black-and-white head shots of unsmiling political celebrities from an earlier era that covered every wall. I ate a club sandwich and drank a glass of unsweetened ice tea before walking back to the hotel.

The lobby was noisier and more animated than when I had checked in. Underneath the sound of laughter, chatter, and the clink of glasses from the bar around the corner, a piano played "The Way You Look Tonight." Most of the couches and chairs were now occupied. I wondered how many were hotel guests and how many were well-dressed people watchers. I walked down an opulent corridor called Peacock Alley, passing a few people taking tea and peeking into ballrooms and salons set up for some upcoming event. One of them looked like someone's wedding reception. Finally I rode the elevator to the seventh floor.

More Beaux Arts elegance in our suite, which was decorated in regal shades of scarlet and gold. Someone had placed my suitcase on a small mahogany bench with a red-and-gold-striped satin cushion. Rebecca's suitcase occupied the matching bench next to it. A floor-length, one-shoulder black evening gown hung in the closet next to my garment bag. In the bathroom her makeup—mostly Chanel and La Prairie—spilled out of a Vera Bradley cosmetic bag on the marble countertop. Among the blush, lip gloss, and eye shadow was a package of birth control pills.

She'd left her red leather planner, closed and bristling with papers, in the middle of the desk in the sitting room. Next to it, bound in green cloth with gilt-edged pages, was a very old copy of

The Poetical Works of Alexander Pope. I opened the cover and saw that she had inscribed the flyleaf to me.

> *For Little.*
> *May you come to know these poems and treasure them as much as I do. Big*

I brought the book over to the gold damask sofa and sat down to look at it. The second dedication—to her—was on the title page and had been crossed out, though I could still read what had been written.

> *For my darling Rebecca,*
> *"Where'er you walk, cool gales shall fan the glade / Trees, where you sit, shall crowd into a shade: / Where'er you tread, the blushing flow'rs shall rise, / And all things flourish where you turn your eyes."*
>   *With all my love, Connor*

Underneath, Rebecca had written her own message:

> *Our passions are like convulsion fits, which, though they make us stronger for a time, leave us the weaker ever after.*

Presumably the words were originally written by Alexander Pope—Connor's declaration of love and Rebecca's bitter recrimination. But there, in a nutshell, was their affair and the breakup. I closed the book feeling like I'd violated her privacy, though obviously she meant for me to see it if she were giving it to me as a present. I put it back on the desk as someone knocked on the door to the suite.

A woman about my age wearing a businesslike white oxford blouse and a slim-fitting navy skirt stood there, long tapered fingers playing with her cell phone. Heart-shaped face, delicate winged eyebrows, English rose complexion, light brown hair pulled up into a chignon, she wore almost no makeup except for lipstick in Madonna red.

When she saw me, she frowned. "Ms. Montgomery?"

She had to be hotel staff since no one else knew I was here. Maybe they needed a credit card on file, after all.

"Yes. You're with the Willard?"

She looked taken aback. "Good Lord, no. I'm Olivia Tarrant. Sir Thomas Asher's personal assistant."

Tommy Asher seemed to surround himself with beautiful young women. Somehow I expected that his personal assistant would be a man—someone older who'd been with him for years. A private secretary or a faithful butler.

"What can I do for you?" I asked.

"I'm looking for Rebecca."

"She had an errand in George—"

Olivia Tarrant cut me off. "I know that. She should have been back here two hours ago. I can't reach her anywhere and she's not answering her phone. I spoke to Dr. Shelby. He told me she kept her taxi waiting while she picked up a package for Sir Thomas and Lady Asher. Rebecca didn't spend ten minutes there."

I opened the door wider and gestured to the room. "I don't know what to tell you, but she's not here, either."

"May I?" Olivia sailed past me before I could answer.

She walked over to one of the two windows overlooking Pennsylvania Avenue and pulled the sheer privacy curtain aside as though she expected to find Rebecca hiding there. I wondered if she planned to look under the beds as well.

"You were with her before she left for Georgetown?" She didn't turn around.

"Yes."

"When was that?" She released the curtain and faced me.

"I met her at one o'clock at the Lincoln Memorial. We did some sightseeing."

"What time did she leave?"

"I don't know. Probably around two, maybe a little before. I didn't check the time."

"Did she say anything else, about where she might go?"

In a moment, I figured Olivia Tarrant would read me my rights. "No."

She fiddled with her phone some more, turning it over and over. "I don't know what I'm going to tell Lady Asher."

"Maybe Rebecca met someone for coffee or a drink afterward."

The winged eyebrows arched in annoyance. "First of all, she was supposed to return directly here. Second, if that's what she did then she shouldn't have turned off her phone."

"Hey," I said. "I'm not Rebecca or Lady Asher. Go tell them."

Her mouth dropped open, then she said, "I'm sorry. I shouldn't have snapped at you. But you have no idea how valuable that package she retrieved is."

I don't have a good poker face. Everyone tells me that. I tried, anyway, to look like I had no idea what she was talking about.

"Rebecca is very responsible. I'm sure everything's fine and she'll show up any minute."

Olivia Tarrant crossed her arms, sizing me up. "How well do you know her?"

Right now I could have told her I wasn't so sure anymore and that would be the truth. Instead I said, "Do you always ask so many questions?"

For the second time she looked taken aback. "I suppose I do. It's part of my job. You can't imagine how many people want my boss's time and attention . . . and money. It's my responsibility to know who he's dealing with."

She seemed to relish the power of her position as gatekeeper and all-roads-pass-through-me. Sir Thomas may have made the *Forbes* list of billionaires every year for the past decade and was well-known for his philanthropy, but he still put his pants on one leg at a time just like every other man I knew. I wasn't as impressed with him as she was.

"I don't want any of those things and I'm an old friend of Rebecca's. She invited me to be her guest for the weekend."

"You're in investment banking as well?"

"I own a vineyard."

She did a double take and said, "So you flew in from the West Coast?"

I hate it when people think the only place anyone makes wine in America is California.

"I drove here from Atoka, Virginia. It took me about an hour," I said.

"Atoka," she repeated. "Is that near Middleburg or Upperville?"

"It's in between. Why do you ask?"

"Sir Thomas's brother just bought an estate there. Upperville, I think it was."

"He's moving to Virginia?"

"No." Her smile was tolerant. "It'll be a weekend place when he's not at one of his other homes."

Her phone rang before I could reply.

"Yes, sir?" Olivia turned away from me and walked back to the window. "No, I'm sorry. She's not in her suite, either. Yes, sir. Right away."

She tapped her phone and I heard the *click* of a disconnected call.

"I have to go," she said.

"That was Sir Thomas?"

She ignored the question and walked to the desk, bending over to write something on a hotel notepad. She tore off the page and handed it to me.

"My number. Please call me if you hear from Rebecca. And for God's sake, tell her to call me and get the hell back here," she said. "I'll see myself out."

I folded the paper and threw it on the desk. Somehow I didn't think I'd be calling Olivia Tarrant.

I spent the rest of the afternoon reading a book on canopy management—pruning, spraying, and how often to do it—and trying not to glance up at the door to the suite every five minutes as though I expected Rebecca to waltz in with some breezy tale of a drink with another friend in Georgetown.

Where was she?

The book wasn't a page-turner, but I forced myself to concentrate because it was a subject I needed to know more about. A lot of people think owning a vineyard means living a glamorous life of days spent wandering among the grapevines sipping champagne and admiring God's handiwork. The reality is that it's backbreaking, mind-numbing, tedious work, often in withering heat or the damp chill of a wine cellar. During harvest, we put in eighteen-hour days for weeks on end. Tempers are short because no one gets much sleep and we're usually racing against the clock and the weather. A good day is when only a few things go wrong. As for glamour, I wouldn't like to say how much scrubbing it took to get most of the dirt out from under my fingernails before I showed up here today. Dark red nail polish did the rest. Luckily, my clothes concealed the Technicolor bruise on my thigh from banging into a metal rack when one of the five-hundred-gallon wine barrels slipped in the middle of turning it. That said, I love what I do.

By six o'clock Rebecca still hadn't turned up. I tried her number one more time and it again went to voice mail. No point leaving a third message. Next I called Quinn Santori, my winemaker, to see how things had gone at the vineyard today. This time of year we were gearing up for spring, which meant the beginning of weeding and planting new vines. For a few more weeks, though, it would still be relatively quiet in the winery until we began bottling in May. Lately we'd been doing wine trials—blending wine in varying ratios from different barrels and stainless-steel tanks to decide how we'd make the wine we eventually bottled.

Quinn and I didn't see eye to eye on this—in fact, lately, we didn't seem to agree on much of anything. Eight months ago we broke our long-established rule of not mixing personal and professional relationships and had gone to bed together. Foolishly, I thought we could handle what happened the next morning and the mornings and days after that.

He was a passionate and exciting lover, and reliving that first night and the handful of others that followed, still made my face go hot. Then in December his mother passed away in California. As far as I knew, she was the only family Quinn had left since he kept a monastic vow of silence about his life before he came to work at Montgomery Estate Vineyard three years ago. My father had hired him shortly before his death without doing much of a background check. Quinn never bothered to fill in any of the blanks.

He remained in San Jose for a month after his mother's funeral, leaving Antonio, our new farm manager, and me to run the place. When he returned from California, something was different. *He* was different. Not quite distant, but remote, I guess. Or restless maybe. By unspoken mutual agreement, he stopped showing up at my house at night anymore. We never discussed the reason, but the fallout was that we didn't spend much time in each other's company during the day, either, unless it was business. Personally, I was miserable. I had no idea how he felt.

His phone, like Rebecca's, went to voice mail.

"Hi, it's me," I said, after his message. "Just checking in. No need to return the call unless something's come up. See you tomorrow."

Then I took a long shower and got ready for the gala.

At six forty-five Olivia Tarrant knocked on my door again. She'd gone from buttoned-up to siren, glamorous in a red satin gown with a plunging neckline. A black cashmere evening coat and a black sequined purse were draped over one arm. This time she wore plenty of makeup—theatrical smoky eyes, rouged cheeks, and that Madonna red lipstick that made her look like some doll on the cover of a '50s pulp novel—except for the phone that she still clutched in one hand and the vexed expression on her face.

"I guess you haven't heard from Rebecca," I said, "or you wouldn't be here. You look very nice."

She looked me over and seemed surprised by what she saw. My own dress came from an upscale consignment shop called Nu-2-You where I occasionally bought clothes since I always needed something for one of the many formal parties and charity events we hosted at the vineyard. This dress was my favorite—silk black-and-gray large floral print, low, square-cut neckline, beaded shoulder straps, and a deeply pleated skirt that swirled gracefully when I moved.

"That dress," Olivia said, "is absolutely stunning. And no, we haven't heard from her. We're contacting cab companies in D.C. to see if we can find out who picked her up and where they dropped her off."

"Why didn't you ask that professor what cab company she used?"

She pursed her lips. "Are you kidding? He couldn't even remember the color. Said he didn't really pay attention."

"What about contacting the D.C. police?"

"Sir Thomas has his own security people looking into this. He isn't ready to involve the police yet. Rebecca's actually more AWOL than missing. So far."

"What about the fact that she picked up something quite valuable?" I asked. "She's nearly four hours late now. Maybe someone followed her and robbed her. I know Rebecca. She'd put up a fight."

Olivia didn't look happy that I appeared to have some knowledge of why Rebecca had gone to Georgetown. I had a feeling she was dying to ask me how much I knew. Instead she changed the subject.

"Our people are checking all the hospitals. If she's anywhere, we'll find her." She pulled on her evening coat. "I have a car waiting downstairs to take me to the National Building Museum. You're welcome to join me if you'd like."

I didn't feel much like going to the gala under the circumstances, but Olivia and Sir Thomas would be the first to hear if their security people found Rebecca, and that's where they'd be. It was a quick ride from the Willard to the Building Museum—though I still thought of it by its former name, the Pension Building—but Olivia, who never seemed to tire of asking questions, continued to quiz me about Rebecca.

"How did you two meet?"

"In college."

"What was she like back then?"

"Smart, ambitious. Like she is now."

"She never talks about her family, but I have a feeling she didn't come from money." Her tone of voice implied that this was a major character flaw.

"Oh, really?" I'd had enough of being grilled and Rebecca's private life was none of her business. "You know, the only person we haven't talked about since we met is you. How'd you get this job, if you don't mind my asking?"

"I . . . well." She sat up straighter. "I've known Sir Thomas all my life. My father manages several private investment funds and he and Sir Thomas do business together. When my predecessor moved to our London office five years ago, he asked Daddy if I'd be interested in the position."

I'd never called my father anything but "Leland," which is what he wanted me to call him. He wasn't a daddy kind of dad.

"Thomas Asher Investments is a family business," Olivia went on, emphasizing the word "family."

"Sir Thomas and Lady Asher take care of us like we're their children. As a result we're a pretty tight-knit group—we party together, take vacations together, that sort of thing. That's why we're so well run and successful. Everyone's incredibly loyal to them. Outsiders just don't get that. Sir Thomas watched me grow up and he knew I'd understand the world he lives in. Knew I'd understand what would be involved in working as closely with him as I do."

She was starting to sound like an infomercial . . . or a cult member.

"Rebecca is part of the family, too?"

Olivia hesitated. "Of course she is. She, ah, . . . well, yes."

Maybe only because Rebecca was Tommy Asher's protégée. It didn't sound like much love lost there. Perhaps Olivia was jealous.

Her phone rang and she turned away to answer it. I heard a series of "uh-huhs" as our driver pulled up in front of the redbrick Pension Building. Though it was a full city block long, the curbs were choked with limousines, taxis, and cars with official or diplomatic license plates. Police directed traffic as men with wires in their ears scanned the crowd.

Then Olivia said, sounding grim, "Sure, I'll tell him."

She disconnected.

"What's wrong?" I asked.

"Rebecca's cab dropped her off in front of some restaurant in Georgetown after she retrieved Sir Thomas's package," she said. "Near the corner of Wisconsin Avenue and P Street, wherever that is. The cabbie said she stood there as though she were waiting for someone to pick her up."

I thought about Rebecca and her trysts at school with Connor. Both of them had managed to keep their affair off the radar for more than a year until someone spotted her slipping into a motel room and recognized his car in the parking lot with its faculty-parking sticker.

"What time?" I asked.

"Around three." She checked the clock on her phone. "That was four hours ago."

"Perhaps she's still with her friend."

Olivia's eyes flashed as she flounced out of the car. "Then she's got a hell of a lot of explaining to do. A few of us are ready to kill her."

She sounded like she meant it literally. I wondered who else at Thomas Asher Investments was on the list of people who did not like Rebecca . . . and where she was and with whom on a cold, dark evening when she was supposed to be at her boss's star-studded gala. The sleek black dress hanging in the closet in the Willard, her invitation to me to be her guest—Rebecca meant to be here.

If she wasn't, it was because something or someone had detained her. And I didn't think it was willingly, either.

CHAPTER 3

⚬⚬⚬⚬

The staid exterior of the Pension Building gave no clue that inside the Great Hall, with its massive Corinthian columns and double-tiered arcaded galleries lining the football-stadium-sized atrium, would be so spectacular. The galleries, columns, and an enormous terra-cotta fountain in the center of the hall were stage-lit a soft yellow. Pinpoint spotlights in jewel reds, yellows, or blues shone on hundreds of tables set for dinner with matching colored linens. The rest of the huge room was bathed in a burnished bronze light.

An enormous screen hung behind a raised stage that had been erected between two columns. Currently the screen was dark and the stage empty, though it looked like the band had set up for later. If they wanted to host the opening ceremony for the Olympics or maybe the coronation of the Holy Roman Emperor after we were finished, it would have been no problem.

"I must find Sir Thomas." Olivia shrugged out of her evening coat. "Get yourself a drink and mingle. There are seating charts on easels next to each of the bars, and staff will help you find your table. You're sitting at Rebecca's table with some of the other analysts from the firm. I checked."

"Thanks," I said as an attendant in a tuxedo took my coat. "I guess I'll see you later."

But she had already disappeared into the crowd, which seemed to swallow her up. I looked around hoping to catch someone's eye, maybe find a companion to talk to. In my business, I meet strangers all the time and it's my job to put them at ease, show them a good time. But Washington is a different kettle of fish. Here people are more interested in who they're seen with than whether they're enjoying themselves. When I worked for an environmental nonprofit the summer before my accident, I'd finally realized that the reason no one ever looked you in the eye when talking to you at a Washington cocktail party was that they were really looking over your shoulder in case someone more interesting or important came into view.

Why had I come? Rebecca wasn't here. Would Olivia notice if I left before dinner?

"Lucie?"

I turned around. Former senator Harlan Jennings, boyishly handsome in a tuxedo, stood there grinning at me, a roguish glint in his eyes that conveyed both gravitas and let's raise hell.

"I thought it was you." He leaned forward and took my arm, brushing my cheek with his lips so I caught the scent of his musky aftershave mingled with the trace of another woman's perfume. "You look absolutely beautiful in that dress. Not that cute roly-poly little girl I remember from visiting your parents' winery when it first opened. You're gorgeous, darlin'."

My heart gave a small leap. The days of the schoolgirl crush were over, but Harlan's Irish charm and the promise of mischief in those bright blue eyes still seduced me. Vanity made me wish he'd forgotten my roly-poly era, but he was right that I'd changed. He, on the other hand, had not. The crow's-feet and laugh lines had deepened, but otherwise he was magically unscathed by the years. Dark haired and handsome in a rugged, Kennedyesque way.

"Thank you," I said. "Glad you recognized me without the puppy fat. And just when I thought I didn't know a soul here."

Harlan burst out laughing. "Stick with me. Let's get a drink and I'll introduce you to a few people. You shouldn't be on your own tonight."

He held out his arm and I took it. "I'd like that. And speaking of the vineyard, why don't you stop by with Alison? Come over some evening to watch the sunset on the terrace over a bottle of wine."

We walked toward one of the many bars that lined the room along the arcades.

"That sounds wonderful." He sounded wistful. "Lately I've seen more sunrises than sunsets I'm so busy with work. How's life treating you now that you've taken over the winery?"

"Pretty well," I said. "We just won the Governor's Cup for one of our brand-new wines. Viognier."

He whistled. "The Governor's Cup? I'm impressed. Top wine award in Virginia. Good for you. But what is VEE-ohn-YAY, anyway? Never heard of it."

"You will. It's French; been around for ages, though it's new to the U.S. Wait and see. It's going to be big in Virginia."

"Guess that means I'll have to try it."

"Well, you could start with mine. Modesty should prevent me from telling you it's an absolutely fabulous vintage, but it really is."

He laughed. "I have an irresistible urge to tousle your hair like I used to when you were little."

"Please don't. The result will scare us both."

He grinned some more. "I'll think of something else, then. So tell me about your prize wine. Ali likes her Chard and we're like old dogs when we find something we enjoy drinking. You think I'll like it?"

"I think so. It's a challenging grape to grow—one of the most expensive because it doesn't produce a huge crop. They say the name translates to 'road to hell,' but my winemaker says that's because of what he goes through to make it."

Harlan's smile was rueful. "Sounds like my last election campaign."

"Your opponent was a moron. Cameron Vaughn? I still can't figure out how he won."

"He got more votes."

My turn to smile. But it had been a stunning upset. Everyone had expected Harlan to win reelection, but Vaughn hammered away at Harlan's absence during a critical vote affecting Virginia, claiming he'd been on a pleasure trip to Europe. The mud stuck and his campaign never regained momentum.

"I saw Vaughn on television the other day," I said. "He's still a moron and he's in love with himself."

"How novel for Washington. Let me buy you a drink, pretty lady. Can I interest you in a glass of champagne? That scrum around the bars is too deep to wade into."

Harlan hailed a passing waiter holding a silver tray filled with champagne flutes. He handed one to me and took one for himself.

As we touched glasses he said, "Drink up. It's Krug."

I raised an eyebrow and sipped champagne. The price for a bottle of Krug began at around $150 and kept climbing.

"I hear Alison has been advising the Ashers on the collection they're donating to the Library of Congress," I said. "It sounds fabulous."

He nodded. "She loved putting that together. Tommy and Mandy gave her a blank check and she went to town. Mind you, Tommy knew what he wanted. He's always been a history nut, and the wars where the Americans and the Brits fought each other fascinate him. He jokes that the reason he became an American citizen was that he can't stand to lose at anything. Now he can say he's on the winning side of both the Revolutionary War and the War of 1812."

I smiled. "You seem to know Sir Thomas quite well."

Harlan gulped some champagne. "If only you know how ironic that was—Sir Thomas. When Tommy and I met we were a couple of hell-raising teenagers in London. His father was a driver at the embassy when Dad was Ambassador to the Court of Saint James's. Tommy took me on my first pub crawl when I was fifteen. He was eighteen and had just bought his first news kiosk." He swung out his arm with the champagne glass to encompass the Great Hall. "And now look where he is. Amazing the way life turns out sometimes, isn't it?"

"I think it's amazing you're still together after all these years."

"Yeah, business associates now. Blood brothers, still thick as thieves."

Harlan reached for another flute as a waiter passed by and raised an eyebrow indicating my glass. I shook my head as he said, "So what brings you here?"

"I came as the guest of someone who works for Asher Investments."

"Really? Who?"

I hesitated, wondering if he was aware that she was missing. "Rebecca Natale."

Harlan looked startled. "You know Rebecca?"

"We were friends in college. She said she was coming to D.C. for the weekend and invited me to this gala."

He nodded, but he still seemed taken aback. "She is one smart lady. Going places if she sticks with Tommy." He looked around. "So how come you're not with her?"

"She, ah, got delayed."

"Harlan, a word please?" Tommy Asher stood at Harlan's elbow, placing a hand on his shoulder. His eyes fell on me. "Sorry, my love. I need to borrow him."

Sir Thomas dressed and looked like the man he'd become—British peer, world-class adventurer who enjoyed the good life, and brilliant financier with an unerring knack for making money—though after what Harlan had just revealed about him I could see traces of the scrappy street kid who got the ambassador's son drunk and juggled odd jobs to save money to buy his own news kiosk. Though the rough edges had been polished smooth, they were still there if I looked hard enough, in his deeply tanned pockmarked face, the jagged scar above his lip, and his dark, intense eyes. For all his wealth, fame, and privilege, I'd bet money Tommy Asher's past still rose up before him like a wraith, making sure he never forgot where he came from.

"Of course you can borrow Harlan," I said now.

"Tommy," Harlan said. "Let me introduce you. An old friend of the family, Lucie Montgomery. Lucie, Sir Thomas Asher."

"How do you do, my dear? I hope you're enjoying yourself. My apologies for stealing him. Harlan, something's come up. A small problem."

The apology was perfunctory and he'd taken no more notice of me than if I'd been one of the waitresses serving drinks. He excused himself again before I could say nice to meet you, too, leading Harlan to join two men in dark suits and a stunning, statuesque raven-haired woman I recognized from the society pages as Miranda Asher. The daughter of a Greek shipping tycoon, she came from a

family of four beautiful and talented sisters, three of whom married
into European aristocracy. The stories in the press were that Miranda's father forbade his youngest daughter to marry a working-class
commoner, disowning her when she eloped with Tommy. After he
built his financial empire and received his knighthood, Sir Thomas
brought his wife's sisters' husbands into the business—excluding his
father-in-law, who still thought Tommy was trailer trash, even if he
now had money.

I finished my champagne and watched the earnest conversation
among the little group. They were talking about Rebecca, I was sure
of it. I caught the shocked expression on Harlan's face as one of the
dark-suited men spoke, gesturing broadly with his hands. Then
Harlan put his arm around Miranda and clapped Tommy on the
back and the meeting broke up. I wondered where Alison Jennings
was—unless she was involved in the search for Rebecca and, presumably, the missing Madison wine cooler.

"Ladies and gentlemen, good evening and welcome."

A male voice over the public address system repeated the greet-
ing until the crowd quieted down. The screen behind the stage now
showed a beguiling larger-than-life-sized photograph of the Ashers,
heads thrown back in delighted laughter as they knelt beside the
wheelchair of a young girl who was also laughing. As I watched, the
words "A Tribute to Tommy and Mandy: A Lifetime of Service"
appeared, superimposed on the photo.

We were asked to take our seats for dinner, where we'd find our
programs for the rest of the evening. The tribute—speeches followed by a short film—would begin as dessert was being served.
Dancing to live music afterward.

I found my table near the stage and within viewing distance of
the head table where Harlan sat with the Ashers. I spotted Alison
Jennings, sultry in a mint green satin gown that looked perfect
against her alabaster skin and flame-colored hair, as she slipped into
a chair next to her husband and whispered in his ear. He replied,
kissing her hand, and she shook her head. By the looks of things,
Rebecca still hadn't turned up.

"May I?" A short, solidly built man with thinning hair
pointed to the chair to my right as he mopped his forehead with a

handkerchief. "That is, unless you were saving this seat for someone?"

"I . . . no. Please, help yourself."

He tugged on the collar of his shirt. "Hate these monkey suits,"
he said. "Feels like I'm wearing a straitjacket."

He sat down as the rest of our table arrived together—five men
and two women, all in their twenties or thirties. One of the men
cradled an open bottle of Krug. Their glazed eyes, giddy laughter,
and risqué barbs made it clear it wasn't the first one they'd drunk
this evening. They took their seats, leaving the chair on the other
side of me empty. We introduced ourselves. Everyone but my dinner
partner, a lawyer named Ben Goldberg, worked in the New York
office of Thomas Asher Investments. I gave my name and decided
not to mention that I owned a vineyard.

"Who's missing?" one of the women asked.

"Rebecca." The man who'd brought the Krug spoke up.
"What do you bet she's personally delivering the goods to some
client?"

Everyone snickered. I picked up my water glass and drank, avoiding looking at any of them. Did he mean what I thought he did?
Did Rebecca still have a predilection for off-the-radar trysts? In the
background a band slid into a samba and the rest of their conversation was lost in a wash of music.

Maybe the list of people who didn't like Rebecca was longer than
I thought.

Ben Goldberg glanced at me. "You work with them?"

"No. I'm a friend of someone who does."

"The missing Rebecca?" he asked.

I nodded. "How'd you guess? Do you know her?"

A waiter set down bowls of soup.

"I don't. But you don't seem like you belong with those guys,
either. That was a crass comment." He stirred his soup with a spoon.
"What's in this?"

"Didn't you get a menu card? It's potato, leek, and sorrel soup," I
said.

"Oh." He set down his spoon and picked up the breadbasket.
"Roll?"

"No, thanks. Oh, come on, try the soup. It's delicious," I said. "So tell me how you ended up here."

"My firm represents Asher Investments here in D.C."

"That must keep you busy."

"Right now that would be an understatement."

"What do you mean?"

"I'm surprised your friend Rebecca didn't clue you in. Some two-bit prick managed to light a fire under the junior senator from Virginia, who happens to chair the Senate Banking Subcommittee on Security, Insurance, and Investments." He spread thick butter on his roll.

"Cameron Vaughn?"

"Yeah. Him. Vaughn took this jerk seriously enough that he's planning to hold a hearing to look into the business practices of Thomas Asher Investments next week."

"What about their business practices?"

Ben snorted. "He seems to think Sir Thomas might be inflating his numbers on how well his portfolios are doing. Claims there's no way Asher can produce the consistent profits he does without some kind of hanky-panky going on inside the mother ship."

I said, shocked, "Is that true?"

"It's my job to prove it isn't." He'd answered the question like a lawyer.

"Who's the guy making the accusations?"

"Ian Philips. A pissed-off ex–investment analyst," Ben said. "He got fired from the last place he worked and now he's got an axe to grind with Asher for some reason. Personally, I think he's jealous of Sir Thomas's success and mad the firm is so tight-lipped about its clients and where it invests. I still can't believe Vaughn took him seriously. It's been in all the newspapers and on the Internet, but so far it's just a back-burner story."

"What are you going to do?" I asked, as he refilled my champagne glass. I was starting to feel light-headed.

"Swat a fly." Ben finished his glass and stood up. He seemed a little tipsy himself. "I think I'll go look for another bottle. Let's live it up."

Ben drank more of the rest of his meal than he ate and what littler conversation passed between us as we were served course after course was mostly small talk. Just as waiters placed our dessert plated in front of us, someone took the stage and announced that it was time for the tribute to Tommy and Mandy Asher to begin.

The film homage had been put together by a Hollywood friend who had won an Emmy. Slick, with soaring music and heartrending montages, it seemed packaged to bring a tear to the eye of everyone in the room. Dozens of photos of the Ashers over the years, separately and together, handing a check to a hospital administrator surrounded by young cancer patients, working in a soup kitchen, hugging kids in a Malawi orphanage, and holding shovels at the groundbreaking ceremony of a school in Haiti flashed on the screen. Then came the images of Sir Thomas at the tiller of his yacht, on safari in Africa, at the summit of Everest. Others showed Lady Asher with her glamorous sisters at what looked like an enviably happy family reunion. The finale was a scrolling list of more hospital wings, university buildings, endowed scholarships, and numerous other charities bearing their name—ending with a preview of the exhibit at the Library of Congress. By then, all the guests were on their feet, yelling and applauding, as Sir Thomas and Lady Asher made their way to the stage. His speech was brief, acknowledging the outpouring of adulation in the room and clearly reveling in it. On the jumbo screen, the two of them bowed to more thunderous applause, their smiles radiant as their hands fluttered over their hearts and Miranda Asher blew kisses.

"I'm out of here," Ben said, as the band appeared on the stage. "I need my beauty sleep."

"Me, too," I said. "I think I'll go back to the Willard and wait for Rebecca."

"Too bad she never made it tonight. Share a cab?" he asked. "The Willard's on my way."

"Thanks. That would be great."

But when the taxi pulled up in front of the hotel, Ben draped an arm around my shoulder. "I could come up to your room," he said, nuzzling my neck. "Maybe we could order another bottle of champagne, get to know each other better?"

"I think we've both had enough to drink tonight." I moved his hand away from where it dangled near the neckline of my dress. "Besides, I'm sure Rebecca will show up in our suite at any moment. Good night, Ben. Thanks for the cab ride."

He withdrew his arm and fumbled in his pocket, pulling a card out of his wallet. "Call me and we'll have dinner. Maybe I'll come out and visit your vineyard."

I moved away so his kiss landed near my ear instead of on my lips. A hotel doorman opened the cab door and helped me out.

"Everything all right, miss?" he asked.

"Just fine. Thank you."

The clock above the front desk read eleven thirty as I walked into the quiet lobby and headed for the bank of elevators.

"Natale. N-A-T-A-L-E. Rebecca Natale. I know she's staying here. I've been trying to reach her all afternoon. If you'd just give me her room number—"

He was tall and lanky and had his back to me, addressing the male clerk on duty in the too-loud voice of the slightly inebriated. I didn't recognize him, but maybe he, too, had just returned from the Ashers' gala and was loaded on Krug—though he wasn't wearing a tuxedo.

I changed my route to the elevators so I passed by the front desk as I heard the clerk say, "I'm sorry, but that information is confidential. Unless Ms. Natale gave you her room number or asked us to share it with you, I can't help you."

"Ha, so she is staying here," he said. "I knew it."

The clerk looked irritated as he realized he'd just fallen for the oldest con in the book. "May I call you a cab, sir?"

"You can call me whatever you want," he said. "In the meantime, I think I'll have a drink in your nice bar and wait for my good friend Rebecca. She's probably still at her fancy party."

He swung around and saw me. Tousled reddish-blond hair, fair skin, freckles that made him look prep school boyish, and a charming smile. He wore his oxford shirt untucked, and his pin-striped suit was rumpled. A tie hung out of the suit jacket pocket and a Burberry scarf was knotted carelessly around his neck. Midthirties, maybe a little older.

"Hello, beautiful." He smiled, swaying slightly as he indicated the clerk. "Look, I'm done here with Mr. Helpful. He's all yours. Maybe he won't tell you anything, either."

"You're looking for Rebecca?" I asked.

He straightened up and seemed to sober up as well. "You know where she is?"

"May I ask why you're trying to find her?"

"You may ask." He seemed to mock me. "As I just told this good man, we're friends. Used to work together. She told me she'd be in town for that over-the-top tribute to her narcissist boss. I've been leaving messages on her phone for the past week, but she never returned my calls. I thought we were going to get together." He looked me over. "Wait. Don't tell me you work for Asher, too?"

"No."

"My turn to ask," he said. "How do you know Rebecca?"

"We're old college friends."

"You staying in this hotel, too, old college friend?"

"Yes."

"So where is she?"

"I don't know, but she's not here. And I didn't catch your name."

"I didn't throw it. Ian Philips. What about yours?"

The "two-bit prick" who had it in for Thomas Asher Investments. And he used to work with Rebecca, who had contacted him. How interesting.

"Lucie Montgomery. If you'll excuse me, I'm awfully tired."

"I really think you ought to have a drink with me, Lucie Montgomery, while we wait for our pal Rebecca. She ought to turn up before too long. They have a great Scotch bar here. The Round Robin."

"Thanks, but no thanks."

I started to walk toward the elevators, but he reached out and grabbed my arm. "Please."

His grip hurt and I pulled my arm away. "I said, no thanks."

A hotel concierge appeared at my side. "Everything all right, miss?"

"Absolutely. I just told Mr. Philips good night and that I'm going to my room."

"Of course, miss. And, Mr. Philips, may I get a cab for you?"

"No, you may not. I'd like to have a drink in your bar, my good man. I just thought Ms. Montgomery would like to join me."

"Excuse me," I said. "My elevator's here."

I left them in the lobby and, on purpose, pushed the button for the ninth floor in case Ian Philips got clever and watched where I got off. I took the stairs to the seventh floor, looking over my shoulder at the deserted hall until I reached our rooms.

The suite looked as it had when I left, except that the maid had been in to turn down the beds and leave chocolates on the pillows. I sat down on the sofa, kicked off my evening shoes, and rubbed my temples.

Rebecca, Rebecca. Where *are* you? What in the hell are you doing? I lay back against the pillows, closed my eyes, and fell into a deep dreamless sleep.

The telephone woke me and I sat up, wondering where I was and why I'd slept in my now badly creased evening dress. Thin streamers of sunlight from the gaps in the curtain panels striped the carpet. The phone, across the room on the desk, went to voice mail as I remembered Rebecca and that this was the Willard. I flopped back against the cushions as it rang again. This time I answered before the voice mail kicked in. A deep male voice asked if I was Lucie Montgomery.

"Yes." I walked over to the bedroom. Neither bed had been slept in. "Who's this?"

"Detective Ismail Horne with the Metropolitan Police Department. You were with Rebecca Natale yesterday afternoon."

He knew; he wasn't asking. I wondered who had told him.

"You found her?" I pushed back the heavy gold-and-scarlet curtains and blinked in the sudden brightness. Stupid question. Why else would he call at seven o'clock on a Sunday morning? "Is she all right?"

"We haven't found her yet," he said. "But we have some items of clothing that we'd like you to identify."

I felt my throat close. "Rebecca's clothing?"

"That's what we'd like you to tell us."

"Where do I meet you?"

"Fletcher's Boat House," he said. "On the river."

CHAPTER 4

 ━━━∞∞∞━━━

Anyone who's ever been out on the Potomac River knows Fletcher's Boat House, which has been around for over 150 years. Located downstream from the tumbling foment of Great Falls and upstream from where the river widens into a serpentine ribbon as it flows past Washington, Fletcher's is located in a peaceful wooded park where people come to picnic, let their dogs run, throw Frisbees, and sunbathe. If you didn't know better, you could be deceived into believing that here the waters of the Potomac are calm and placid.

They are not.

Beneath the surface, boulders and steep channels form swirling eddies and powerful currents. In some places, the river is thirty to forty feet deep. One false step while fishing on a rocky outcrop along the banks and even the strongest swimmer will be swept away, unable to fight a current that comes at you like a fleet of trucks.

I'd been to Fletcher's before, canoeing with friends on the river and on the adjacent C & O Canal, so I knew where the steep one-car-width entrance was located off Canal Road. The little gravel parking lot overflowed with red, white, and blue Metropolitan Police Department cruisers and emergency vehicles, but I found a spot into which I could shoehorn my Mini Cooper.

I got out of the car and looked around. Rebecca had been here last night? Doing what? Was this the site of a rendezvous gone wrong? Some of the stories—rumors, actually—about where she and Connor met for sex were pretty kinky.

As I crossed the footbridge over the canal, the moss green trailer where the boat rental and concession stand were located came into view. Next to it was an A-frame tackle shack where fishermen stocked up on supplies. A new-looking sign stated that Fletcher's had been taken over by the National Park Service and was now operated by an organization called Guest Services, Incorporated. Good luck getting people to call it that.

Except for a gaudy row of red, orange, and yellow kayaks lined up along the bank of the canal, a blazing yellow forsythia bush, and a clump of daffodils next to the tackle shack, most of the scenery was tinted the browns and dull yellow greens of late winter. Even the sky was a washed-out shade of blue. Occasionally a filigree of pink cherry blossoms or green buds enveloped a lone tree like a mist, but otherwise as far as the eye could see there was only dense brush and skeletal trunks and branches bent toward the light and water. As for the river itself, it was murky and brackish at low tide. Broad mud-flats made the boathouse, with its wilted American flag, look as if it were marooned on a small island.

In summer, the place is so lush with vegetation the Potomac all but disappears from view, but today I could see clear to the other shore. An occasional flash of movement at the crest of the steep, wooded ravine several hundred feet above the river came from cars zooming along the George Washington Parkway. Otherwise, that side of the river was not a hospitable place for fishermen—or for anyone to walk or hike. If Rebecca had come here, she had done so the same way I did.

A uniformed officer stopped me as I walked down the gravel path toward the boathouse. When I told him why I was here, he let me pass. On the river, a marine search boat with FAIRFAX COUNTY, VIRGINIA stenciled on the side moved into view. The knot in my stomach tightened. They were looking for Rebecca in the Potomac.

I stepped onto the boat shack gangway, which rocked back and forth so crazily I had to use my cane to keep my balance. Half a dozen red rowboats with FLETCHER'S and numbers stenciled on the sides lay overturned at the end of the pier. It looked like fishing and boating had been canceled for the day.

A female officer told me to wait by a wooden locker filled with oars while she told Detective Horne I was here. She walked over to a tall, slim man with ebony skin, close-cut salt-and-pepper hair, and the bearing of an ex-marine, and spoke to him. He nodded and came over, cradling a cup of coffee the color of the river water. His badge was clipped to his belt next to his gun, and he wore khakis, a plaid dress shirt, and a black all-weather jacket with the department logo embroidered on it. He also looked dead tired, like he might be working his second shift of the day.

"Appreciate you coming," he said, after shaking my hand and introducing himself. "I understand you're sharing a suite at the Willard paid for by Rebecca Natale. And one of her colleagues said you were with her yesterday afternoon before she disappeared."

"That's right," I said. "But I have no idea why she'd be here."

"That's what we're trying to find out. Like I said on the phone, we have some clothes we'd like you to take a look at. They're over here. See if you recognize anything."

Each item was in its own brown paper bag, neatly laid out in a row on the dock. Horne showed them to me one by one. The shawl. The blazer. The jeans. The silk blouse. Even her shoes. There was something else, too. Blood on the shawl and the blouse.

"Take your time," he said. "Be sure."

Thank God I hadn't eaten anything. I felt like I was going to be sick.

"I don't need to take any time. These are Rebecca's clothes. She was wearing them yesterday. Why is there blood on them? Where did you find them?"

"A park service employee discovered them this morning out on the river during a routine check. They were in one of her boats."

"A boat? Where's Rebecca?"

Horne cleared his throat. "I'm sorry, Ms. Montgomery. We're looking for her right now. I've got officers walking a grid and the marine squad is searching the river."

As he spoke, two men in wet suits with tanks rolled backward off the side of the police boat into the muddy water, disappearing with a small splash.

"I don't believe this," I said.

Horne led me back to the oar locker, away from the evidence bags.

"I have a few questions," he said. "When you were with Ms. Natale yesterday, did she seem depressed or upset about anything?"

"No, not at all."

"She say anything about an argument with someone—boyfriend, coworker, anyone?"

"Nothing. No one."

"Any reason to believe she might contemplate taking her life?"

"Look, Detective, you're way off base if you think Rebecca committed suicide. She's not the type. Besides, when she left me she was on her way to Georgetown to pick up an antique silver wine cooler that belonged to President James Madison. An errand for her boss."

Horne nodded when I mentioned the wine cooler, so I guessed he knew about it now, too.

"Go on," he said.

"She was wearing diamond-and-sapphire earrings and a matching necklace and carrying a Coach purse. Where are those things? Plus her identification and credit cards? What makes you so sure this wasn't a robbery that went bad?"

He studied me. "Right now I'm not ruling out anything. A robbery homicide is one possibility. It's also been my experience that a woman doesn't remove her clothes before deciding to take her life, but that doesn't mean it couldn't happen—that this isn't some weird kind of suicide. What about a boyfriend? She have one?"

I thought about the birth control pills back in the hotel. "She didn't mention anybody."

"But?" He prompted me.

There was no reason not to tell him. "I hadn't seen Rebecca in almost twelve years until yesterday. We spent about an hour together doing some sightseeing and then she said she needed to take care of that errand. I saw her birth control pills on the bathroom counter when I got back to our hotel room at the Willard, but I have no idea about a boyfriend."

"You know if she's monogamous?"

"I . . . no."

"What you're saying is you didn't really know her that well," Horne said.

"I used to. But that was a long time ago."

He drank some of his dishwater coffee, then flung the rest of it into the river.

"Okay, thanks. That's it for now. I don't have any more questions, but I might be talking to you again depending on what happens." He pulled a business card out of an overstuffed wallet that looked like it was about to split at the sides. "Call me if you think of anything else. And if she gets in touch with you, tell her to call me and make it quick. The chief gets cranky when we spend taxpayers' money searching for someone who isn't missing anymore."

I nodded. "How long will you keep looking?"

"Hard to say. But right now the suspicious circumstances surrounding her disappearance and that missing White House wine holder mean we'll keep at it for a while." He paused and scratched his head. "Though I'll be interested to see what the lab says after we get that blood analyzed."

"What do you mean?" I asked.

"You learn a lot from blood spatter. Whether it could have come from, say, a gunshot, or whether she merely cut herself and bled on her clothing. Either accidentally or on purpose."

The implication of what he'd just said sunk in. "On purpose? Why would she do that?"

"I don't know right now. But I mean to find out. Good day, Ms. Montgomery. Thanks for coming by. I'd better get back to work."

"Good day, Detective."

He returned to the group of men he'd been talking to when I arrived. A light breeze rustled the edges of a sheaf of papers attached to a clipboard on top of the locker. Boat rental tickets. Next to the clipboard sat a red plastic coffee can that had been converted into a tip jar. The cheery hand-drawn sign with jumping fish on it read, IT'S TIME TO FISH.

I stared at the coffee can. None of this made sense.

As I left the dock, a woman wearing a gray T-shirt with THE BOATHOUSE AT FLETCHER'S COVE stenciled on it in red sat on a large rock by the path to the boat rental trailer, smoking like her life depended on it. Horne said a woman found the rowboat with Rebecca's clothes in it.

I changed direction and headed toward her.

She gestured to the dock with her cigarette. "Friend of yours, baby?"

I nodded. "You're the one who found the boat?"

She wore a bucket hat secured under her neck with a cord that hid her hair and shaded most of her face. I couldn't guess her age, but her voice was burred with years of smoking and her skin was nut brown and sun weathered.

"Yup. Out this morning around six putzing around when I saw it. Hung up on one of the Three Sisters. This one was weird, though."

The Three Sisters were an outcropping of rocks downriver. Boaters watched out for them at their peril.

"Weird how?"

"Don't see too many suicides folding their clothes before they jump." She pulled a smashed pack of Marlboros out of her back pocket. "And she didn't leave no ID. You go to all the trouble of killing yourself, you want someone to *know*. You don't do it for the hell of it."

"The clothes were folded?" I'd thought whoever bagged them had done that.

"Yep. Neat as a pin." She paused to light up. "Didn't leave her underwear. Maybe she was modest."

"That detective says women who plan to commit suicide don't usually take off their clothes," I said. "Anyway, Rebecca didn't kill herself. She had no reason to."

"Don't kid yourself, baby. People come down her all the time to die. Happens more often than you think." She shrugged. "People with problems just can't take it no more. You'd be surprised how many times I've found a body."

I swallowed hard. "There is no body."

"Yeah, sometimes it happens that way, too," she said. "I know a couple cases where they never found nothing. It's real hard on the families. Course this time those divers could get lucky. River's cold, so it acts like a refrigerator. If she tied something heavy to herself, she'll sink. She'd be well preserved. Possibility number two is all you get are the bones. They'll wash up on shore, whatever's left after the catfish and critters get to her."

"Please," I said, "don't."

"Sorry, baby." Her eyes grew soft. "I talked to that detective, same as you. Maybe somebody killed her and made it look like suicide. Could even be one of the homeboys living around here."

"Living . . . where?"

"The woods. Where d'you think? I don't see no hotels, do you? Lots of people set up camps and call it home. Some of these dudes are okay, but some will scare the living crap out of you." She twirled a finger next to her ear.

"Rebecca had no reason to come here," I said.

Or did she? I really didn't know.

"Then there's the last possibility," the woman said. "Behind door number three."

"Which is?"

She let out a stream of dragon smoke. "Maybe she's fakin' us all out. Staged the whole thing and ran away somewhere. Sippin' a latte someplace, laughing her fool head off at all of us."

CHAPTER 5

———∞∞∞———

I was most of the way up the one-way gravel road leaving Fletcher's when a black Lincoln Town Car turned off Canal Road. I waited, but the other car didn't intend to let me exit. Then I saw the New York license plate: TAI1. Thomas Asher Investments.

I gave in and reversed the Mini, too numb to care about winning a game of chicken. A chauffeur sat behind the wheel of the Lincoln, but I couldn't make out who the passenger was—or passengers. Possibly Sir Thomas himself. At the bottom of the hill two MPD cruisers backing out of the parking lot boxed in the big car. I scooted around all three of them and zoomed up the drive feeling vindicated.

Of course Horne would question Tommy Asher since the Madison wine cooler vanished when Rebecca did and she was his employee. Once the press got wind of this—Rebecca's disappearance, her bloody clothes in that rowboat, and the details of the stolen silver intended to be returned to the White House after two centuries—the story would be all over the place in no time. And since Washington leaked worse than a bad sieve and was runner-up for gossip capital of the country after Hollywood, we were probably talking about hours or even minutes.

When I got back to the Willard, a self-possessed woman in a navy pantsuit met me in the lobby, told me she was the day manager, and accompanied me to my suite. The place had been searched and

Rebecca's suitcase and her clothes were gone. It was all nice and legal; the police showed up with a warrant and the hotel cooperated. The manager assured me she'd been present the entire time.

The first thing I did was check the desk. Rebecca's planner and the book of Alexander Pope's poems were missing. The dedication and our private names for each other—Little and Big—would have meant nothing to the D.C. police. But maybe some officer had read the crossed-out love poem from Connor and decided the book was relevant to their investigation.

Connor O'Brien, PhD, currently of Wyoming. Had Rebecca picked up the phone and called him, just as she'd called me, luring him to Washington? Had she met him after she retrieved the Madison wine cooler? And if it had been Connor, how long before he became a person of interest to the police? The bitterness and resentment Rebecca had nursed for twelve years had boiled over yesterday. Had she been angry enough to want payback for an old hurt? Then what happened? Nothing good—Rebecca was missing and her bloody clothes had been found in a rowboat.

I fingered Detective Horne's business card in my jacket pocket. Rebecca wanted me to have that book of poetry and it now seemed important to get it back. As soon as the D.C. police were finished with it, I would explain to Horne that it was mine. I hoped he'd see things my way—though I had my doubts that would happen.

I put the top to the Mini down for the drive home to Atoka, as much for the weather, which had warmed up, as the need to clear my head. A sweet breeze ruffled my hair and the harsh winter sunshine with its pale shadows had vanished, replaced by the slanted golden light of spring.

Though Atoka is only a little more than an hour's drive from Washington—give or take—coming home is like traveling to another country. I headed west on Route 50, Lee-Jackson Memorial Highway, as the city and its sprawling exurbs receded. After a while the road dwindled to a winding country lane lined with Civil War–era stacked stone walls and post-and-board fences behind which prizewinning Angus cattle and expensive thoroughbreds grazed.

By the time I passed the turnoff for the Snickersville Turnpike,

I'd shrugged off Washington like a snake shedding its skin. Out here, Route 50 became Mosby's Highway in tribute to the Gray Ghost who used to ride through this territory with his band of Partisan Rangers looking for Union soldiers. Dead ahead the Blue Ridge Mountains, with their comforting dowager's hump profile, appeared on the horizon.

At Middleburg, I slowed to twenty-five, passing a sign for an upcoming point-to-point sponsored by one of the local hunts. Next to that sign hung another of a cheeky red fox in a hacking jacket lounging next to the words RELAX, YOU'RE IN THE VILLAGE.

But as I turned down Atoka Road and saw the vines and the split-rail fence that marked the beginning of my land, the image I'd been trying to push out of my mind for the past few hours came rushing back—Rebecca, floating like a limp doll in the Potomac River. Why hadn't I insisted on going with her to Georgetown? Maybe if I had, she'd still be alive.

I turned into my driveway as guilt and remorse wormed their unwelcome way inside my head.

Katherine Eastman called my cell phone while I was getting my bags out of the Mini. Kit and I had known each other for twenty-five years, meeting during a kindergarten recess where we'd built an elaborate sand castle that we gleefully stomped flat as soon as it was finished. Our friendship proved more resilient than that castle, and we'd remained best friends ever since. In all that time, I could count our disagreements on the fingers of one hand.

I had a feeling this call was about to trigger one of those rare occasions, especially because Kit was a reporter for the *Washington Tribune*. A few months ago she leaped on a temporary assignment to work on the Metro desk in D.C., leaving her job out here as Loudoun County bureau chief. That meant Rebecca's disappearance was now her beat.

I shoved open my front door, cradling the phone between my shoulder and my ear as I wrestled with the bags and my cane and said, "Hey."

"Hey, yourself. Where've you been? I've got some news."

"Oh, yeah, what?"

Maybe this wasn't about Rebecca. Last winter Kit's fiancé, a detective with the Loudoun County Sheriff's Department, had been deployed to Afghanistan for a second tour with his reserve unit and Kit finally moved her mother, now descending into the twilight world of Alzheimer's, into assisted living. Maybe she had something to tell me about Bobby or Faith.

"It's about your ex-friend Rebecca Natale," she said. "You won't believe this. The police found her clothes in a rowboat on the Potomac this morning with blood on them. They're searching the river for her right now. I thought you'd want to know."

This wasn't going to go down well.

"I do know," I said after a moment. "I'm the one who identified the clothes."

The silence on her end of the phone went on so long I wondered if she'd disconnected.

Finally she said in a quiet voice, "Care to explain that?"

Kit knew Rebecca. I'd introduced them when she visited me at school, and she'd disliked her from the moment they met.

When I'd asked why, she'd said, "I just don't like her, that's all. I can't put my finger on it, but there's something about her. Something . . . fake."

I didn't want to say what I really thought: You're jealous of my friendship with Rebecca. Instead, I tried to get Kit to come around, but she wouldn't have it. Later, when Rebecca would no longer return my calls or answer my e-mails, Kit said she wasn't surprised and had seen it coming.

"She's only out for herself, Lucie. You're better off without her. Forget her and move on."

Now I said to Kit, "Rebecca called me a few weeks ago and asked me to meet her in town for the weekend."

"And you said yes. Jeez, Luce. *Why?*"

"I don't know. Curiosity, I guess."

More silence.

"Are you covering the story?" I asked her.

"No." Her voice was flat. "My boss asked, but I knew I couldn't be objective about this one. I'm sorry she's missing, but I still think she treated you like dirt all those years ago."

"I know," I said. "Look, it's complicated."

"I suppose you went to that shindig last night for Tommy Asher and his wife since that's probably why Rebecca was in town?"

"Yes."

"You know Cameron Vaughn is holding a hearing in a couple of days to look into her boss's questionable business practices. I think he plans to turn over a few rocks and see what crawls out."

"I heard."

Ian Philips, as far as I was concerned, would be among those crawling out.

"Look," she said, "I've been at Mom's all weekend trying to get her taxes in order. I'm not going back to D.C. until tomorrow morning. How about getting together for dinner? Maybe we should talk."

"I didn't get much sleep last night, Kit. I'm kind of beat."

"I've got the cubicle next to David Wildman in the newsroom, you know. He's been digging around Asher Investments for the past few months. If half of what he's uncovered is true, Rebecca was up to her neck in muck," she said. "And now she's missing. Sure you don't want to have dinner at the Inn?"

She waited.

"I'll make the reservation," I said. "How about seven?"

"I'll be there," she said, "with bells on."

Kit's Jeep pulled into the parking lot of the Goose Creek Inn at seven o'clock sharp just as I was climbing out of the Mini. Though the sun wouldn't set for another half hour, a path of luminarias along the flagstone walk and fairy lights woven through the branches of a flowering dogwood cast a soft light on the whitewashed half-timbered building so it took on the enchanted aura of a fairy tale.

I walked up the path and waited for Kit by the front door. She bounded up the walk dressed in skin-tight jeans, a hot pink sweater, a Concord grape corduroy jacket, and a lime green silk scarf. Lately she'd developed a taste for wearing violently hued outfits—the brighter, the better—which she said never failed to get her called on when she raised her hand at a press conference. Since she was also forty pounds overweight, dyed her hair Marilyn Monroe blond, and applied makeup like war paint, she was hard to miss even without the bright clothing.

"You look like something they forgot to shoot." She leaned in, giving me an air kiss. "Try aromatherapy, kiddo. Works wonders for me."

"Nice to see you, too. New outfit?"

She grinned. "You like?"

"Phosphorescent colors look good on you. Does that sweater glow in the dark?"

She burst out laughing and held the door. We stepped inside to the fragrant aromas of my cousin Dominique Gosselin's cooking and the comforting sounds of conversation, laughter, and the clink of dishes and glassware. In the forty years since Fitzhugh Pico, my godfather, founded the Goose Creek Inn and Dominique inherited it after he passed away, the place had won every major dining award in the Mid-Atlantic, earning a reputation as the region's most romantic restaurant. Dominique, who'd seen her share of high-profile clients show up with their "secretaries" asking for a discreet table for a special lunch or dinner, often said she knew more Washington secrets than the CIA and Secret Service put together.

The maître d' waved us to the front desk and led us himself to the main dining room and my favorite window table with its view of Goose Creek. He promised my cousin would stop by as soon as she cleared up a momentary crisis in the kitchen.

"Something only she can handle?" I asked.

He winked as he gave me an elaborate Gallic shrug. "Would she have it any other way? They're all crises only she can handle. *Bon appétit, mesdemoiselles.* Gilles will be with you *dans un petit instant.*"

We sat and, though the window was closed, I could hear the creek below us as it rushed over rock-strewn rapids on its way to the Potomac. Soon it would be too dark for the police to continue their search. I wondered whether Detective Horne had already called it off for the day.

"They still haven't found her," Kit said, reading my mind. "I checked with the desk before I left the house."

"*Bonsoir, ma chère Lucie, Mademoiselle Eastman. Quel plaisir de vous revoir.*" Gilles, the headwaiter, lit the hurricane lamp on our table and filled our water glasses. "Cocktails? The usual? *Deux kir royals?*"

Usually he and I bantered in French, but tonight I didn't feel like chatting or drinking champagne. "*Bonsoir,* Gilles. I'll just have a glass of white wine, please. The house white's fine."

"I'll take a vodka martini. Straight up, very dry, with a twist," Kit said. "Nice to see you, as always."

"I'll bring those right away." Gilles switched to English and shot me a concerned glance as he left.

Kit picked up her menu and studied it in silence. I did the same. We ordered dinner and a bottle of Oregon Pinot Noir as soon as our drinks came.

"May she rest in peace," Kit said finally as we touched glasses.

"She's not at peace, that's for sure," I said. "The detective who questioned me this morning about her clothes, Horne, promised to let me know when they find her. If they find her."

"Are you talking about Ismail Horne . . . Izzy Horne?" Kit asked as I nodded. "I know him. He's a good guy. No nonsense, doesn't screw around. He'll find whoever did this, Lucie—if it's a homicide."

"It's not suicide. I'm sure of it."

Kit watched me as she reached for a piece of baguette from the breadbasket and slabbed herbed butter on it.

"Her underwear was missing," I said. "It wasn't with her clothes."

Kit hesitated. "Either she kept it on when she went in or, if it was a homicide, maybe he took it. Some sicko with a fetish."

I gulped my wine and considered what she wasn't saying. That maybe Rebecca had been raped, too.

"Look, until the cops find her, we're just speculating," Kit said. "Do you even know what was going on in her life these days? Remember how secretive she was? Evasive? How long did she keep that affair with the chairman of your English department off the radar? A year, wasn't it?"

"Nearly eighteen months."

"See?" Kit took a large bite of baguette. She said, through a mouthful of bread, "So what'd you two talk about when you got together yesterday?"

A sommelier opened our wine and poured some for me to taste. I nodded and he filled our glasses.

"She felt bad about the way she treated me after she left school. Said she wanted to apologize."

"Just like that?" Kit was incredulous.

"That's what she said."

"Then a few hours later she vanishes?" Kit waved her index finger back and forth. "No, no, no. She planned this. Sounds like she was putting her affairs in order before she ended it."

"Oh, come on!" I said. "You forget, she was carrying the . . ."

I stopped abruptly. Kit didn't know about the Madison wine cooler. As far as I knew, Detective Horne had kept that information away from the press. No one was aware of it except the police and a few people in Sir Thomas's inner circle—and me.

"Carrying what?"

"A purse with a wallet, credit cards—her identification. She was also wearing a pretty flashy diamond-and-sapphire necklace and earrings. None of that stuff was in the rowboat. She didn't jump overboard with a Coach purse."

"Sweetie," Kit said, "you do know it's me you're trying to con, don't you? Your nose just grew two inches. Carrying what? Where were you, anyway? I want to hear it all."

Gilles arrived with our dinners, wok-charred salmon for me, roast duck with plum sauce for Kit—new Asian dishes on the menu in tribute to cherry blossom season.

Kit didn't pick up her fork. "I'm waiting," she said. "I don't care if my dinner grows stone-cold, even if it is your cousin's fabulous duck. Give it up, Luce."

Our eyes met across the table. Hers were troubled, and I knew what she was thinking. Where did my loyalties lie?

In twenty-five years of friendship, Kit had never let me down. Rebecca, on the other hand . . . well, let me count the ways.

"All right," I said. "But you have to swear that you won't say anything about this to anyone. Not even a hint, especially to your buddy. The one writing the story on Tommy Asher."

She crossed her heart with her steak knife.

"The reason Rebecca went to Georgetown yesterday afternoon

was to pick up something for her boss. One of Sir Thomas's ancestors was a soldier who stole a silver wine cooler from the White
House right before the British burned Washington during the War
of 1812. Asher apparently had no clue it was in his attic or on some
dusty shelf for the past two centuries, but once he discovered it and
learned its provenance, he planned to return it to the president and
first lady. On Monday."

Kit's mouth hung open. "You're not making this up, are you?
Because that's an unbelievable story."

"Which you can't print."

"I know, I know . . . but word will get out. You wait and see."

"Yes, but I'm not going to be the source of the leak. I'm not even
supposed to know about it. The only reason I do is that Rebecca
wouldn't let me go to Georgetown with her. Finally she showed me
a photo of the thing on her phone and told me it was a hush-hush
errand."

Kit dunked a large piece of duck in plum sauce, popping it in her
mouth.

"So you think this was a robbery?" she said, after a moment.

"Like I said, I don't think she jumped overboard with a Coach
purse. And an eighteenth-century wine cooler," I said.

"You really can't take it with you." Kit grinned, then saw my face.
"Sorry. I'm used to Bobby's cop humor. I didn't mean that. But why
go to all the trouble of folding the clothes and leaving them in the
boat?"

I shrugged. "For her killer to buy time to disappear? So he could
confuse the police and let them think it was a suicide until they figured out differently?"

"Bobby wouldn't be fooled for long. No cop would." Kit's voice
was gentle. "I don't think Rebecca's alive, Luce, however it went
down. I'm sorry."

"She was a good swimmer. Maybe she got away."

"The Potomac. April. You know better."

I nodded and picked up my wine, staring into the glass. "I know."

Gilles reappeared to pour more wine and ask if everything was
all right. He left and we ate in silence.

"There's still something weird about the timing," Kit said, wiping up the sauce on her plate with the last piece of bread. "That hearing's coming up this week."

"Do you know anything about it?" I asked. "Some disgruntled out-of-work ex-analyst is going to try to poke Asher Investments and see if anything twitches. That's like me trying to poke someone in a suit of armor with this dinner fork."

"And just how would you happen to know all that? You're a regular font of information tonight."

"The cone of silence has not been raised."

"Tough crowd," she said. "Spill it."

"My dinner partner last night at the gala worked for the law firm representing Asher Investments."

"Dewey, Cheetham & Howe?" She chuckled at her little joke. "Sorry. Couldn't help it. So what did he say?"

"The guy's fishing with no worm on his line. He's got nothing."

"Maybe. Maybe not."

"I met him. I'd go with 'maybe not,' " I said.

"Met *who*?"

"Ian Philips. The star witness at the hearing. Dead drunk, looking like a couple of miles of bad road."

"Are you going to make me drag this out of you? Met him where, for God's sake?"

"At the Willard, after I got back from the gala. He was looking for Rebecca."

Her eyes grew big.

"They used to work together," I said.

"Holy cow." Her mouth fell open. "This gets more interesting by the minute. Were they supposed to meet?"

"I don't know. Ian said he'd heard from her. Apparently he tried to call her back a couple of times, but Rebecca never returned his calls. When I showed up at the hotel around eleven, he was trying to find out our room number. Thank God, the desk clerk refused to give it out. After that he tried to pick me up and wanted me to have a drink with him while we waited for Rebecca. Fortunately, a concierge came to my rescue."

"And the next morning—this morning—Rebecca's gone." Kit propped her elbow on the table and rested her chin on her hand.

"You think he could have gone off in search of her after he left you?"

"Anything's possible, I suppose. But she'd been missing all afternoon and evening. Where would he look—other than the hotel—and where was she?"

"Well, sometime last night she was down on the Potomac River," Kit said. "And she probably wasn't alone."

No, she probably wasn't.

But who was she with? And why had she been there?

CHAPTER 6

————— ∞∞∞ —————

We spoke no more about Rebecca, Ian Philips, or Tommy Asher for the rest of the meal. Kit ordered a slice of the Inn's legendary chocolate cheesecake for dessert—a sinfully decadent recipe concocted by my godfather—and a cappuccino. I had an espresso.

"You know, the next time we have dinner together, we ought to do it in D.C.," Kit said. "Party a little, go clubbing or something. You could spend the night at my apartment."

"Sure." I nodded. "Maybe sometime."

"I'm bowled over by your enthusiasm." She waved her fork at me like a conductor at a symphony. "You are becoming a crashing bore, and if you don't do something fun for a change, you're going to forget how."

"I don't know what you're talking about." I scowled at her. "What do you call the concerts and dinners and parties we have at the vineyard almost every weekend?"

"Work. And tasting wine in the barrel room at midnight with Quinn is not a date, either."

"That," I said, "is a low blow."

"I notice you didn't deny it." She swiped whipped cream off her cheesecake, closing her eyes as she ate. "This stuff is better than sex. Sure you don't want a taste before I wolf the rest of it down?"

"No, thanks. You look like you're having way too much fun. Go for it."

She helped herself to another bite. "Maybe you need to forget Quinn, Luce. Maybe it's time to move on."

I stared at the grounds in the bottom of my espresso cup.

"I'm sorry," she said. "None of my business."

"You want some advice?" I looked up. "Don't ever get personally involved with anyone you work with. It screws up everything."

She pushed away her plate and sighed. The only thing she hadn't done was lick it clean, though I knew she was tempted.

"I hate to see you so torn up over this," she said.

"I'll survive." I signaled Gilles for the bill. Kit reached for it, but I got it first. "My turn. You driving back to D.C. tomorrow morning?"

"I don't know. I'll see how I feel." All of a sudden she sounded defeated.

"What's wrong? You finally started telecommuting?"

"Nope." Her smile didn't make it to her eyes. "Guess you weren't following the news over the weekend or you would have heard. The *Trib* laid off twenty-six people—"

"Oh, God! Were you—?"

"Not this time."

"It's that bad?"

"It's worse than that bad. When the axe falls, it's inhuman. You get called to the boss's office, told you're fired, and by the time you get back to your desk, the moving boxes are there and you've got twenty minutes to clear out. Someone from security watches you the whole time so you don't take your Rolodex or your computer files. Then they escort you out of the building. You're on the street, unemployed, before you know what hit you."

"How can they do that? It's cruel!"

"I presume it's getting easier since this is the third round of layoffs," she said with heavy sarcasm as we both stood up. "The rest of us have to take two weeks of unpaid leave between now and the end of August. A furlough."

"Good Lord. It's already April."

"Don't remind me."

"Is there anything I can do?"

She slung her purse over her shoulder. "If you need help in the vineyard, I can recommend a bunch of people who might be available. Will work for wine. Will work for anything."

It sounded like she was serious.

"Sure," I said. "Just say the word. We can always use extra hands in the tasting room or out in the field."

"I'll pass that on," she said. "Maybe Dominique is hiring, too. I'll have to ask her. Wonder why she didn't stop by tonight."

"She's probably still dealing with that kitchen drama," I said.

But on our way out I spotted my cousin in the bar, her attention—and everyone else's in the room—riveted on a flat-screen television that usually featured some sporting event with the volume set on mute. This time, though, someone had turned on the sound. Dominique saw us in the doorway and gestured for us to join her.

We made our way through the crowded room as I heard the familiar voice of the Channel 3 news weekend anchor announcing the search for Rebecca as the top story. Except for the occasional clink of glasses and the background buzz of conversation from the adjacent dining rooms, the bar was hushed as the picture changed from the newsroom to a live shot of a good-looking young male reporter in front of the dock at Fletcher's. Bathed in the artificial brilliance of television lighting, he looked like he was on a movie set.

Kit muttered something about him that included the words "child" and "twerp" as Dominique leaned over from the bar stool she was sitting on and said in a low voice, "Isn't that missing woman your friend from school?"

I nodded. Like Kit, Dominique hadn't known where I'd been this weekend.

"It's awful," I said, and left it at that.

The picture cut to a provocative photograph of Rebecca in a low-cut turquoise evening dress, a teasing smile on her lips and promise in her eyes as she vamped for the photographer. Behind us someone gave a wolf whistle and a few people shushed him.

"Bet that's not her driver's license photo," Kit said in my ear. "She looks stunning."

There was footage from earlier in the day of the police boat on the Potomac as officers searched the riverbank and finally older films of Sir Thomas Asher, younger looking than when I saw him last night, presumably at his Manhattan office and then with his wife at the dedication of a pavilion bearing their name.

The camera cut back to the reporter. "Somewhere out there in the fast-moving waters of the Potomac River is the semiclothed body of a beautiful young woman whose life ought to have been ahead of her—and more questions than answers about Rebecca Natale."

"Did you see that smirk?" Kit asked. "He didn't have to say that. He's just hyping this story—"

"I'm trying to listen."

"Shhh!"

"Police have called off the search for this evening but plan to resume tomorrow at first light." He paused as the camera focused on the deserted boathouse. "Though they are starkly aware that they are running out of time before their efforts go from 'search and rescue' to 'search and recover.' Keep it here for the latest, and now back to you in the studio."

"Number one story and they gave it to that lightweight. He said diddly in that report," Kit said. "All he's got going for him is a permanent tan, hair gel, and a good orthodontist as a kid. I don't know why Channel 3 hasn't flushed him."

"Because he's cute," Dominique said. "Maybe he isn't the brightest cookie in the jar, but you just want to cuddle him."

Though my cousin had moved to the States more than a decade ago to look after my kid sister when our mother died, American idioms continued to baffle her. Somehow, though, she always made perfect sense.

"Unless you're a real journalist. Then you just want to stuff a sock in his mouth." Kit still sounded grumpy.

Dominique slid off her bar stool. "I need to find somebody. Be back in a minute."

He took her place before I realized he was there, placing his hands on my shoulders and leaning so close I could feel his breath on my neck.

"Fancy meeting you here, love. I haven't seen you for ages. Come here often?"

If I closed my eyes, the familiar scent of his cologne would haunt me with images I would be better off forgetting. Once upon a time Mick Dunne's aristocratic English charm, rakish good looks, and the passion with which he'd courted me had seduced me until I was dizzy with desire.

Not anymore.

I took a deep breath. "Only when I'm sure you won't be around."

Two years ago Mick floated out of my life into the arms of the daughter of an old family friend who happened to be an earl. Since then I'd become the sadder but wiser girl, avoiding him like he was contagious—though it hadn't always been easy. He happened to be my next-door neighbor and he'd planted thirty acres of grapes along our common property line. We had shared business interests, though that, too, seemed to be waning.

It had taken Mick three years to realize he could have skipped the expense and backbreaking labor of establishing a vineyard when all he really wanted was his name on a bottle of wine. For that he only needed to buy the labels and the wine from someone else. His real passion was horses—raising them, racing them, playing polo, or fox-hunting. His second was women, as I found out.

"Aw, come on, Lucie." His mouth was against my ear. "Give a bloke a break. Haven't you missed me?"

I wiggled away from him and removed his hands from my shoulders. "Like a bad habit I finally gave up."

Next to me, Kit cleared her throat.

"You remember my friend Kit Eastman?" I asked.

Mick lifted Kit's hand to his lips and kissed it. She turned scarlet.

"I never forget a beautiful woman. Lovely to see you again." He nodded in my direction. "Do you have any influence with this hussy? Think you could put in a good word or two for me?"

"Here's two words," I said. "Forget it."

I felt Kit's elbow discreetly in my ribs. "I'm sure I could have a little chat with her," she said. "See if she can fit you into her busy social whirl. Don't give up hope."

"We ought to be going," I said. "I'm sure I've got laundry to do at home."

Mick burst out laughing. "I've missed you, Lucie, I really have.

We need to get together again. Dinner or a drink, what do you say? I'll ring you."

"I have caller ID."

"Mick!" Dominique rejoined our group, a hint of wood smoke and the chill of the outdoors clinging to her clothes. "Have you heard from Simon? He's not answering his phone, but after what I saw on the news I'm sure the fan hit the roof and he's probably still in Washington."

Her cheeks were bright pink but I didn't think it was from the cold. Whoever Simon was, he was important enough to trade her standard work attire of black trousers and white blouse for a haute-couture outfit she bought on her last trip to Paris—caramel cashmere sweater with a sexy diagonal neckline, tobacco-colored wool skirt with a side slit, and a striking leather bow belt. She also wore more makeup than usual and there were new russet highlights in her spiky auburn hair.

"Speak of the devil," Mick said. "Look who just walked in."

My cousin looked radiant as a lean, wiry man with dark blond hair, the wind-burned skin of a sportsman, and sharp features that reminded me of a hawk strode across the room. He took her hand and kissed her cheek. I wouldn't have described him as handsome, but there was something mesmerizing in his quicksilver smile and the light in his eyes as he stared at my cousin. The look that passed between them, as though there were no one else in the room, sent a pang through my heart. Dominique was captivated.

"Sorry I'm late, darling," he said. "Mickey, old man, let me buy you a pint and some champagne for this beautiful lady."

An Englishman, like Mick. He drummed his fingers lightly on the bar and scanned the crowd as though he were searching for someone. His eyes fell on Kit and me. I heard Kit's sharp intake of breath, and Dominique suddenly seemed flustered.

"Simon, I'd like to introduce you to your cousin and my friend." She seemed oblivious to her garbled pronouns. "Lucie Montgomery, Kit Eastman. Meet Simon deWolfe."

"How do you do?" That dazzling smile again as his eyes, an unusual yellowish green, lingered on me. "Have we met before?"

"I don't think so," I said. "I'm sure I'd remember if we had."

"Please join us for a drink." He took the champagne flute from Mick and handed it to Dominique. Then he picked up his beer. "God, what a bloody awful day."

"Thank you just the same," Kit said, "but we were on our way out."

"Oh, come on, love. Just a quick one." Simon winked at her and smiled. "We won't keep you long. Promise."

Kit dug her elbow into my ribs again. "We really have to go. Don't we, Lucie?"

"Uh, yes. We do. Nice to meet you, Simon. Good-bye, Mick."

I kissed my cousin. "Call me," I said.

She murmured, "I meant to tell you about this. You could have knocked me over with a fender when I met him. I never expected to fall in love again."

"I'm happy for you," I said.

Eighteen months ago her fiancé had walked out on her after a messy affair. She'd thrown herself into her work, more than usual, trying to get over him and claiming she was done with men.

"Come on." Kit tugged my arm. "Let's get out of here."

We didn't speak until we reached the parking lot.

"You mind explaining what that was all about?" I asked.

"You were the one who couldn't wait to get away from Mick, remember?"

"I had my reasons. You were downright rude to Simon deWolfe," I said. "What's going on? Do you know him from somewhere?"

"Yeah, the news," she said. "Remember that comment your cousin made? Do you know who her new boyfriend is?"

"Obviously more than some friend of Mick's."

"Tommy Asher's half brother, that's who. He's the muscle guy for Asher Investments. Tommy takes care of him and keeps him on the payroll in return for Simon making sure he's protected at all times."

I stopped walking and stared at her. "What do you mean, 'muscle guy'?"

"Security. Protection. Keeping people Sir Thomas doesn't want around away. You know, shoo . . . scat . . . scram? That kind of protection. From what I hear, Simon's not someone you want to mess with if you get in his brother's face. That charm he was oozing in there is only skin deep. He can turn it off like that." She snapped her fingers. "Ask my colleague David Wildman."

Olivia Tarrant had said that her boss had "people" out looking for Rebecca last night. If Simon deWolfe handled security for his half brother, then that meant that he had been one of those people.

I thought of those hypnotic yellow green eyes and his captivating way with Dominique. I could easily imagine him flirting with Rebecca—and more. Had Simon deWolfe been with her before she vanished in the Potomac River? And did he know something about where she was now?

CHAPTER 7

⊶⊷

Monday morning's *Trib* ran a front-page article about Rebecca's disappearance that was nearly as lurid as the report on Channel 3 the evening before. Somewhere they found a gorgeous color photo of her flashing that siren smile and wearing a skin-tight knit top that hugged her like a lover. Next to her picture was another of a younger, unshaven Sir Thomas in Katmandu with a garland of marigolds around his neck as he posed before leaving for the Everest Base Camp, cocky and confident about the upcoming expedition to the summit. The article took up half a page below the fold and continued inside with more photos—Tommy and Mandy Asher at a hospital ribbon-cutting ceremony and aboard their yacht, the *Arbitrage,* hoisting drinks for the camera. The headline said it all: MYSTERIOUS DISAPPEARANCE OF TOP ADVISER TO BILLIONAIRE ADVENTURER & PHILANTHROPIST BAFFLES POLICE.

Still no direct reference to the missing Madison wine cooler Asher had intended to return to the White House today. I could imagine the lid the police and the Asher camp were keeping on that information and how much hell would break loose when it leaked out. Kit had kept her word; there was no hint of it in the *Trib.*

Reading about Rebecca, whose beauty, career, and personality had been thoroughly parsed along with theories about her disappearance, took away my appetite for breakfast. I dumped the eggs I'd made in the trash and finished my coffee as the phone rang. When the display showed Quinn's number, I answered before the second ring.

"I just got back a few hours ago," he said. "Frankie told me about your friend. I'm sorry, Lucie. You okay?"

Back from where? He hadn't mentioned a trip, though he knew I planned to be in D.C. Last winter, after three straight years of working flat out, we finally agreed to take weekends off to recharge our batteries before the season started in the spring. Besides, in one of my more brilliant career moves, I'd hired Frankie Merchant, a part-time employee who had become so indispensable we brought her on full-time to run the tasting room. Before long she took over planning our events calendar and asked for more staff to help as we grew busier. Quinn joked she was probably gunning for his job, maybe even mine. Truth was she could probably handle both of them with one hand tied behind her back.

Still, if either he or I left town, the other one was supposed to be available in case something came up in the barrel room or Frankie needed us. I wondered if Quinn's trip had been a last minute impulse and he'd decided that Antonio, our new farm manager, could handle things. If that was the case, he should have let me know he was taking off. I still ran the place.

"I'm all right," I said to him now. "Just trying to deal with everything. I didn't know you were going out of town. What happened? An emergency?"

"Nope. Just a trip."

A couple of his former girlfriends lived in the area. I had no idea whether he kept in touch with any of them or dropped by for an occasional visit. Though to be honest, I didn't want to know.

"I hate to bring up work when you've got so much on your mind," he said.

"Bring up anything. I'm going crazy."

"I want to start bench trials for the new Viognier," he said. "And we've got one barrel that smells funky."

"You mean our award-winning wine that just won the Governor's Cup?" I asked. "I crowed about it all weekend at that gala they hosted for the Ashers."

"I heard. We already had a call from Alison Jennings. She's going to stop by later and talk to you about it. Wants to order a couple of cases for some party. She specifically asked for you," he said.

"Oh." I had seen Alison the other night with Harlan, but we never managed to speak. Odd that she hadn't called me directly about the wine. "No problem. I'll be around."

"When are you coming over here? We'll start the trials as soon as you show up," he said.

"Give me ten minutes."

A bank of clouds hung in the sky like dingy laundry, obscuring the Blue Ridge and matching my mood as I drove over to the winery. Last night the temperature had dropped to one degree above freezing. Grapes could survive in the cold as long as the mercury didn't dip below thirty-two, but people were different. Rebecca's odds had grown exponentially bleaker after two nights outdoors with almost no clothing on—presuming she'd survived the river's currents. Still, miracles happened. Until they found her, I could keep hoping.

I walked into the barrel room and saw Quinn through the plate-glass window of our new laboratory. He was sitting at the workbench, probably figuring the ratios for the Viognier. Over the winter we'd modernized and upgraded this part of the winery, which hadn't changed since my parents built it twenty-one years ago. A brand-new catwalk ringed most of the Olympic-pool-sized room and we'd added a second-story loft where the new lab and an adjoining office were located. Originally we planned to build a staircase with landings between the two floors until Frankie found an antique wrought-iron spiral staircase at a marine salvage depot that fit perfectly and took up less space. The other option for reaching the loft was my favorite—the scissor lift, a kind of open-air elevator.

Quinn threw down his pencil as the lift reached the catwalk and I climbed out. He pushed his reading glasses up on his salt-and-pepper hair, which he'd let grow so that it now curled over the collar of his flannel shirt.

"I finished calculations for the first batch of trials." He squinted at his paperwork. "And we need to talk about that barrel of funky wine. It smells like your worst nightmare in high school chemistry lab."

We had only seven barrels of Viognier; three in brand-new French Allier oak that would give the wine a strong oak flavor and four in older American ones where the oak would be muted. We also had about five hundred gallons in a stainless-steel tank. One funky barrel was a lot of spoiled wine.

"Which barrel, new or old?"

"New."

"What if we just do nothing and see how it develops?" I asked.

"That's what you want, that's what we'll do."

"Pardon?"

"I said, whatever you want to do."

"You're joking, right?"

"Dead serious. Why?"

"I can't believe I'm saying this, but I think we ought to discuss it. We never agree on anything without an argument—sorry, discussion—first. What's going on?"

"Nothing. There's nothing to discuss. I happen to agree that a minimalist approach would be worth a try. It's no big deal." He gave me a wide-eyed look that I recognized as feigned nonchalance.

I leaned on my cane and waited as he shifted in his seat.

"You've come a long way in the last year," he said. "You're perfectly capable of making smart decisions without me weighing in."

Three years ago, shortly before my father was killed in a hunting accident, he hired Quinn. When Quinn and I finally met, he made it clear he thought that what his new young boss knew about winemaking and growing grapes could be written on the back of a postage stamp with room to spare. As for me, I wondered how to handle a mouthy winemaker with a macho personality who seemed better suited as a bouncer in a bar. A compliment from Quinn was the mountain coming to Muhammad—maybe the whole mountain range.

"Do you want something? A raise?" I asked. "Is that what this is all about?"

"Oh, for God's sake, stop reading into things. All I said was that you know what you're doing. Grab that plastic beaker and the bottle of SO_2." He pointed to a graduated cylinder and a spray bottle next to the sink. "I got the rest of the stuff."

I obeyed, but it felt like I was talking to a stranger. We took the lift down together in silence and I followed him into one of the bays as he flipped on the low-wattage lights. We generally kept this part of the barrel room completely dark since nothing kills wine faster than light, air, and bacteria. The sulfur dioxide spray was something new learned at a winemakers' conference a few months ago. By spraying the top of a barrel before we opened the bunghole—where most of the germs were located—we prevented bacteria spreading from one barrel to another.

He found the one he was looking for and used the SO_2. Then he took a wine thief and siphoned the liquid with his mouth. He released the straw-colored wine into the beaker and passed it to me. Our fingertips brushed and his eyes met mine.

His were opaque and unreadable, but I couldn't hide my confusion and misery. He pulled me close. "I'm trying to work out a few things. All I'm asking for is some time and space by myself. That's why I took off this weekend."

Working a few things out. Time and space by himself. I said things like that. Quinn, who thought real men worked out their problems with a bottle of Scotch or in a barroom with the guys, did not.

He kissed my hair and I leaned my head against his chest. "Are you talking about us?"

"I thought we'd backed off 'us.'" His voice was soft. "It got pretty intense for a while, remember?"

I didn't want to feel what I was feeling, didn't want to have this conversation right here, right now.

"We never talked about it," I said. "Backing off just kind of happened."

He didn't reply.

"So how long do you need?"

"Lucie—" he began.

Already I knew I was not going to like his reply, but before he could finish the winery telephone rang in the main part of the barrel room.

"I got it." I hated the relief in his voice at the reprieve.

I followed him into the other room. We weren't done yet. He

said, "Hey, Mick. Yeah, long time no see. Sure, she's right here.
Hang on."

He held out the cordless phone and said in a toneless voice, "It's
Mick Dunne."

"Thank you." I took the phone and tried to keep my expression
as deadpan as he was. "Hello, Mick."

"Morning, love. Just wanted to call to see how you're doing. I
was hoping you'd stick around a little longer last night at the Inn
once Simon showed up. Too bad your friend wanted to push off so
soon."

Quinn's mouth twitched. He'd heard that "love" and the mention of last night. I walked over to the row of stainless-steel tanks
where the humming of the cooling system and the gurgling of gly-
col moving through the tank jackets as it chilled the wine gave me
some privacy.

"I'm all right, thanks."

"Simon told me about your friendship with Rebecca Natale. I
didn't realize you'd been with her just before she disappeared. No
wonder you seemed so upset."

I probably shouldn't have been surprised that Simon deWolfe
knew about my relationship with Rebecca since he handled security
for his half brother. Had Olivia Tarrant told him? Who else in Sir
Thomas Asher's circle knew about the two of us?

"I hope they find her soon. I'm going crazy wondering what happened to her."

"Simon's in constant contact with the D.C. police while this is
going on. He'll probably be one of the first to know when something new develops. I promise I'll pass along anything I find out."

"You seem to know him quite well."

"Of course. We met through Tommy and Mandy," he said. "At
their place in West Palm. All of them come down every year for
winter polo. We used to party together when I was living there."

Before Mick moved to Virginia, he owned a pharmaceutical
company in Florida that he sold for a bundle of money after growing bored with it. I had sensed that same restlessness and what
seemed like an incessant need for a new distraction when we were
seeing each other. It wasn't long before he moved on from me to

the earl's daughter. That's when I'd realized it was only a matter of time before he tired of his life in Virginia as well and left for the next adventure. With Mick the future was an ever-shifting horizon.

"So you've known Simon for a while?" I asked.

"Yeah, we're mates. We go hunting together. Now that he's buying a house here I expect I'll see more of him."

So Simon deWolfe was a hunter, too.

"Look, I was serious last night about dinner," Mick went on. "I know you may not be up for it with what's just happened, but why don't I call back in a day or two? I need to see you, Lucie. You know I'm not going to stop asking until you say yes."

He'd said "need." What was going on? "Mick—"

"I mean it."

"Okay," I said. "But give me a couple of days."

"Whatever you want."

I disconnected and I walked over to the long pine table we used for winemaker's dinners. Quinn pulled out a chair for me.

"You all right?" He took the seat next to mine.

"Fine. Why?"

"No reason. Here, try this." He pushed a glass of wine over to me.

"Mick knows the Ashers," I said. "Kit and I ran into him last night at the Inn with a guy called Simon deWolfe. Turns out he's Sir Thomas's brother. Half brother, actually. Mick just wanted to see how I was holding up with all the news about Rebecca."

"Nice of him to look out for you. You don't owe me an explanation, Lucie. Mick's a good guy."

I took a deep breath. "It's not what you're thinking."

"I'm thinking a friend called to comfort you on a tragedy involving another friend. Is it something more than that?"

"No."

"Okay, then. Bottoms up."

I swirled the wine, then held the glass to my nose before I drank. He did the same. Back to business. Fine by me.

"It's okay," I said. "Good nose, smooth finish."

"It's a fifty-fifty blend from the barrel with the South African yeast and the wine in the tank with the American strain."

It was the blend we used for the Viognier that won the Governor's Cup.

"This time around it doesn't taste like wine that would win a prize," I said. "It's good but not fabulous."

"That's why we're doing trials." He shrugged. "Okay, how about the same ratio with the Rhone strain?"

"All right. Or maybe a different ratio of South African to American."

"Sure. Sit tight and I'll get it."

He disappeared into the bay like a shadow vanishing into the night, and I felt as though a glass curtain had descended between us. He was shutting me out of whatever was really going on in his life. I didn't know whether to be hurt or angry or both.

A phone rang, but this time it was my cell. A Washington, D.C., number, no caller ID.

"I'm looking for Lucie Montgomery." The male voice sounded familiar, but I couldn't place it.

"Speaking."

"Detective Horne here."

I licked my lips and tasted Viognier. The road to hell. "You found Rebecca?"

"I'm afraid not, but we've located her purse and ID. We've also got a person of interest temporarily in custody." Horne still sounded beat and I wondered how much sleep he'd gotten since I saw him yesterday. "A homeless guy living down in the woods by the river. A pawnshop owner in Georgetown called nine-one-one when he showed up trying to sell that wine cooler you told us about. And some jewelry. Can you describe what she was wearing?"

I did. Then I said, "Do you think this man killed Rebecca?"

Horne snorted. "He said he didn't. He claims some dude showed up in his tent and just gave him all her stuff. Told him to sell it and use the cash for food and a warm place to stay. It was like Robin Hood stopped by."

Rebecca still missing and someone giving away a priceless antique and her jewelry? No way. "Do you believe that?"

He sighed. "Like I told you, I don't discount anything. Sometimes the most bizarre thing you hear turns out to be what really happened. Look, did Ms. Natale mention meeting anyone once she picked up that package for her boss? A man, maybe? A date with anyone?"

"No. No one."

"All right. Thanks for your time."

"Before you go," I said. "Are you looking for this other person? Robin Hood?"

"We'll follow up," he said. "If he exists. But to tell you the truth, the number one person I'm looking for is Rebecca Natale. I got her clothes, her jewelry, and that wine holder. What I don't have is a body."

CHAPTER 8

Quinn and I went our separate ways after the bench trials. He took one of the all-terrain vehicles out to the vineyard, saying he needed to check some trellises, and I pretended to believe him. If one wanted time and space, a good place to find it was the churchlike solitude of acres of bare vines where the only sounds were the whistling wind and the sweet cries of the first birds of spring.

I, on the other hand, sought company that I knew I'd find in the ivy-covered villa my mother had designed for our tasting room. Last fall after harvest, Frankie had planted winter pansies in the halved wine barrels that lined the courtyard portico between the barrel room and the villa. As I walked along the portico I deadheaded white, yellow, and plum-colored blossoms to distract me from thinking about a winemaker who wanted to get lost and a friend who hadn't been found.

More pansies—lilac and white—bloomed in the border gardens around the villa. A straw basket with gardening tools sat by the door next to a tidy pile of weeds. Frankie must have been cleaning the beds and decided to take a break. I called to her as I walked inside the airy, light-filled room and felt the familiar heart tug as I thought of my mother who had chosen this place for her winery because of its breathtaking view of the vineyard framed by the layered Blue Ridge Mountains.

The room still bore the unmistakable stamp of her style and

flair—her oil paintings of the vineyard on the walls, the cheery Pro-
vençal fabrics she loved on the sofas and chairs, and the brilliantly
hued Turkish carpets brought from my grandparents' home in
France. Frankie wasn't here, nor was she in the small galley kitchen.
I found her in my office, pink cheeked and mud spattered, perched
on the edge of my desk watching television, her garden gloves in a
heap on the floor.

"Hope you don't mind." She twisted her blond windblown hair
into a knot and stuck a pencil through it. "A friend called to tell me
to turn on CNN so I came inside. The D.C. police are holding a
press conference about an antique silver wine cooler that belonged
to James Madison. They said Rebecca Natale had it with her when
she went missing and that Sir Thomas Asher was supposed to return
it to the White House today."

So the news about the wine cooler finally leaked out.

"When did the press conference start?" I asked.

"About five minutes ago. Look, there's Asher and his wife next
to the mayor and the chief of police. She looks really upset, but he
seems like he's handling it pretty well."

I threw myself into my desk chair and stared at the screen as the
D.C. police chief, the mayor, and Tommy Asher answered questions
ranging from serious to borderline lewd asked by a packed room of
reporters and photographers. Frankie was right. Miranda Asher, pale
and ghostlike, looked as though she hadn't slept much recently, but
her grim-faced husband answered questions put to him with calm
stoicism. Detective Horne was there, too. He must have called me
from that auditorium.

"Boy, Asher is like the Rock of Gibraltar," Frankie said.

"Isn't he?"

As the press conference wore on, the questions kept coming back
to an almost prurient interest in Rebecca's clothing found folded in
the rowboat and the fact that she was now nearly nude. The subject
of rape was raised and someone else asked about a possible sexual
ritual. The mayor and the chief exchanged glances, and it seemed
clear neither he nor she wanted to go down the kinky road. Instead,
the chief brought up the man Horne had referred to as Robin Hood.

"We're asking for the public's help in locating this individual," she said. "Sir Thomas Asher has generously pledged a one-hundred-thousand-dollar reward to be paid to the person or persons who provide information leading to an arrest and conviction in this case."

There was another barrage of questions about Robin Hood and how much longer the search for Rebecca would go on.

"Thanks, folks," the mayor said. "I think we've worn this subject out. This is all we have for you now."

The chief and the mayor drifted away from the podium as one last question concerning the stolen wine cooler and referring to the British soldier who took it as a thief was picked up by a live microphone. Sir Thomas Asher, on his way out the door, turned and strode across the room to the podium.

"Who asked that question? Who referred to that British soldier as a thief?" His mouth was a thin, angry line. "Identify yourself please."

"Boy, somebody pushed his hot button," Frankie said.

The press room was as silent as death. A hand finally went up in the crowd and the camera panned to a familiar face.

"Oh, God, it's that reporter from Channel 3 who was down on the river last night," I said. "Kit thinks he's a jerk."

"I'd hate to be in his shoes," Frankie said. "Look at Asher. Like a volcano about to go off."

"Shh . . . listen."

"My wife and I have donated millions of dollars to charity in this country and around the world." Asher's clipped British voice was calm, but there was no mistaking his outrage. "Next week we plan to give the Library of Congress one of the largest gifts in its history, outside of the Jefferson library and the Lessing Rosenwald rare book collection. That anyone should question my integrity and the integrity of my family is personally offensive. The Madison wine cooler will be returned to the White House as soon as the police release it from evidence. I hasten to add that I had no idea it was in my family's possession, no clue about its provenance, until Dr. Alison Jennings, a historian who works with me, discovered it and did some investigating. Had I known what it was, it would have been returned long ago. I find the word 'thief' insulting and reprobate, and I expect an apology from your network, sir."

He turned abruptly and left the room as the place erupted. A moment later the picture flashed to the shell-shocked reporter. I picked up the remote and hit the mute button.

"Now I know why they call him 'Tommy the Barracuda,'" Frankie said. "He ate that kid for lunch."

"If he'd let it go, no one would have focused on it," I said. "Why didn't he ignore it? Now it's going to be a story of its own."

"Probably because the kid hit a nerve." Frankie bent and picked up her gloves. "That'd be my guess."

"Well, his ancestor did steal the wine cooler," I said. "He didn't borrow it for two centuries. I don't think Channel 3 owes him an apology at all."

"He's probably pretty strung out over this whole thing with Rebecca," Frankie said. "And lost his cool. It happens."

A bell went off in the hallway outside my office.

"We've got company," Frankie said. "I'll see who it is."

She was back a moment later. "Ali Jennings wants to see you. Someone else who looks kind of strung out, if you ask me."

"A lot of that going around." I stood up. "I think she's here about wine."

I found Alison Jennings outside on the terrace with her back to me and gripping the railing so tight her knuckles showed white. I didn't know her as well as I knew Harlan, though our paths crossed occasionally at parties, community events, or the Middleburg shops. It was known around town that she was the rock of her family, devoting herself to her twin sons after Harlan lost his Senate seat and more or less moved to their Georgetown pied-à-terre so he could build a client list for his new consulting firm. It was Alison who made the long commute to her university job in D.C., coming home each evening to supervise homework, cheer the boys at sporting events, and bake cookies for their school fund-raisers. After the twins left for boarding school, her life increasingly revolved around her teaching and research, but she still remained Middleburg based. I'd heard from Mick that she'd taken up foxhunting again, riding with the Goose Creek Hunt. People said she was a crack shot.

"Alison?"

She turned around. Frankie wasn't kidding. I'd never seen Ali Jennings look anything but smart and pulled together, even if she were only picking up a quart of milk at Safeway. Today without makeup she looked haggard, as though she had aged years since Saturday night. Her beautiful red hair, pulled into an unflattering ponytail, betrayed that she was overdue for an appointment with her colorist and her riding clothes were dingy and shapeless.

"Can I get you something?" I asked. "Coffee? A glass of water? Wine?"

"Maybe a glass of water. I've got a fierce headache."

"Come on." I held one of the terrace doors open. "Let's go inside. You're shivering. By the way, I heard the police found the Madison wine cooler. Sir Thomas mentioned your name at a press conference just now."

Her smile was forced as she followed me into the tasting room and sat down on one of the bar stools. "Did he?"

I slid the glass of water and a bottle of ibuprofen across the bar. "Try this. Are you feeling all right? You could have just called me about the wine, you know."

"Thanks, but I thought it would be better to do this in person." She held the glass with both hands. "The wine is for Harlan's birthday party next week. A surprise, or at least I hope it is, so please don't mention it to him. I thought I'd get two cases of your Viognier. He said you raved about it the other night."

I smiled. "It won the Governor's Cup. I didn't know his birthday was coming up."

"I'm having the party out here, so I need to figure a way to lure him from our place in Georgetown." Her voice seemed to waver. "He spends so much time there now."

"I'm a little surprised you aren't spending more time in Georgetown yourself now that the boys are gone," I said. "I'd forgotten what a commute it is from Middleburg until I drove to D.C. last weekend. It wasn't even rush hour—"

The pain in Alison's eyes stopped me. Sometimes I should just keep my mouth shut. What had I missed? Were there problems between her and Harlan?

"It's the horses. I stay out here for them."

"Of course. I forgot about the horses."

"I saw you at the gala. Talking to Harlan."

Surely she wasn't hinting about something between her husband and me? I looked her directly in the eyes. "Yes, that's right. The only familiar face in the crowd."

"Except for Rebecca Natale, if she'd been there." Her voice grew harsh. "I didn't know you were old friends from college, Lucie. She's the one who invited you the other night, isn't that right?"

It sounded like an accusation.

"Yes," I said, "it is. What's wrong, Ali?"

Alison drained her glass and set it down on the bar.

"When you and she were at school together, Rebecca had an affair with the husband of a colleague who happens to be my best friend. Jill O'Brien." She brushed a tendril of hair off her face with a swift flick of her hand. "She's Jill Walsh now and she teaches in the history department with me at Georgetown. I'm sure you knew all the sordid details of what happened with Rebecca since the two of you were such good friends. Jill said it was the talk of the campus for months."

So that explained why Alison was here in person.

"I tried to ignore the gossip and, believe it or not, Rebecca and I never spoke about it," I said. "I'm sorry. I had no idea it involved a friend of yours."

"Jill called her a scheming little vixen. Lured poor Connor into the affair and then threatened to expose him if he didn't continue to see her."

She folded her arms and waited for my reply. Ali was sure it was all Rebecca's fault. But Connor's dedication to Rebecca in the volume of Pope's poetry hadn't exactly read like an older man pushed unwillingly into a relationship with a beautiful coed. Then there was Rebecca's remark the other day about no one giving a damn what Connor had done to her.

"I'm sure there are two sides to every story. Even this one."

"Rebecca destroyed their marriage. What other side could there be?"

Ali banged her hand on the counter. Something else was going on here that I was missing. Then she filled in the blanks.

"I suppose you've been seeing her when she came to D.C. on all those so-called business trips?"

"All what so-called business trips?"

"Come on, Lucie. I know about it, so you don't have to pretend, okay? Rebecca's been traveling to Washington every few weeks because Tommy manages a couple of Harlan's funds." Her voice wavered. "Jill warned me what might happen."

I got it now. Harlan and Rebecca.

I opened the small wine refrigerator under the bar and found a half-full bottle of Viognier, splashing it into two glasses. It wouldn't do much for her headache, but it was her heart that really hurt.

"I had no idea." I set one of the glasses in front of her. "Honest to God. The first time I saw Rebecca since she graduated twelve years ago was last Saturday. Were Harlan and Rebecca . . . seeing each other?"

Alison threw back her head and drank. Her eyes were anguished.

"A quaint way to refer to an affair," she said. "Yes, they were."

"How did you find out?"

"The usual. A note in the pocket of his suit trousers when I was sending it to the cleaners. I still take care of his dry cleaning. So stupid, isn't it?" she said. "I confronted him and he told me he'd ended it. The note I'd found, about meeting her, was to break it off."

"Did he?"

"Of course. He gave his word." Alison set her glass down for a refill. "Unfortunately, Rebecca called Harlan Saturday afternoon after she picked up the Madison silver and said she had to see him. Said it was urgent, a matter of life or death. Could he come get her in Georgetown so they could talk? He went to meet her and she told him she wanted to go back to our place."

"What happened?" I asked.

Alison shrugged. "Harlan says she clammed up as soon as she walked through the door. Wanted a drink so he gave her one. Only one. Then he told her she had to go. He tried to call a cab for her, but she wouldn't hear of it."

"What did she want to talk about?"

"He has no idea." She took a long swallow of wine. "Now he feels like he should have pushed harder, made her talk about what was bothering her. He feels responsible for what happened to her."

I drank my wine, trying to recall the time line Saturday afternoon after Rebecca left me at the Vietnam Veterans Memorial. According to Olivia Tarrant, Rebecca's cab driver said he dropped her off in Georgetown and thought she was waiting for someone. He'd been right: Harlan. But then where did she go after she left the Jenningses' Georgetown home?

As though she read my mind, Alison said, "After Rebecca left, that's the last time Harlan saw her. She told him she wanted to walk for a while and clear her head."

"Do the police know that?"

She laughed. I couldn't tell if it was derision or hysteria.

"Do they know? Oh, you bet they know. They've been to the Georgetown house and searched it with tweezers and a microscope. My God, there was nothing too minute that didn't fascinate those evidence people. Wait until word gets out about this."

"But if nothing happened and Rebecca left—"

"Harlan had to tell them about the affair, Lucie. He wasn't going to lie about that, even if—" She looked into her glass.

"Even if it gave him a motive for murder?" I said.

She pressed her lips together. Her expression was bleak.

"Do you have any idea where she went after she left our place? Did she say anything, drop any hint? Please, if you know anything . . ."

I shook my head, and the light drained out of her eyes.

"The police have been all over that with me, Ali. I wish I could help you, but to be honest, I'm still trying to work out why Rebecca called me out of the blue and wanted to get together. That doesn't make sense, either."

"Without something concrete for the police to go on, it's Harlan's word against no one's that she left our place that afternoon. It's like she vanished into the ether. Except for her clothes in that boat and this Robin Hood, or whoever he is, who handed over her things to that homeless man."

"Have the police charged Harlan with anything?"

"They brought him in for questioning and then released him.

Apparently he's not considered a flight risk." She drank some more wine. "But they believe he had motive and opportunity."

"He didn't do anything, Ali."

"Of course he didn't. It's too ridiculous to even consider."

I thought about Harlan joking with me at the gala, his little kiss, our banter about his election campaign, and his wistful interest in watching a sunset at the vineyard with Alison. There was no way he was so cold-blooded and calculating that he would show up at a party hours after killing an ex-lover, flirting and acting like he didn't have a care in the world. At least I couldn't believe he was capable of doing so—even though his story sounded a little far-fetched. I wondered if Ali thought it did as well but didn't want to admit it. Though I did believe there was more to what had gone on between Harlan and Rebecca than what he'd told his wife or the police.

I wondered what Harlan was covering up. I also wondered if Rebecca were alive or dead—and if Harlan knew something about that, too.

CHAPTER 9

Frankie showed up in the tasting room as Alison finished paying me for the Viognier for Harlan's party. Her eyes flitted between the two of us as I handed Ali her credit card.

"How are the boys, Ali? I don't see you so often anymore now that our kids aren't together at school." She smiled her serene smile, ignoring the gloomy fug that hung in the air.

Frankie was the person you wanted on your side in a hostage crisis or a nuclear standoff because she could defuse tension in a room faster than anyone else I knew. It was an inside joke among the tasting room staff that she heard more confessions than the priests at St. Stephen's in Middleburg—from both customers and employees. Everyone talked to her, trusting the compassion in those clear blue eyes.

Alison seemed to brighten. "They're doing great. Boarding school agrees with them. How about yours?"

"Looking at colleges. Can't believe we'll be paying double tuition soon."

"I know what you mean. We're so blessed my father-in-law invested in blue chips way back when and that Harlan inherited his dad's good head about money," she said. "Speaking of money and investing, did I hear that Quinn is looking to buy some farmland?"

Ali was looking directly at me. I saw Frankie's imperceptible nod out of the corner of my eye.

"Why, yes, he is," I said. "What makes you ask?"

"Harlan and I have some acreage we'd like to sell," she said. "To the right buyer. It's adjacent to our property, so we'd like the new owner to continue to use it for agriculture—cattle, horses, farming. If Quinn's planning to put in a vineyard, that would be even better."

Frankie closed her eyes slowly and opened them. Another yes.

"That's his plan," I said.

"Terrific. I'll talk to Harlan and make sure he gets in touch with Quinn."

The moment the door closed behind Alison, I said to Frankie, "How long have you known about Quinn looking for land?"

"Lucie, calm down."

"I am calm."

She pulled out a bar stool for me.

"Sure you are," she said. "I can tell. Look, I found out over the weekend. A couple of the Romeos dropped by for a drink just as we were closing yesterday. I'm not sure how they heard about it, but it's obviously no secret if Ali knows."

"Quinn probably dropped a hint someone overheard and brought up over morning coffee at the General Store," I said. "Meaning Thelma found out and told her partners in crime, the Romeos. Which is why everyone knows about it from here to Richmond—except me."

The Romeos, whose name stood for Retired Old Men Eating Out, were the second worst source of gossip in Atoka after Thelma Johnson, who owned the General Store. Between them they vacuumed up every scrap of news—real or imagined—and then spread it to the four corners of the county and beyond.

"You were out of town," Frankie said.

"Why didn't he tell me?"

"Maybe he was trying to find the right time."

"I knew he inherited some money from his mother after she passed away, but it wasn't a lot," I said. "How's he going to finance something like this?"

There's a sad-but-true saying among vineyard owners that the fastest way to make a small fortune growing grapes and selling wine is to start with a large one. Quinn, as near as I knew, didn't even have a small fortune.

"Maybe he's got a couple of partners who are willing to invest with him."

I nodded, stunned. "He always said he wanted his own place. I guess I thought we'd combine forces. It would be something we'd do together."

"Oh, Lucie." Frankie's eyes were full of sympathy. "Don't beat yourself up over this. You know Quinn and how ambitious he is. It's sort of a natural progression, don't you think?"

Maybe she was right. Maybe it was, but I hadn't wanted to see it.

"Sure. Of course it is. Hey, thanks for telling me. At least I found out from you and not the Romeos or Thelma. That would be gossip fodder for a month of Sundays."

"He'll tell you himself, you wait and see." She picked up her gardening gloves and patted me on the shoulder. "Guess I'd better get back to those beds. Are you going to be all right? When I came into the room, Ali looked like hell and you didn't look much better."

I stood up and went behind the bar. "You know something about that, too?"

"Not directly, but I can add two and two. Mac Macdonald was one of the Romeos who came in for a drink," she said. "You know how close he is to his money. Made sure I wouldn't charge him for a glass of water before he drank it."

Mac was a teetotaler and a querulous old dear who owned an upscale antiques store in Middleburg. One of my parents' oldest friends, his penny-pinching went beyond zealousness. If anyone were going to figure out a way to take it all to the eternal reward that awaited in the afterlife, it would be Mac.

"He'll never change," I said.

"Did you know Harlan Jennings manages his portfolio?"

"No," I said. "I didn't. I thought Mac kept his money in his mattress."

"Apparently he goes to D.C. regular as clockwork to check up on how his investments are doing." Frankie gave me a significant look. "He bumped into your friend Rebecca a couple of times. Thought she worked as a secretary for Harlan, who never disabused him of the idea. Then he saw her picture on the news and found out she was Sir Thomas Asher's golden girl. So he wondered why Harlan didn't explain who she really was."

"Is there something you're trying to say?" I asked. "Or not say?"

"Okay," she said. "You asked. Ali's got a lot of friends who think she got a raw deal when Harlan abdicated his responsibilities out here and moved to town. All that nonsense about needing to be in Washington because that's where his clients are. Please!" She waved a hand like she was shooing a pesky fly. "As if she doesn't make that same drive every day. She loves Harlan so much she's blind to . . . well, let's just leave it at blind."

"She's not blind. But she does love him more than anything else in the world." I thought of the surprise party she was planning, even after the tawdry situation Harlan had dragged her into over Rebecca.

Frankie traced a finger around a cabbage rose on one of her gloves. "Ali would go to the ends of the earth for him or the boys. You're right about that."

She went outside, leaving me to mull over what she'd said. Just how far would Alison Jennings go to protect Harlan? What would she do to preserve her marriage and his upstanding reputation in the community?

She'd been in Washington on Saturday, arriving late to the gala— plus she would have realized Rebecca would be in town for such an important event honoring her boss. An athlete and a good shot, Ali was probably strong enough to take on Rebecca if she needed to do so. How hard would it have been to find out from her historian colleague that Rebecca planned to drop by earlier in the day to pick up the Madison wine cooler?

And of course, Alison already knew about the affair.

The police had questioned Harlan about Rebecca's disappearance. But so far, it seemed no one suspected his wife. Was she setting things up to protect herself?

Had Ali just played me to cover up a murder—that she'd committed?

On Tuesday morning, my cell phone rang as I was pouring a cup of coffee in the galley kitchen in the villa. Another D.C. number, but I didn't recognize this one.

"Who is this?" a male voice asked when I answered.

"You called me. Why don't you go first?"

"Don't I know you?" he said. "I'm sure I do."

I disconnected and dropped the phone on the counter as though he could detect my location if I held on to it. He called back twice. Each time I let the call go to voice mail, but he never left a message. Was it a prank caller? Persistent wrong number?

Shortly before noon, Frankie showed up in my office with the mail. "You might want to take a look at this. I wasn't snooping, but I couldn't help noticing it when I was sorting through everything."

She set a postcard in front of me. The Lincoln Memorial at night.

"It's from Rebecca," I said. "Postmarked yesterday. I don't believe this. She's *alive*."

There was no mistaking Rebecca's sprawling handwriting: *"To err is human, to forgive divine."* And a phone number.

"She bought this postcard when we were together on Saturday," I said. "In fact, she bought several. All the same. She made a point of showing them to me."

"Is that her phone number?" Frankie asked.

"No." I picked up my phone and scrolled through the calls. "It belongs to this guy, whoever he is. He called me three times. I bet he got a postcard with my number on it."

Frankie sat down in a red-and-white flame-stitched wing chair across from me and folded her arms across her chest.

"Do you know who he is? What's going on? And what's up with the Shakespeare quote?"

"I don't think it's Shakespeare. I bet it's Alexander Pope." I ran my thumb over the postmark. "It was mailed yesterday in Georgetown. What do you bet Rebecca's alive and hiding somewhere?"

"It was *postmarked* yesterday. She could have dropped it in a mailbox on Saturday knowing it wouldn't get picked up until Monday. Maybe it was sort of insurance in case anything happened to her— which it did." Frankie's forehead creased with worry. "What are you going to do? Whatever's going on, it's getting dangerous."

"I'm going to call the guy who has been calling me and find out what he wants. He didn't know who I was—and I didn't know who he was until I got this." I tapped the postcard and picked up my phone. "Rebecca sent these for a reason. I need to meet him and find out why and what happened to her."

He answered in the middle of the second ring. "You finally decided to return my call, did you?"

"I got a postcard, too," I said. "What does yours say, besides my telephone number?"

I heard a long expelled breath on his end. "'Fools rush in where angels fear to tread.' That's Alexander—"

"Pope. Mine says, 'To err is human, to forgive divine,'" I said. "You're Ian Philips, aren't you?"

"And you're Rebecca's college friend. Lucie Martin."

"Close enough. Montgomery."

"I think we should talk," he said.

"Where's Rebecca?"

"Somewhere in the Potomac River. Haven't you been watching the news?"

"What if she's not?" I said. "I was with her when she bought these postcards on Saturday just before she disappeared. She planned to send them to us. I'm sure of it."

"I'm not following you."

"She's setting up something—actually, she's setting us up for something. What if she faked her death and vanished?"

Frankie's eyebrows went up and I shrugged. Wasn't it possible, as the woman at Fletcher's had suggested? An image of Rebecca, laughing her head off drinking a latte in some exotic café, popped into my head. Right now, it seemed as plausible as any other explanation.

"I don't think so," he said. "I think she sent these as backup, in case anything happened to her."

"You mean as insurance?" I said as Frankie nodded her head and mouthed "yes."

"Exactly. Look, I don't think we ought to continue to discuss this over the phone. How'd you like to take a walk around the Tidal Basin and enjoy the cherry blossoms? They're nearly at their peak today."

I looked at Frankie, whose normally untroubled face was lined with concern. Whatever was going on, I wanted to keep it as far away from the vineyard as possible.

"I can be in Washington by two. Where should we meet?"

"You know the FDR Memorial?"

"It's huge. Spans Roosevelt's life and the entire three-term presidency."

"Since you obviously know it, how about meeting me at the blocks? I'm sure you know what I'm talking about."

A set of what looked like life-sized child's building blocks hewn out of granite. I knew what was carved on them. Roosevelt had initially tried to remain neutral during World War II, but the Japanese attack on Pearl Harbor provoked America into finally entering the war.

"I hate war," I said. "Those blocks?"

"See you there," he said and hung up.

CHAPTER 10

I recognized Ian Philips leaning against the "I Hate" block when I showed up at the FDR Memorial. Unshaven, wearing faded jeans, an untucked shirt, a leather jacket, and the same knotted Burberry scarf he had on the other night, he had an impressive-looking Nikon digital SLR slung over his shoulder. A cigarette hung out of a corner of his mouth.

He straightened up when he saw me and blew a smoke ring. "We meet again."

"Yes, we do."

He pointed to my cane. "I didn't know about that. You weren't using it the other night."

"Don't worry, I have it on a leash. It won't bite."

He was right about not seeing it on Saturday. I'd forgotten it in the hotel suite in my rush to leave when Olivia Tarrant offered me a lift. In fact, I'd needed it less than I'd expected that evening at the gala—which had been a pleasant surprise.

He looked startled before his face broke into a smile. "Good, because I don't have all my shots."

I leaned against the block with "War" carved into it. "You ought to do something about that."

He took another long drag on his cigarette. "Kidding aside, would you rather just stay here instead of walking around the Tidal Basin?"

"No," I said. "I wouldn't. Would you?"

He drew his head back as though he were reassessing me.

"I can see why you're a friend of Rebecca's." It sounded like a compliment. "Okay, then let's go. How'd you end up needing a cane, if you don't mind my asking?"

"A boyfriend drove into a stone wall one night in the rain. I was in the passenger seat."

"That's rough." He dropped his cigarette and squashed the butt under the toe of a highly polished brown oxford. "You bring your postcard?"

I took it out of my purse. "Where's yours?"

He picked up the butt and flung it in a trash can. His postcard was in the back pocket of his jeans. He pulled it out so we could compare. Same bold scrawl, same bright green gel pen.

"Anybody follow you here?" he asked.

For a moment I thought he was joking. He wasn't.

"I don't think so. Is somebody following you?"

"I haven't spotted anyone. But I have gotten a few warnings, so I figure it's possible someone's watching me."

I caught my breath. "What kind of warnings?"

He took my arm. "Try not to look like you've come to drop off the ransom money for the kidnapper." He gave my hand a light squeeze. "We're here to enjoy the cherry blossoms, okay?"

"Sure."

We walked down a couple of stairs. As sobering and surreal as this meeting was, it was hard not to be enchanted by the lovely tableau of thousands of pink-blooming trees framing the Washington Monument and the Jefferson Memorial as we joined the slow-moving crowd navigating around the Tidal Basin. The afternoon sun glinted off the water, reflecting an azure sky and pale pink flowers that Monet would have painted. The statue of Thomas Jefferson limned by sunlight slanting through the memorial columns reminded me of a relief on a bronze coin.

Ian and I turned left so that we took the long way around to the Jefferson Memorial, blending into the sea of tourists, lovers, and amateur photographers. I buttoned my coat and turned up the collar as a raw wind gusted off the water. He reached in his jacket pocket and took out a balled-up navy blue knitted cap, pulling it over his reddish-blond hair.

"What kind of warnings have you gotten?" I asked again.

He raised his camera and aimed it across the water, firing off a few shots. "Phone calls I can't trace. Someone waiting on the other end until I finally hang up. They usually call around two or three in the morning."

"Have you told the police?"

He shrugged. "That I've got a heavy breather calling? Nah, what could they do?"

"If someone's following you, they won't want to be photographed."

"You catch on fast. Keep an eye out, will you?"

He panned the crowd and snapped more pictures. "Smile," he said to me. "Pretend we're having a good time."

I obeyed, trying not to grimace. "How come you don't believe Rebecca is alive? Or that she didn't set up this meeting between us like some offstage puppeteer?"

His camera continued to whir as he shifted his lens to the Washington Monument, framed between two gracefully arched branches heavy with cherry blossoms.

"I didn't say she couldn't be alive or couldn't have orchestrated us getting together," he said. "But she may have underestimated the people who don't want me to testify. I don't plan to make a similar mistake. You're very photogenic, by the way."

I ignored that. "You said people. Are you talking about Sir Thomas?"

"I'm not talking about the tooth fairy. Sir Thomas is one of them."

"Who else?"

We resumed our stroll. I had forgotten there was no safety railing between the path and the Tidal Basin so that it was possible to lose one's footing or be jostled, ending up in the water. Ian slipped behind me and maneuvered himself so he was closer to the edge.

"A lot of people have a vested interest in me keeping my yap shut," he said. "They need the rest of the world to think everything's hunky-dory at Asher Investments when it's not. The company uses feeder funds that his investors don't know about as a source of cash for his own funds. Asher keeps quiet about it, but it's made a bunch of small-time investors very rich and their clients superhappy. If only they knew his numbers are bogus. The guy's faking it."

"Come on, who would fall for that in the post-Madoff era?" I asked. "Everyone has wised up."

Ian stopped walking and snapped a few more shots of me. "An endangered species," he said. "I need to take a picture. Are you really that naïve? Catching one slimeball doesn't put an end to greed, sweetheart. There are plenty more where he came from. Think P. T. Barnum, not Barney the purple dinosaur."

"Knock off the sarcasm, okay?" I said. "I didn't say it couldn't happen anymore. All I mean is that maybe it's a lot less likely to happen right now."

"Open your eyes, baby. Tommy Asher's got deep pockets and people like Harlan Jennings watching his back here in D.C. You went to that suck-up gala the other night. Surely you don't need me to spell it out for you?"

"All right, then, what are you going to tell that Senate subcommittee when you testify? You have proof to back all this up?"

He pulled down a low-hanging branch full of blossoms. "These really are pretty, aren't they? Like pink snowballs."

"You didn't answer my question."

"As it happens, I don't have ironclad proof." He released the branch. "More like a case of 'where there's smoke, there's fire.' "

Meaning he had nothing. Two days before he testified in front of Senator Cameron Vaughn's subcommittee he was hanging out on a limb as fragile as the flowers on that branch he'd just examined.

"Which is where Rebecca comes in? Or came in?" I looked sideways at him. "What happened? Why were you looking for her Saturday night?"

Ian shrugged and jammed his hands in his pockets. "Rebecca, bonny, bonny Rebecca. We worked together, had a little fling once. Then she found some rich old guy like she always does and that was the end of it. Went to work for Tommy Asher three years ago. I told her he stunk like a rotting corpse and she told me to go to hell."

I heard the wistfulness of a jilted lover in his voice. He still carried a torch for her.

"Rebecca only says things like that to people she cares about," I said. "She ignores everyone else."

He raised an ironic eyebrow. "She never told me about you. Wish she had."

"Moving on." I felt my cheeks go hot. "You were saying?"

"I was saying. God, I could use a cigarette."

"Show a little willpower. Come on, this is important."

He grinned like a blue-eyed devil. "You're a pain but I like you."

I looked away. He was enjoying making me uncomfortable. "Can we get back to Rebecca?"

"Sure thing, baby doll." He took my elbow and we moved into the crowd again. "Rebecca. You know what they say, 'No love like an old love,' especially when you've been thrown over. It became sort of a personal crusade to dig up whatever dirt I could find on Sir Thomas and prove to Rebecca that I was right."

"You mean to tell me all this is about getting even? A vendetta?"

"Not with Rebecca." Now he was the one whose face turned red. "But once I found out what I did, I suppose I wanted Asher to pay for what he's done. Maybe you're right and it is a vendetta. Every trader on Wall Street gets compared to Tommy Asher's whiz kids. After a while you get sick of it, especially once you find out it's all lies. I wanted to stop him."

"What are you talking about?"

He spread his hands and gave an eloquent shrug. "When all's said and done, he's running nothing more than a goddamn Ponzi scheme. No arbitrage, no split-strike conversion, nothing complicated or fancy like I originally suspected. Just robbing Peter to pay Paul. Easy-peasy. Works as long as new clients keep feeding the beast and nothing triggers too many people to ask for their money back at the same time."

"As simple as that? The whole pyramid thing?"

"Yup. As simple as that. At least that's how I figure it."

"Which brings us back to the fact that you have no proof," I said. "*If* it's true."

"*If* it's true?" His voice cracked. "It's a lonely old world out there, Sancho. So many windmills to tilt at. Thought you'd be right there by my side."

"Ian—"

He dropped my arm. "I figured you were Rebecca's friend, so you'd at least hear me out. Thanks for your time, Lucie."

"Don't. Wait a minute," I said. "What did Rebecca say? Did she believe you?"

"If I don't get a cigarette I'm going to go nuts."

"Okay, okay. But not here."

We moved off the path away from the crowd and stood under one of the older trees, its trunk twisted and pockmarked with age, branches reaching toward the sky like the arthritic arms of old men.

He lit up and eyed me through the flame of his lighter, speaking in a cloud of smoke.

"Rebecca was furious at first when I told her what I suspected. Didn't believe it, told me to go to hell, stay out of her life. Yada yada. That was a couple months ago."

"She changed her mind since then?"

He sucked on his cigarette. "I think I told you she called me and left a message at the beginning of last week. Said she wanted to talk, then never returned any of my calls. That's why I tried tracking her down at the Willard. And now she's gone and we get these."

He palmed his postcard again.

"What are you saying?" I asked.

"I think she was going to pass me information I could use for my testimony," he said. "And I think she got caught. That's why she sent the postcards. In case something went wrong."

Something had gone wrong. Rebecca was missing. "What about the story that she was robbed and killed by whoever took her jewelry and that wine cooler? What about her folded clothes in the rowboat?"

"Somebody went to a lot of trouble to cover their tracks. Threw in a little of everything. Let people wonder if maybe it was a robbery or maybe she committed suicide." He shrugged.

"She still could have set this up," I said. "Left you the information you needed and then disappeared because she knew it was like handing over a lighted stick of dynamite."

"And be on the lam for the rest of her life? No way. Not our girl. Rebecca's too high profile, too flash, to ever do something like that.

Can you see her working as a waitress in some diner in Podunk to stay off the grid?"

"Well . . ."

Ian's phone rang from somewhere inside his jacket. He answered and spoke in monosyllables while I tried to remember the name of the piece of music he used as a ring tone. Something my father used to listen to.

Finally he said, "Yeah, sure. Not tonight, unfortunately. I'm . . . with someone. How about tomorrow? Right. Later."

"What's that ring tone?" I asked as he shoved the phone back in his pocket.

He raised an eyebrow. "You like it? It's Mozart. *Dies Irae.*"

Day of Wrath. Judgment Day and the Second Coming. How fitting. I'd nearly forgotten it. Leland had liked it, too.

"Suits you."

He laughed. "How about a drink?"

"I shouldn't."

"Oh, come on. We still have things to discuss and it's getting cold. Besides, we're a team now. Whatever Rebecca wanted me to know, she brought you into it, too."

We trudged in silence to my car on Ohio Drive.

Maybe Rebecca had tied me to Ian, but she'd also written each of us a quote from a poem by Alexander Pope, which, it seemed to me, warned us about what we were getting into: *Fools rush in where angels fear to tread.* Ian's message.

And especially for me: *To err is human, to forgive divine.*

What mistake had she made?

Exactly what was I supposed to forgive?

CHAPTER 11

━━━━∞∞∞━━━━

I expected Ian to take me to a relatively secluded restaurant, some-place where we could talk quietly about Rebecca and what she'd dragged us into. Instead we went to the Tune Inn.

The Tune is located a few blocks from the Capitol at the end of a strip of Pennsylvania Avenue populated by crowded bars and ethnic restaurants catering to the appetite and thirst of a young Hill crowd, along with Library of Congress researchers and Supreme Court clerks. As bars go, it's in a class by itself: dark, earthy, noisy, a taxi-dermist's paradise where dozens of stuffed animal heads—and one derriere—line paneled walls and look down on an eclectic clientele. Locals who claim their own seats at the bar, off-duty marines from the nearby barracks, and Hill staffers jammed like sardines in the scarred-up booths drinking pitchers of Miller as if the brewery was going out of business forever—these are the Tune's habitués. The only music on the jukebox is break-your-heart country; the wide-screen televisions are all sports. A sign by the cash register says, IF YOU'RE DRINKING TO FORGET, PLEASE PAY IN ADVANCE. The place is as comfortable as a ratty old sweatshirt, as familiar as family.

When we walked in, the bartender waved at Ian and said, "Hey, man, how's it going?" Obviously, Ian was a regular. When he flirted with the waitress who showed us to a booth and called her by name, I knew for sure this was his hangout.

I slid into a cracked leather banquette across from him. "I haven't been here for years. This place never changes. What do you suppose that animal is above our booth?"

"Dead," he said. "If the place changed, people would riot. How about a pitcher and some fried pickles?"

"I've got to drive home," I said. "Maybe just a glass of white wine. I'm not much of a beer drinker."

He ordered the pitcher anyway, and my wine. When our pony-tailed gum-chewing waitress brought our drinks, he poured himself a glass and clinked it against my wine.

"Mud in your eye. Why did Rebecca send us each postcards with pithy quotes from Alexander Pope?" he asked.

"I don't know, but she also planned to give me a book of Pope's poetry," I said. "She'd signed the flyleaf and left the book on the desk in our hotel suite in the Willard. Unfortunately, the police now have it."

I decided to leave out the part about the other dedication and that the book had originally been a gift from a previous lover.

Ian leaned back against his seat and narrowed his eyes. "Don't tell me you think she left another message to go with the postcards? What is this, a treasure hunt? I don't get why she's jerking our chains."

"I don't know, either, but I wouldn't be surprised if there's something we're supposed to find in that book."

"Beautiful. A hidden message in a poem written by an English guy who died a couple centuries ago. And we don't even have the goddamn book anymore." He threw up his hands. "Did you see anything when you looked through it before the cops took it? A piece of paper? List of names, phone numbers, bank accounts—something?"

"Come to think of it, I did. It was neon and had blinking lights." I glared at him. "Don't you think I would have told you already? No, I didn't find anything—though that doesn't mean there wasn't something to find."

"We've got to get hold of that book," Ian said.

"The police won't let it go until they're ready to," I said.

Our waitress was back. "You guys want anything to eat besides the pickles?"

Ian looked at me. "Hungry?"

I nodded. "I missed lunch. I'm so hungry I could eat a horse."

Ian grinned. "I wouldn't say that in this place or you may get the tail end of Trigger up there."

"Aren't you the wise guy," the waitress said.

We ordered burgers and their famous basket of fries.

"How are we going to find out what she meant without that book?" Ian said. "Maybe there's something else. Maybe she told you something you didn't realize at the time was important."

I sipped my wine. "I was only with her for about an hour. We met at the Lincoln Memorial, where she bought the postcards. Then we went to the Wall."

"Why did she pick the Lincoln Memorial to meet? That could be significant." He looked hopeful. "Some kind of hidden symbolism."

"You mean, like people claiming the face of Robert E. Lee is secretly carved in the hair on the back of Lincoln's head? I doubt it. It would have to be something tangible."

"Why'd you visit the Wall?"

Our burgers arrived. Ian drowned his fries in ketchup and his sorrows in alcohol. He was halfway through his second beer. I'd drunk about half a glass of wine. Rebecca had asked me not to share with anyone why we'd visited the Vietnam Veterans Memorial, but that was then. Now she was gone—dead? on the run?—and I'd already had my doubts about the veracity of her story about her "biological" father whose name I never found.

"Rebecca wanted to leave a bouquet of flowers for a man she said was her real father. Told me her mother had an affair out of wedlock and then he died at the end of the war before they could marry. She claimed she only found out about him recently," I said. "She left the flowers where the first and last tablets meet, and that was that. Didn't look for him because she was in a rush to get to Georgetown. After she was gone, I checked the names."

"Let me guess. You couldn't find him?"

"At the time, I thought I'd just missed it somewhere."

Ian said, through a mouthful of fries, "What do you bet she made it all up? What'd she say the guy's name was?"

"Richard Boyle the Fourth."

He wiped his hands on a paper napkin and pulled out his phone. "Let's see who he really is."

He poked at the screen for a few minutes and frowned. "Richard Boyle, fourth Earl of Shannon. British politician of the Whig party in the 1800s. Doesn't sound like our guy."

"She left a message on a little card that was attached to the flowers," I said. "I'm trying to remember it."

Ian looked up, disgusted. "You waited all this time to tell me she wrote something on a card she left for a bogus guy she claimed was her father?"

"Something about 'the absent.' Forgiving them, I think. I'll bet it was Pope."

Ian typed some more on his phone. " 'Never find fault with the absent'?"

"That's it."

He snorted. "That's code, all right. 'To err is human, to forgive divine.' 'Never find fault with the absent.' Rebecca did something and she doesn't want to be blamed for it."

"And the fools rushing in would be us," I said.

"Story of my life. I'm always rushing in to something I regret."

I smiled. "So what doesn't she want to be blamed for? Betraying her boss by helping you? Her way of asking Tommy Asher to forgive her?"

Ian set his phone on the carved-up table as a rambunctious group of soccer players in muddy uniforms piled into the semicircular booth opposite us. Our waitress showed up with a fistful of pitchers for them and the volume went up. I had to lean closer to Ian to hear above the din.

"Maybe she was the fool rushing in," he said. "She knew that what she was doing was dangerous."

"But who does she want to forgive her?" I asked.

He shrugged. "I think that should be sort of obvious. She wrote it to you, didn't she? Bringing you back into her life after so many years."

He sat back and watched me, letting the words sink in. I felt like I'd been punched in the gut.

"I wondered why she called me out of the blue."

"My guess would be that she trusted you. Knew you'd see it through."

The noise receded and the room blurred. Rebecca had said just that: I'd stuck by her through the scandal of the affair with Connor and hadn't judged her—the reason she wanted to see me was to thank me after all these years.

What she'd left out was that she was about to ask me to do it all over again. This time in absentia. Good old loyal me. I didn't know whether to mourn a friend who was killed while trying to right a wrong or to be furious with her for running away and hiding, leaving me to finish what she hadn't.

Ian covered my hand with his. "Let's go back to my place."

I tried to extract it from his grip. "I think you've got the wrong idea about me."

He laughed and squeezed my fingers.

"Give me a break, will you? I'd be much smoother if I was asking you to go to bed with me." He threw some money down on the table and polished off the beer in his glass. "My eyes are crossing trying to type on my phone. I need to use a proper computer. And you and I still have work to do."

He waited for me to slide out of the booth before leading the way through the packed restaurant. On the jukebox, Toby Keith crooned about wishing he didn't know now what he didn't know then. Perfect exit music. When I met Rebecca last Saturday I had no clue about the tangled web she'd woven me into before she disappeared. Part of me wished I'd never gotten involved. The rest of me wanted to know where this was going.

Ian stopped in the doorway and I stumbled against him. I heard him say, "Well, well, look who's here."

We stepped outside to a small patio where a wrought-iron fence corralled half a dozen empty bistro tables with chairs around them.

"Lucie, let me introduce you to Summer Lowe," Ian said. "Summer, meet Lucie Montgomery. Didn't think this was your kind of place, sweetheart."

We were blocking the entrance to the restaurant, forcing people to maneuver around us as Summer Lowe, a tall, slender woman with a tawny mane of hair like a lion and patrician features, regarded

Ian with the grace and favor of something she'd scraped off the bottom of her shoe.

Her eyes slid over me, before fixing on Ian. "You smell like beer. You'd better not show up hungover on Thursday, got that, hotshot?" She glanced around at the passersby on the street. "I can't be seen with you."

"Lucie's a friend of Rebecca Natale's." Ian's tone made it clear he'd ignored everything she just said—probably deliberately to infuriate her. "We both think she might have been trying to help me with my testimony before she disappeared. You've been watching the news, haven't you? See you Thursday."

He took my elbow and steered me through the open gate onto Pennsylvania Avenue.

"What the hell's that supposed to mean?" Summer called after him.

He turned around and hollered back at her. "Thursday. You'll find out then."

"What's going on and who is Summer Lowe?" I asked as we walked to my car.

"The staff director of the subcommittee I'm testifying before. She thinks this hearing is a load of crap and that I'm some disgruntled ex–fund manager with an axe to grind. My, uh, old man's a good friend of Cameron Vaughn's." He reddened but shrugged like it was no big deal. "Summer thinks this is my way of settling scores with some people in New York."

"Is it?" I asked.

"No." He kept his voice level. "It's not. If it was, we'd probably be having drinks with Rebecca tonight, wouldn't we?"

I let him open my car door for me without answering. Whatever I was getting into, there was no turning back anymore.

CHAPTER 12

Ian lived in a town house on North Carolina Avenue not far from the Tune Inn. He directed me to an alley paralleling the street and showed me where I could wedge the Mini into a gravel bay next to the high wooden fence surrounding his postage stamp backyard. The padlock on the back gate groaned when he unlocked it and pulled it open. Inside, a pretty garden looked like someone cared for it. Off a wooden deck on the back of the house a large covered hot tub had prominence under a vine-covered pergola.

"An old classmate from Wharton owns the place," Ian said. "She's on sabbatical for a year, teaching at LSE. Some guy takes care of the yard for her."

"That's generous. What's LSE?"

"London School of Economics." He waved his thumbs. "Give me a plant, I'll kill it within weeks. Two brown thumbs."

"Looks like you and that gardener are doing okay so far."

He opened the back door—double locked—and flipped on the lights. We were in a compact, attractive kitchen small enough that I could almost stretch out my arms and touch both walls. Mexican-tiled floor, glass-fronted maple cabinets, granite bar with bar stools for dining. Next to a cappuccino maker was the untidy exception to the neat-as-a-pin room—a large collection of bottles of booze.

"Want a drink?"

"I'm all set, thanks."

He reached for a half-empty bottle of Laphroaig and waved it at me. "You sure?"

"Nothing hard. I'll take some water, please."

He opened the refrigerator and shoved aside a six-pack, reaching for a bottle of Perrier. I didn't see much food in there.

"The hot tub's nice at this time of night." He took two glasses from a cabinet. "I could turn on the lights in the backyard and we could talk there, chill a little. It's like fairyland."

"I don't have a bathing suit and you said this was going to be about work."

"You don't need a bathing suit and it could still be about work."

"Knock it off, please."

"Let me guess. You've got a boyfriend?"

"Where's your computer?"

"Is that a no?"

"Ian—" I gave him a warning look.

"Okay," he said. "It's in my bedroom."

"That's it. I'm leaving."

He reached out and grabbed my arm. "No, don't. Please."

"I shouldn't be here—"

"Yes, you should." He took both my hands in his. "I'm sorry for acting like an ass. You don't need to go, I mean it. I'll get my laptop from the bedroom and bring it downstairs. Okay? Why don't we sit in the living room? We need to figure this out. I don't want to do it alone."

I nodded. "All right. I'll stay for a while. Where's the living room?"

He looked relieved. "Upstairs."

The second-floor living room was as appealing as the kitchen. The centerpiece was the floor-to-ceiling bookcases filled with books, art, and sculpture on either side of a Victorian fireplace. A modern sofa upholstered in tangerine canvas and two barrel arm-chairs in chocolate brown leather were pulled around a large piece of driftwood with a glass top that served as a coffee table. The art on the walls included Andy Warhol and Roy Lichtenstein prints and a couple of modern oils.

Mail lay fan-shaped on the floor by the front door where it had been pushed through the brass mail slot; the curtains had not been drawn in the bay window. I liked that about cities and towns where houses practically sat on the street—the chance for a quick glimpse through a lighted window while driving by, a flash of someone's life, a vignette of family.

Ian turned on a torchère next to the front door and two brass table lamps on either side of the sofa. He didn't bother to pick up the mail.

We sat next to each other, elbows touching, as he turned on his computer.

"Why don't we search for Richard Boyle *and* Alexander Pope?" I said.

"That was my next idea." He tapped the keyboard and whistled. "Bingo."

I caught my breath as I looked at his screen. " 'Epistles to Several Persons: Epistle IV, to Richard Boyle' by Alexander Pope. So it's not Richard Boyle 'the Fourth.' This has to be the right guy. I wonder who he was?"

"Who cares? Let's read the damn epistle. That's what we're looking for."

"It might be important to know."

"I doubt it. Hang on, here it is . . . thank God for the Internet . . . damn. Why couldn't he have written a limerick? Five lines. This goes on for pages. I don't suppose you were an English major." He scrolled down through multiple screens.

"French and history. Exactly what I need to run a vineyard."

He gave me a sideways grin. "So what does all this stuff mean? The beginning is in Latin. All I speak is pig."

"If he wrote, 'Caesar divided Gaul into three parts,' I can translate that, but otherwise forget it." I took the computer from him and set it on my lap. "Let's go through the English verse, line by line."

After half an hour he leaned back and stretched. "I give up. It's about architecture . . . buildings. It's like a letter in verse to this guy—Richard Boyle—admonishing him about gardens and nature and . . . stuff. If there's a clue in this, I'm not getting it."

"Maybe the clue is who Richard Boyle was," I said. "Like I suggested."

"If you're right, you're going to rub it in, aren't you?"

"Of course."

I wasn't right. After more searching all we knew was that Richard Boyle, third Earl of Burlington and fourth Earl of Cork, had been known as "the architect earl" because of his role in reviving Palladian architecture in England, making it the generally accepted style for country houses and public buildings. The poem itself was ostensibly about gardening, but it also poked fun at the vulgar and ostentatious estate of a rival.

"Palladio," Ian said. "Now we're talking about a sixteenth-century Italian architect. We keep going further and further back in history, for God's sake. Next we'll find some link to the Stone Age."

I sat back and rubbed my temples. My head had started to throb.

"I have no idea, except that Palladio's ideas were grounded in classical Greek and Roman architecture," I said. "And he in turn influenced the men who designed and built the city of Washington."

"Bully for him." Ian sounded irritated. "And this relates how to Rebecca turning over information about Tommy Asher?"

"I don't know. But she did say that the Asher Collection—which is all about the design and planning of Washington—was displayed in their New York offices and that her boss often brought historians in to talk to his employees about it."

"Meaning she knew about Palladio and the difference between Ionic and Corinthian columns and what an architrave is?"

"Right."

"And if, say, it's a key ring flash drive that could be downloaded onto a computer, we'd be looking for something about two inches long and half an inch wide," Ian said. "That narrows it down to just about any-freakin'-where in the city."

"Maybe just the public monuments. Or gardens." I rubbed my eyes. This was getting to be insane.

He shut the laptop and picked up his empty glass. "I need another drink."

"If you're going downstairs, how about walking me to my car?" I said. "We're not going to get anywhere tonight with this, and my head's about to split apart from thinking so much."

"You're not ditching me?"

"We have one more day. Why don't we start again in the morning?"

"I say we stick with it until we figure it out."

His words had grown thicker as the evening wore on, the accumulated consequence of a couple of beers and a tumbler of Scotch.

"Ian, I need to go."

"Please?"

"I'm sorry, but no."

I stood up and reached for my cane. He pulled me back down on the sofa and kissed me. "Stay." His voice was low. "I want you."

"No." I struggled to push him away from me. "Don't do this. I mean it."

"It's okay, baby."

He tried again and this time I pushed harder.

"Stop it!"

He released me and I saw the two red blotches on his cheeks. "Sorry. I'm not really an oaf most of the time. I just got carried away. You're beautiful, you know. I could fall for you in a heartbeat."

I looked away. Tomorrow he wouldn't remember this. "I think you should walk me to my car. Now, please."

He had to unlock the kitchen door from the inside before he let me out into the cool evening. I shivered and he put his arm around me, rubbing my shoulders. At the back gate he unlocked the padlock. When we got to my car, he leaned down and kissed me again.

This time I let him do it.

"Why don't you call me when you get home?" His words were lightly slurred. "I wanna know you got there safely."

"I'll be fine. Maybe you should get some sleep and we'll talk in the morning."

He stood there, watching me back out of the parking space and head down the alley. As I turned the corner, he raised his hand in a good-bye salute, an eerie specter, his silhouette outlined by moonlight and the red taillights of my car.

I pulled out onto North Carolina Avenue and thought about calling him to remind him to double-check the locks to his doors after what he'd said about being watched. An MPD cruiser passed me, heading east as a siren wailed in the distance. At least his neighborhood was patrolled. And he probably didn't need me mothering him.

In spite of what I'd told him, I called his cell an hour later as I walked through my front door—as much to check on him as to let him know I was home. He didn't pick up so I hung up and tried again. He'd probably passed out either in bed or on the sofa with the Laphroaig. After the fourth call I left a message.

In the morning, I found out just how much trouble I'd gotten myself into by doing that.

CHAPTER 13

⊶⊷

Ian Philips still didn't answer his phone Wednesday morning when I called after breakfast. Quinn showed up at the villa as I was in the kitchen dialing Ian's number yet again and making coffee.

"I think I remember who you are." He took the carafe from me and filled it with water. "Don't you own this vineyard?"

I hit End Call and picked up a bottle of wine on the counter. "I believe that's my name on that label. It appears I do."

"Well, then, where the hell have you been? You're disappearing on me all the time lately. I thought we were going to do more bench trials on the Viognier yesterday. What'd you do? Shut off your phone and play hooky?"

He poured the water into the coffeemaker as I resumed scooping French roast into the basket.

"I'm sorry. I had to run into D.C. It was sort of last minute—and weren't you the one who wanted time and space? I gave it to you."

He ignored that. Convenient.

"You went to Washington? Again? What for, if you don't mind my asking?"

"I met a friend of Rebecca's."

"They still haven't found her?"

"No." I punched the Brew button. "They haven't."

"What's wrong?"

He leaned against the counter and folded his arms. This morning he wore an old gray sweatshirt that stretched tight across his chest, faded jeans, and work boots. I did not want to search for any subtext in his concern or fool myself that we were anything but friends and coworkers. Especially since I knew he was contemplating pulling up stakes and moving on. What happened between us before was finished; God knows he'd gotten over me just fine.

How could men do that? Switch off their emotions so abruptly, ready for the next adventure. Like catching a bus. Another one would be along and it would get you there the same as the previous one. I just . . . couldn't.

"Nothing's wrong."

Maybe it was time I started putting some distance between us as well. In the past I would have confided in him, but now I wasn't so sure.

"I know you." He raised an eyebrow. "I know when you're keeping something from me."

I turned and found two mugs in the cabinet. With my back to him, I took the carafe off the hot plate and poured coffee into one of the mugs.

"Talking about keeping things from someone, I heard you're looking to buy land. Ali Jennings says she and Harlan have some acres they might like to sell. Here's your coffee."

I slid it across the counter and set the carafe back in its place, waiting for it to refill.

"Uh, thanks," he said. "And, uh, thanks for passing that on. I'm, uh, sorry you had to find out from someone besides me."

"Don't mention it," I said. "It'll take me some time to find a new winemaker. Maybe I should start looking now. How soon do you think you'll leave?"

He went pale. I poured coffee in my mug, adding sugar and milk, while I waited for his reply.

He cleared his throat. "It's still up in the air. I've got some financial stuff to figure out. But I was hoping in about two months."

I put my lips together because I did not trust my voice. He placed a hand on my shoulder as my phone rang. I moved out of reach of his sympathy and his touch. It was Kit, calling from work.

"Hey," I said.

"Boy, you don't sound too good. I guess you heard already, huh?"

"Heard what?" I turned my back on Quinn and blinked hard. "What are you talking about? Have they found Rebecca?"

"No, no . . . nothing like that. David Wildman just told me some news. You know who he is, don't you? My colleague who's working on that story about Asher Investments."

"I remember. What is it?"

"Remember that guy you said tried to pick you up Saturday night at the Willard? Ian Philips?" She waited. "Lucie?"

"I'm here."

"David was meeting one of his contacts at the MPD for breakfast this morning to talk about Rebecca when the detective got called out on a possible homicide on Capitol Hill just as they sat down in the restaurant. He let David ride along so they could keep talking. You'll never guess who the homicide was. Ian Philips."

For a long moment I stood there listening to the slight hissing of the coffeemaker and the slow, hard slamming of my heart against my ribs.

I closed my eyes. "My God, not Ian, too."

"What are you talking about, 'too'? Don't tell me you actually met up with him?"

"It's complicated. What . . . happened?"

"David says it looked like he passed out in a backyard hot tub and drowned. The cops found an empty bottle of Scotch right there, so he could have been really plastered when it happened. I guess they won't know whether it's an accident or a homicide until the autopsy results."

I still couldn't believe it. "Did it look like anyone broke into his house?"

"The back gate was unlocked, so someone could have walked in. It led to an alley. But the house looked fine, nothing disturbed or out of place." I could hear her shrug through the phone. "David said the cops think he had company, though. They found a couple of empty glasses on the living room coffee table."

"He did have company," I said. "Me."

Quinn must have heard Kit's shrieked expletive through the phone, because he planted himself in front of me and mouthed, "What?"

I shook my head at him and said to Kit, "I guess I'd better call Detective Horne and tell him myself. My prints are there, anyway. Plus I called a bunch of times and left Ian a message."

"Damn right you should call him, Luce. What the hell were you doing at Ian's place, anyway? Are you out of your mind?" Her voice was still shrill. "First Rebecca, now Ian Philips. Why'd you see him?"

"He called and asked me to meet him. One thing led to another. We had dinner at the Tune Inn, then ended up back at his place."

"You mean, a date?" Kit sounded incredulous.

"No," I said. "Nothing like that. Look, I can't talk about it now."

"Why not?"

"Uh . . ."

"Someone's there?"

"Yes."

"Call me after you talk to that detective. You're probably going to have to go down to headquarters on Indiana Avenue and give a statement."

"I know."

"You'd better be careful, kiddo. Otherwise you're going to end up in a hole so deep you may not be able to climb out."

I set my phone on the counter after she disconnected, heaping sugar in my coffee.

"Having sugar with your coffee? You already did that," Quinn said. "Who's Ian?"

"A friend of Rebecca's," I said. "The police found him this morning. It looks like he drowned in a hot tub sometime last night."

"You were with him last night?"

I nodded.

"What's going on, Lucie?"

"I don't know. But I don't think he drowned."

I left Quinn in the kitchen and called Detective Ismail Horne from my office. As Kit predicted, he issued a personal invitation to come down to Indiana Avenue and explain my side of the story. If I chose not to do so, Horne promised he'd send someone to fetch me, with a matching pair of bracelets to accessorize my ride. And they probably wouldn't roll out the red carpet when I arrived if we did this the hard way.

"Do I need a lawyer?" I asked, shaken.

"You're not being charged with anything," he said. "We just want to talk with you. That's all. But if you do lawyer up, then we need to read you your rights and it starts getting complicated. Your choice."

"Ian Philips was alive and well when I left him last night," I said. "But he'd been drinking. I called him several times when I got home and he never answered, so I figured he'd gone to bed and I left a message on his machine."

"I know," Horne said. "I heard. That's why it looks better that you called me than me calling on you. Come on in here. Later this morning would work just fine for me."

On my way out, I walked by Quinn's office. His door was ajar and he was talking on the phone, his deep voice carrying into the hallway.

"Sure, Ali . . . thanks . . . yeah, I'd love to see it. Give me a call when it's convenient."

My heart gave another unwelcome lurch. He hadn't wasted any time calling Alison Jennings about their land. Was he really going to go through with this? I had just slipped past his door when he called my name.

"You leaving again?" He stood in his doorway, hands in his pockets as he leaned against the jamb.

I couldn't read the expression in his eyes, but I could sense a new energy in him, anticipation about the possibilities that had opened up since he'd come into that inheritance—a chance to put his own stamp on a vineyard, his name on a wine label. I wanted to be glad for him. Really I did. But how could I not have noticed his restlessness before this?

"I'm going into D.C. Again. Sorry, but I'm not sure when I'll be back. Can we put off the bench trials another day?"

"Sure. Your call. Want me to come with you? You're talking to the police, aren't you?"

I nodded. "And you're going over to the Jenningses' place to see their land."

He reddened. "Not for a while. Look, I'm not going to jump

ship tomorrow, okay? And if this works out, it's not like I'm leaving Atoka. I'll still be around. We'll still see each other." His smile was self-conscious; he knew he wasn't conning me, but I played along.

I tried to smile, too. "I know."

"You understand, don't you? You know I'm not unhappy here. That's not why I'm doing it."

Sure, I understood. I just didn't want him to leave. And it wasn't about the wine, either. "You caught me by surprise, that's all."

He flashed a cheeky grin like a kid who hooked a big fish with nothing but string and a worm. "If you want to know the truth, it surprised me, too. But financially things are looking up so I think I can pull this off sooner than later. With the recession, it's a good time to buy land. Prices are down."

"You're talking about the money from your mother's estate?"

"That and a few investments."

"I'll miss you," I said.

"What are you going to miss? I told you I'll still be by to give you grief, like I always do."

"Something to look forward to." I hooked a thumb in the direction of the door. "I'd better get going. They're waiting for me."

"You never said whether you want me to come."

"Thanks, anyway, but I can handle this on my own."

He seemed surprised by the rebuff, but all he said was, "Sure. I know you can."

As I closed the door I thought I heard him say, "I'll miss you, too, sweetheart. I'll miss you, too."

Perhaps I imagined it, but I thought he sounded wistful and even a little melancholy.

It took me almost as much time to find a parking place near D.C. police headquarters as it did to drive from Atoka to Washington. Finally I gave up on meters and found a garage a few blocks away. Once I got inside the building it took another twenty minutes to get past security to the third floor where the homicide division was located.

I'd obviously watched too many television cop shows because I was expecting to be interrogated in a large room with a grungy table, a couple of beat-up wooden chairs, a mirrored window—where someone would watch me from the other side—and a legal pad and pencil for me to write it all down. Instead Ismail Horne ushered me into a space slightly larger than a freight elevator, containing only a laminate table and two molded plastic desk chairs. No window. I glanced up. Of course, a surveillance camera. This was real life, not television. When he closed the door, I felt claustrophobic.

We sat across from each other.

"Suppose you start from the beginning," he said.

So I told him about Ian and the postcards, and something flickered in his eyes that made me realize he'd found the one Rebecca had sent Ian, though he said nothing.

"We met at the Tidal Basin," I said. "That was Ian's suggestion."

"First time you met?" he asked.

"No. I encountered him at the Willard hotel on Saturday night. He was looking for Rebecca and didn't know her room number."

"Encountered?"

"He asked me to wait with him in the hotel bar when he found out I knew Rebecca. He'd been drinking and sort of made a pass at me so I said no. A hotel concierge escorted him out, or at least I think he did. By then I'd taken the elevator to my room."

I took Horne through the rest of it—dinner at the Tune Inn, running into Summer Lowe, and finally ending up at Ian's place trying to figure out whether Rebecca had somehow given us a coded message as to where she'd left information that could help Ian in his testimony before the Senate Banking Subcommittee.

If trying to find a clue in a poem written in 1731 by Alexander Pope had seemed far-fetched last night, the expression on Detective Horne's face as I continued talking made me wonder if he thought he was listening to someone who was waiting for her mother ship to return from her planet.

"So," he said, leaning closer to me, "did you figure out this secret code, Ms. Montgomery?"

He emphasized "secret code" ever so slightly and I blushed. Maybe he did think I was nuts.

"No, we didn't. Look, Detective, I know it must seem completely loony to you, but here's what's absolutely true: Rebecca Natale sent Ian and me identical postcards that she bought at the Lincoln Memorial on Saturday with our phone numbers on them and a quote from Alexander Pope. She left flowers at the Wall for a man named Richard Boyle, whom she said was her biological father, but there's no Richard Boyle listed as having been killed in 1975. There is, however, a poem written by Pope to Boyle, and Rebecca planned to give me a book of Pope's poetry, which she'd inscribed to me. I assume you've got it since you confiscated all of her things when you searched our hotel room."

Horne stood up. "Stay right here."

He was back in five minutes with the book, which he slid across the table. "Be my guest."

I flipped to the index and found the page with the epistle to Richard Boyle. After a moment, I looked up.

"She's marked two passages: 'Oft have you hinted to your brother peer, / A certain truth, which many buy too dear.' "

"Go on."

"This is from a different part of the epistle." I cleared my throat and continued:

No artful wildness to perplex the scene;
Grove nods at grove, each alley has a brother,
And half the platform just reflects the other.
The suff'ring eye inverted Nature sees,
Trees cut to statues, statues thick as trees;
With here a fountain, never to be play'd;
And there a summerhouse, that knows no shade.

"Very nice." He was no longer bothering to hide his skepticism. "What the hell's it mean?"

"According to what we found out last night, Pope used this poem to poke fun at the ostentatious home of a nobleman he knew, calling it vulgar and over the top. The guy figured out Pope was mocking him and it got Pope in hot water," I said. "This passage refers to that estate—or the gardens on the estate."

"And the estate of this—what'd you call him?—'nobleman' fits into your puzzle how?" He sat back in his chair, which creaked. "This house is in England, isn't it? And all those people are dead?"

"Yes, but perhaps she was referring to some place in Washington," I said. "Some place where there's a dry fountain and manicured gardens. A park, perhaps."

"And what, exactly, would we find there?"

"I don't know. Something that would have buttressed Ian Philips's testimony. Documents. Evidence on an external computer drive."

Horne reached over and closed the book, sliding it to his side of the table.

"We'll look into it," he said. "In the meantime, I've got one homicide with no body and a suspicious death that doesn't look like murder but smells bad. Fountains and parks are kind of low priority on my list."

I swallowed hard and nodded. He thought I was going to tell him about little green men next.

"What about me?" I asked. "Am I free to go?"

"Your story checks out, so yeah, you can go. A neighbor saw you leave from that alley when you said you did. She said Philips stood out there and waited until you'd gone."

"Really? I never saw anyone."

"Be glad she was there. Gave you an alibi."

"I am. But I don't understand why Ian didn't lock the gate after I left. He had to unlock it to let us in when we got there and again when I left."

"Maybe he was so wasted he forgot. Or he opened it to someone he knew and never got a chance to lock it again," Horne said. "Did he say anything about more company coming by later on?"

"No," I said, "but he did say he'd been getting phone calls in the middle of the night from someone who never said anything. Just waited on the other end."

"We're checking his phone records."

Detective Horne stood up and opened the door. "Thanks, Ms. Montgomery. If there's anything else, I know where to reach you."

I retrieved my cane and my purse.

"What happened to the homeless man you arrested?" I asked. "Can you tell me anything else about the search for Rebecca?"

"I can't discuss an ongoing investigation," he said. "As for your friend, I can tell you that yesterday the operation went from search and rescue to recovery. I'm sorry, but there's no way she survived four days in that river. We're just looking for her body now."

I imagined divers and boats plying the Potomac looking for remains, rather than a person, after the catfish and critters had gotten to her, and felt ill.

"Do you think you'll find her?"

"Eventually." His voice was kinder. "They usually turn up. The river doesn't keep 'em forever, except every once and awhile."

Horne walked me to the bank of elevators and left me there. We'd passed a clock as he took me through the squad room. I'd been here just over an hour and a half, but it felt more like years.

Were Rebecca and Ian's deaths linked? And what about Rebecca? I still wasn't sure that she hadn't faked her own death and fled somewhere. The common link between them was Thomas Asher Investments.

But what, exactly, was that link?

CHAPTER 14

It was just after noon when I left police headquarters. In a nearby courtyard, a hot dog vendor was doing a brisk business with the lunchtime crowd. Now that the butterflies in my stomach were gone, I was starved. I joined the queue of men and women in business suits and officers in uniform. This part of D.C. wasn't for tourists; everyone waiting in line worked in the nearby courts or for the local government or at MPD.

"Lucie?"

It had been a dozen years since I'd seen Linh Natale on the Mother's Day weekend of her daughter's graduation. She had been etched in my memory as the joyous, exuberant woman who looked and acted more like Rebecca's older sister than her mother. Now her beautiful dark hair was streaked with gray and her face was pinched with age and grief. For a moment I thought Rebecca's spirit had returned from the future.

"Mrs. Natale? I'm so sorry—"

Her eyes filled. I put my arms around her and felt her shoulders shake as she clung to me.

"I should have called," I said into her hair. "I feel awful."

She didn't speak. After a long moment she squared her shoulders and took a deep breath.

"It's okay." She wiped her eyes with the back of her hand. "I'm glad to see you, my dear. A familiar face. It's been too long."

"Where's Mr. Natale?" I asked. "You're not here by yourself, are you?"

"He's at home. Boston. He's not well." Her hand rested on her heart. "This dreadful news hasn't helped."

"Is there anything I can do?"

She shrugged with the weary resignation of someone running out of options. "Pray for a miracle. I think that's all we have left."

She looked me over—including the cane. I saw the same fleeting look of shock that had been in Rebecca's eyes.

"Why are you here? Is it about Rebecca?" she asked.

There was a faint note of hope in her voice. I smiled, feeling bleak, unwilling to be the bearer of more bad news. If Rebecca had gone out with Ian for a while, I suspected Linh Natale would know him.

"Not exactly."

She reached in the pocket of her coat and pulled out a crumpled tissue. "Then what is it? Please, Lucie. Anything you can tell me will be of help."

The queue at the hot dog stand had advanced.

"Are you in line?" A dark-haired man in a sharp suit tapped me on the shoulder.

"Yes." I turned to Mrs. Natale. "Have you eaten? Can I buy you a hot dog and perhaps we could talk somewhere?"

She gave me a blank look and said, "You know, I'm famished. I'd love a hot dog. But can we please get away from this place and go somewhere else? I've been here every day since . . . well, since."

"I'm parked in a garage a few blocks away. Let's get a bite to eat and then we can find somewhere with more privacy where we can talk."

"I know a place," she said, "but it's not nearby. I would very much like to see the bonsai gardens at the National Arboretum. I don't suppose you would like to visit it?"

"I'll take you anywhere you want to go, Mrs. Natale. But maybe we should eat our food before it gets cold."

"Call me Linh," she said. "Please."

"Linh."

We sat on a park bench and ate our hot dogs and drank the Cokes I'd bought.

"There was a botanical garden in Saigon, but the war destroyed it," Linh said in her carefully accented English. "It was beautiful. I went there often as a young girl. Now it's gone, all gone."

"We can spend as much time at the arboretum as you wish," I said.

"Thank you, dear. You're very kind. I need to calm my soul." Her voice broke and my heart ached for her. "It's unbearable to think of life without my daughter. The police have no news . . . nothing. The waiting is torture."

"I know," I said. "Come, let's walk to my car."

I couldn't remember the last time I'd visited the arboretum, but it was so long ago that I had to check the map for directions. The twenty-minute drive was a straight shot out of the center of the city, over railroad tracks and through a blighted industrial area to the pretty 450-acre park tucked away in the far eastern reaches of Washington.

I drove through the front gate, and the pollution and noise of the city faded. Dogwood and flowering cherry trees bloomed along the winding drive to the Bonsai and Penjing Museum. Here the warm spring air smelled fresh and clean.

"There is no one except us," Linh said. "It is so quiet."

"It's a weekday," I said. "Looks like we might have the park to ourselves."

"In Saigon our gardens are always filled with people," she said. "They find tranquility in nature."

"In Washington it's our buildings that are filled with people," I said. "Government workers. And there's no tranquility."

She smiled. "I prefer the ways of my country."

"What is 'penjing'?" I asked.

"An older form of bonsai. From China."

I pulled into a gravel strip parking lot by a low pavilion next to one other car. In front of us at the crest of a hill surrounded by meadows nearly two dozen Corinthian columns rose like a ruined temple transported from ancient Greece. Blindingly white against an azure sky, they made a spectacular tableau in the middle of nowhere.

"How beautiful," Linh said. "What is it?"

We got out of the car and I went over to read a brown-and-white park sign.

"The Capitol Columns," I said. "They used to be part of the East Portico of the U.S. Capitol. It says here they were removed and put in storage in 1958 when some expansion work was done on the building. Moved to this site in the late 1980s and dedicated in 1990."

"Perhaps we can walk up there after we see the bonsai," Linh said.

We crossed the parking lot and entered the outdoor pavilion of the bonsai exhibit through a Japanese-style wooden gate that led to a path called the Cryptomeria Walk. Linh fell silent as we toured the grounds, fingers pressed to her lips as she paused to contemplate each of the ancient miniature trees from Japan and China, some several centuries old. Her breathing seemed to slow, as though their mysticism and timelessness did, in fact, calm her troubled spirit.

Though I tried to connect to her Zen-like serenity, I couldn't. Instead I felt restless, edgy. I had questions I wanted to ask, but it would be wrong in this almost sacred place. Perhaps when we visited the columns.

"Rebecca loved gardens. Did you know that?" Linh asked.

We had come to the North American pavilion, the last of the outdoor exhibits, where more bonsai were displayed in rustic simplicity on weathered wooden tables. The afternoon sunshine cast silhouettes onto the white stucco walls, transforming the miniature trees into bizarre shadow puppets.

"No, I didn't."

"We used to visit some of the grand estates together. Biltmore, Winterthur, Longwood. She loved doing that."

I thought of the passage referring to a garden that Rebecca had marked in the epistle to Richard Boyle. Would Linh find some significance in it that Ian, Horne, and I did not?

"My mother also loved gardening," I said. "We went to those same places and she brought me here to the arboretum many years ago. But her favorite place was Monticello. She followed *Thomas Jefferson's Garden Book* like a bible."

"I've never been there." Linh faced me, folding her arms across her thin chest. "Do you want to tell me what's bothering you, Lucie? It's about Rebecca, isn't it?"

"Yes."

We passed under the branches of a gnarled cherry tree as a sudden breeze blew the puffball clusters of blossoms, sending petals like fat snowflakes swirling around us and making a pale pink carpet on the ground.

Linh bent her head and, for a moment, I wondered if she were praying. When she looked up, her eyes were again bright with tears.

"What do you want to know?"

I wanted to know things that were really none of my business, things that were intensely personal that Rebecca had perhaps not shared even with her mother. But Rebecca had dragged me into the middle of this. Whether or not she was still alive, Ian was dead and I couldn't help but think his death was somehow related to her disappearance.

"I don't want to upset you," I said.

"There is little chance of that." She tilted her chin. "I knew my daughter, Lucie. Flaws and all. And I loved her. She was my life. You know that."

"I know. And I know she loved you just as much."

Linh linked her arm through mine. "Ask your questions."

"Let's talk while we walk to the columns," I said.

"This isn't too difficult for you?" She indicated my cane.

"I can do everything I used to do. It just takes me longer. Though my running and cross-country days are over."

She pressed her lips together again. "You, too, have had your share of problems."

The dirt footpath had been worn smooth into a narrow meandering trail that led to the grassy knoll where the enormous columns stood like an ancient ruin. They had been placed on a foundation made of stones taken from the east side of the Capitol. A constant wind whistled across the wide-open scrubby meadow as we made our way like pilgrims journeying to a holy site. Except for the flowering trees and a budding magnolia, everything else in the surrounding woods was brown and bare, just as it was back home in Atoka.

"You know Rebecca and I hadn't seen each other since she graduated," I said. "Until last weekend. The only time I heard from her was when she sent me flowers in the hospital."

"I was aware of that, yes."

"Do you know why she wanted to see me, out of the blue, after all these years?"

"Perhaps because she wanted to connect with an old friend?"

So Linh didn't know.

"I, uh, think it might have been more than that," I said. "I think there was something she wanted me to do . . . or something she wanted me to know."

Linh tugged my arm and we left the path so she could admire an enormous flowering cherry tree. Across from us a young couple sat talking on a wooden bench, absorbed in each other.

"And you don't know what that is?" Linh asked.

"I think I'm beginning to have an idea. Did Rebecca ever mention someone named Ian Philips to you?"

"Yes, of course. They worked together before she left to join Asher Investments. They went out a few times, I believe. But when she moved on, their relationship ended. I think he was angry with her for leaving. Perhaps a little jealous of her advancement."

"Rebecca got back in touch with Ian recently," I said. "She called him the week before she disappeared, but they never managed to connect. Then she sent Ian and me identical postcards with each other's phone numbers on them. They came yesterday. Did you know he was scheduled to testify on Capitol Hill tomorrow about possible improprieties at Asher Investments?"

We began walking again. "No, I did not. Why did you say 'was'?"

"I'm so sorry, Linh. I didn't want to tell you. Ian was found dead this morning at his row house on Capitol Hill. He'd been drinking last night. It seems he drowned in his hot tub."

Linh made a brief sign of the cross and kept her hand over her heart.

"That poor boy! How did you find out?" She turned to me. "That's why you were at police headquarters, isn't it?"

We had nearly reached the top of the knoll. Set in the middle of the plaza where the columns rose to the sky was a dry fountain. In the summer, a channel flowed from the fountain down a small hill where it fed a shallow rectangular pool at the base of the columns. It reminded me of the Reflecting Pool in front of the Lincoln Memorial and I wondered, suddenly, if Rebecca had been here recently and this was the place she was referring to in the passage of Alexander Pope's epistle.

Except this small fountain and the shallow pool had been drained for the winter and would be turned on again once there was no chance of freezing weather. The Pope verse described a fountain "never to be played" in a park that was well manicured, not untamed as it was here.

"Lucie." Linh shook my arm. "What's going on? Did the police question you about Ian's death?"

I nodded. "I was with him last night. Probably only a few hours before he died."

Linh leaned against one of the massive sandstone columns, her slight shadow crossing mine. In the distance, the couple that had been sitting on the bench made their way to their car and drove out of the parking lot. We were now completely alone, with only the noise of the wind and birdsong from the trees in the surrounding woods for company.

"You think Ian's death and Rebecca's disappearance are related?" she asked.

"I think," I said, "that Rebecca may have been trying to pass Ian some documents or information about illegal business dealings at Thomas Asher Investments."

The color drained from her face. "What are you talking about, illegal?"

I told her, but I stopped short of using the words "Ponzi scheme."

"Ian told Rebecca what he suspected a few months ago. At first she didn't believe him and even got angry with him. But it seems she might have discovered something recently that changed her mind," I said. "It's possible Rebecca planned to hand Ian the proof he needed for his testimony and then disappear. One scenario is that this is all an elaborate hoax and she's alive and well somewhere."

Linh's voice was hoarse with disbelief and hope. "Scenario? You think she faked her death?"

"The story about a mysterious stranger—Robin Hood—giving the Madison wine cooler and Rebecca's jewelry to a homeless man down by the river sounds a little far-fetched, don't you think?"

"I don't know." She sounded dubious and I could tell she'd wondered about it herself. "I'm not sure I believe you about these illegal dealings, as you call them, Lucie. Of course I would like to think my daughter is alive, but did you know Sir Thomas is paying for my trip to Washington? He flew me down here, first class. He has taken care of everything for me—a suite at the Willard hotel for as long as I need to be here, all my meals, expenses, everything. I even have a driver at my disposal when I wish. He is a good man. He and Lady Asher do so much for charity. So much good work."

"But if Ian's right—"

"Why would Rebecca run away?" she asked. "*That* doesn't make sense."

"Because she was afraid of the repercussions of her actions," I said. "And if Ian Philips's death turns out not to be an accidental drowning—which I don't believe it was—then maybe Rebecca had good reason to be scared."

"Because someone from Asher Investments murdered Ian, or had him killed to keep him from testifying?" Linh sounded incredulous. "And my daughter set up some . . . some *charade* to convince everyone she was dead—even her own mother and father—because she, too, feared for her life?"

"It's also possible," I said, "that she didn't succeed in getting away. Maybe the homicide is real—though the police haven't found a . . . haven't found Rebecca yet."

Linh walked to the edge of the foundation and stared out at a meadow of untidy rows of tufts of dried fountain grass that stretched to a distant road. Beyond it were more woods. I went over and stood next to her.

"I'm sorry."

"That's what you believe, Lucie?" There was both sorrow and anger in her voice. "Because they have not found my daughter?"

"It's only a theory," I said.

She turned to me. "She was involved with someone. You knew that, didn't you? She seemed so happy this time."

My heart constricted as I thought of Ali Jennings explaining to me that the affair between Harlan and Rebecca was over.

"Rebecca didn't tell me herself," I said, "but I know she was at

Harlan Jennings's home in Georgetown on Saturday afternoon. His, uh, his wife said the affair was over."

Linh looked surprised. "The former senator? That Harlan Jennings?"

I'd let some cat out of God knew what bag. "Isn't that who you were referring to?"

"I didn't know his name," she said, "but whoever it was—Senator Jennings or someone else—Rebecca had a very good reason not to disappear on Saturday."

"What was that?"

Her voice wavered. "Because she was spotted on a surveillance camera at a pharmacy in Georgetown around five P.M. on Saturday. The police found the clerk who waited on her. She bought one of those pregnancy tests. And that's why I'm sure my daughter didn't run away somewhere. Because she thought she was pregnant. And knowing Rebecca, she would be deeply in love with the man who would have been her baby's father."

CHAPTER 15

—⊶⊷⊷⊷—

I drove Linh back to the Willard after that. It was a mostly silent trip—forty-five minutes through Washington's bottlenecked traffic—with each of us absorbed in her thoughts.

If Rebecca were pregnant, that put an entirely new spin on things. Who was the father? Presumably Harlan—which meant that the affair definitely was *not* over. I'd seen Rebecca's birth control pills in the bathroom of our suite at the hotel. Had she been careless, taking them erratically? Or had the decision to get pregnant been deliberate, because she wanted the child of her current lover? Ian told me that he'd been thrown over for an old, rich guy. Harlan was older and he was rich.

Whether the pregnancy had been an accident or not, it gave both Harlan and Alison even stronger motives to want Rebecca out of the way. Especially Harlan, if the reason Rebecca wanted to see him on Saturday was to tell him what would surely be unwelcome news.

But how did this fit in with Ian's death and the postcards? Were they related, or two entirely separate incidents whose timing was coincidental?

I pulled up in front of the hotel. Linh put her hand on the door handle, as though eager to flee. Then she glanced out the car window.

"Oh, no," she said. "Not another reporter with a camera. Be a dear and drive around the corner, will you? I think I'll take a walk before I go inside. Find another entrance."

I turned off Pennsylvania Avenue onto Fifteenth Street and pulled up to the curb. "Are you going to be all right?"

She took oversized sunglasses and a scarf out of her purse. "I'll be fine. Thank you for taking me to the arboretum, Lucie. It was a comfort."

"My pleasure. Will you be staying in Washington much longer?"

"I don't know." She tied on her scarf. "It depends on when they find Rebecca."

I didn't want to say it, but what if there was no one to find because Rebecca was on the lam? Would she contact her anguished mother and let her know she was alive?

"Please stay in touch," I said. "You're more than welcome to come out to the vineyard if you want a break from D.C. I've got plenty of room and it's peaceful and quiet in Atoka. There wouldn't be any reporters lurking on your doorstep."

"That's very kind. I'll call you." Linh donned the sunglasses and I had a flashback to Rebecca, the same gesture, almost the same sunglasses, as she said good-bye to me for the last time at the Wall.

Linh touched my cheek and slipped out of the car. No one followed her. I hadn't thought about her being hounded by the press, but I knew she wouldn't visit me at the vineyard, nor would she call, in spite of what she'd just said. In her shoes—grappling with the loss of her beloved daughter and the obvious media frenzy the story had generated—I wouldn't, either.

Before I pulled away from the curb, I turned on my phone. In D.C. it was against the law to talk while driving; the fines were horrendous. Two messages, one from Kit, demanding that I report in on my session with Detective Horne, the other from Frankie, saying someone named Summer Lowe had been phoning all afternoon trying to get in touch with me.

I called Frankie.

"The fourth time I let that woman's call go to voice mail," Frankie said. "What an annoying person. Who is she, anyway?"

I told her. "Did she say what she wanted?"

"Yeah. You. And she told you to call her; she didn't ask," Frankie said. "You going to talk to her?"

"I think I will," I said. "I probably won't be home until later this evening. Can you lock up?"

"Sure." She paused. "Quinn's not here, either. He, uh, might have gone over to the Jenningses' place."

My stomach churned. Was Quinn ready to make a down payment on their land as soon as he took a look at it? He'd said he figured on being around for two more months. At the speed he was moving, he'd be gone in two weeks.

"He told you that's what he was doing, didn't he?"

"Well, yes. I guess he did." I heard her sigh. "Look, he's going to be staying in Atoka. It's not like he's moving back to California."

"I know."

"Don't worry, Lucie. It'll be all right. You'll find a new winemaker and it will work out with Quinn. I'm sure of it."

"Yeah, everything will be fine. Thanks." I kept my voice light, but she probably wasn't fooled.

Frankie was right that I'd have to find a new winemaker. But I wasn't so sure it would work out with Quinn. We'd drifted apart, not closer. Once he was gone, he could easily turn what was left of our relationship into out of sight, out of mind.

Summer Lowe answered her phone midway through the first ring.

"You're the Lucie Montgomery I met last night at the Tune Inn with Ian, aren't you?"

Last night? It seemed like last year.

"Yes, I am. How'd you find me?"

"How else? The Internet."

"Oh."

"Look, I need to talk to you about Ian. Could you come by my office on the Hill? Today? It's important."

I didn't care for her officious tone.

"Ian," I said. "May God rest his soul. You do realize you were one of the last people to see him alive, don't you?"

"Oh, jeez. I mean, yes. Of course I do. God, what a tragedy. I was so sorry to hear about it . . . him."

I wondered if she believed Ian's death was an accident, or whether it had crossed her mind that maybe it had something to do with sticking his neck out as a whistle-blower who was supposed to testify before her subcommittee. It wasn't her fault Ian was dead, but couldn't she at least sound like the permafrost on her words hadn't yet reached her heart?

"Yes, you sound all broken up."

I heard her draw in a breath like a hiss. "You have no right to judge me." Finally, some real emotion. She was mad.

"You called me. Four times. It's been nice shooting the breeze with you, Ms. Lowe. I've got to go—"

"Wait! Please don't hang up!"

It was the "please" that stopped me. "Why not?"

"I admit I didn't take Ian seriously," she said.

"But now you do?"

"Yes."

"Why?"

"Uh, I'd rather not say on the phone. That's why I want to meet in person."

"I'm at the Willard."

"You could be on the Hill in ten minutes."

"I have to park."

"Oh. Well, half an hour, then."

"Where do I meet you?"

"There's a desk for Senate visitors at the CVC."

"The what?"

"Capitol Visitor Center."

"Wouldn't this be easier if I came straight to whichever Senate Office Building you work in?"

"We're not going to be meeting in my office."

I wondered what she had in mind. "What do I do? Sign in and someone comes to get me?"

"No," she said. "I'll be waiting for you. I suggest you take the tunnel from the Library of Congress, the Jefferson Building, because it brings you directly inside the second floor of the visitor center. Otherwise you have to hassle with the crowds in the Capitol plaza and the tour lines in Emancipation Hall. When you come into the library on the street level, the hallway to the tunnel is on the left. If you get to the Senate desk before I do, whatever you do, for God's sake don't sign in."

The parking situation on the Hill was even worse than it had been around police headquarters. I wedged the Mini into a spot on a residential street behind the Supreme Court and walked the few blocks to the Library of Congress. For some people, Washington, the federal city, conjures images of the monuments or the White House or the Capitol dome on the skyline. For me, it's this place—East Capitol and First streets—where the Capitol, the Library of Congress, and the Supreme Court sit across from one another, their classically elegant façades representing the confluence of law, letters, and justice at a quiet tree-lined intersection.

Security inside the Jefferson Building on the basement level was not complicated—I passed through a metal detector and set my purse and cane on an X-ray conveyor. I retrieved my things and found the corridor to the tunnel just as Summer described it. At the bottom of a flight of stairs the Capitol police had set up their own security checkpoint with more metal detectors and X-ray machines. I nearly asked what they thought I might have acquired to warrant the belt-and-suspenders mentality of double searches within a few hundred feet of each other when I'd never left the library. Maybe it was a territorial thing.

The well-lit marble corridor that led to the Capitol coiled like a snake as it sloped deeper under First Street. At the height of cherry blossom season, I expected this walkway to be cheek by jowl with tourists, Hill staffers, and library researchers heading from one building to the other. Instead, my footfalls echoed eerily as I passed framed posters from the Library's many collections. The only other sound was the steady hiss of the air circulating through the tunnel. Otherwise I was alone, unable to see around the corkscrew curve ahead of me or behind me. It wasn't until I heard a child's laughter and the chatter of her mother and father that I realized I'd been holding my breath—imagining shadows and wisps of voices, and hearing the echo of Ian's remark yesterday that he was being followed.

I was relieved when a set of double doors spilled me onto the upper level of the visitor center with its bustle and noise and crowds. Straight ahead, two men in fire engine red blazers sat behind a large desk. The din on the lower level sounded like an army massing for battle and I leaned over the railing to see what was going on. An enormous white plaster cast of the bronze Freedom statue that stood atop the Capitol dome dominated a light-filled marble room where hundreds of people waited in lines for tours and tickets. Above me through a fretted skylight was the Capitol dome as close as if I were on the roof of the House of Representatives.

A tour guide in a red vest told me I was standing next to the desk for House visitors. The Senate desk was at the opposite end of the corridor.

Summer Lowe spotted me before I reached it. Today her tawny hair was done up in a sleek chignon and she wore a vintage black-and-white houndstooth checked suit with peep-toe heels. She would have looked at home on the set of a Bogart film.

She took my arm and pulled me away from the desk.

"Come on," she said under her breath. "Ladies' room."

Before I could reply, she pushed me into the handicapped stall and followed me in, closing the door behind us and sliding her oversized canvas tote off her shoulder. She reached in and pulled out something.

A Senate ID on a lanyard. I looked at the photo. Someone named Lana Davidson. We looked vaguely alike.

"Put it on and give me your jacket."

"Why are we doing this?" I asked.

She stuffed my jacket in her bag. "So you don't have to sign in. No one knows you're here, except me."

"And presumably Lana Davidson."

"She owed me a favor. Luckily I'd seen what you look like. This'll do."

"Does Lana use a cane?"

Summer's eyes flickered briefly to my leg. "No, but I'm counting on not running into someone who knows her. As for everyone else noticing, anyone can have a temporary injury and you don't drag your foot around like a real cripple. Looks like you just use it for balance."

"Gee, thanks."

Her cheeks turned pink. "That was sort of crude, wasn't it? Sorry."

I eyed her. "Where are we going?"

"The Capitol. My boss's hideaway. Here's how we're going to do this." She reached again into her tote bag, pulling out a sheaf of papers and a softbound book with a green cover that she handed to me.

"Lana Davidson and I are going to leave here and take the escalator to the Capitol. There'll be a bunch of Capitol Hill police by the escalator. They expect to see you wearing either a stick-on visitor's pass or a Hill ID. Otherwise you wouldn't be going anywhere. Once we get past them, no one is going to give you a second look. Just act like you own the place and we'll be fine."

Just act like I owned the U.S. Capitol. I read what was written on the cover of the book she'd given me. "S. 576. A bill to provide rules for the modification or disposition of certain assets by real estate mortgage investment conduits pursuant to division A—"

Summer shook my arm. "Let's get out of here."

We left the ladies' room and headed down a corridor with signs pointing to the Capitol. As she warned me, at the escalator four Capitol Hill police officers watched everyone come and go as they talked among themselves.

Maybe it was my nerves showing or maybe it was the fact that one of them nudged the other to check out the two of us—guys ogling girls—but Summer suddenly said in a loud voice, "It's going to be in markup next week, but God knows when they'll get it to the floor. If it does pass, the Senate version is so different from the House we'll probably end up in reconciliation, anyway."

The officers were still watching.

"Why don't you talk your boss into waiting until you get more support?" I said. "You've got a year and a half before sine die. Bring it up during the second session."

Summer didn't reply, but her mouth twitched like she was trying to control her expression. She waited until we entered the dimly lit

Crypt, which had originally been planned as George Washington's burial place.

"Not bad, Lana. Where did you learn the inside baseball stuff about the legislative process?"

"Thanks for the curveball. Working for a small environmental nonprofit a few years ago. Not one you heard of. My boss sent me to hearings and markups, or else I'd stop by one of the galleries to watch a vote," I said, as she whisked me around the corner to a set of worn marble stairs in a dim corridor. "Yeah, I know. I could have just turned on C-SPAN. But it's not the same as being here."

We entered the Capitol Rotunda and I caught my breath. "I can't believe I'm telling you this, but I watch *Mr. Smith Goes to Washington* at least once a year. It gives me hope."

Summer grinned. "I guess I underestimated you."

"You wouldn't be the first." I stared up at Brumidi's fresco *The Apotheosis of Washington* nearly two hundred feet above our heads.

"Let's go." Her voice was urgent once again. "I can't be gone long. Someone's going to miss me and ask where I've been. We haven't got much time."

She led me down a corridor into the small Senate Rotunda with its columned arcade surrounding a spectacular crystal chandelier.

"You know that chandelier used to be in a vaudeville theater?" she said as we turned down another hallway.

"No. I didn't."

"The things you learn working here. Turn left."

We raced down a corridor of private rooms that was well away from any public tour. Summer pulled a key out of her jacket pocket and stopped in front of a nondescript door with a sign on the wall that read S-206. I'd heard about senators' hideaways and what did and didn't go on inside. There were the legitimate reasons—a quiet place to get work done away from constituents and staff or to hold a meeting. Some hideaways had sofas or daybeds, convenient for when the Senate was in session all night and it was too far to walk back to the Dirksen or Russell or Hart office buildings between votes. That was the aboveboard stuff. Then there was the hanky-panky, most of which involved alcohol and sex.

Summer opened the door. "After you."

Senator Cameron Vaughn's hideaway was a mixture of personal and patriotic, but it was a restful retreat rather than a working office. The walls were painted butter yellow; the woodwork was white. A primitive carved wooden statue of an eagle dominated a fireplace mantel with an American flag folded in the shape of a triangle behind it. The fireplace itself had been freshly laid with firewood and the room held a faint tinge of wood smoke. Silver-framed pictures of Vaughn's good-looking wife and four teenage children adorned the walls and sat atop a credenza, which held bottles of top-drawer alcohol. Law books filled the bookshelves on either side of the fireplace. A yellow-and-white-striped sofa and two patterned upholstered armchairs were grouped around a coffee table, which had a box of Cohiba cigars sitting on it. Through a tall slim window I caught a slivered view of the Mall with the Washington Monument and the Lincoln Memorial in the distance.

"Have a seat," Summer said. "How about a drink?"

She dropped into one of the armchairs and kicked off her shoes. I took the sofa.

"No, thanks; I'm fine."

"I'll have one, if you don't mind." She jumped up and padded over to the credenza, where she fixed herself a gin and tonic. I hadn't noticed the minifridge tucked inside.

She flung herself into the chair again and put her feet up on the coffee table, crossing her legs. I thought she seemed nervous, keyed up.

"Why'd we have to meet like this?" I asked.

"Because as far as anyone knows, you were never here. Neither was I. Lana slipped me the key. Hopefully the senator won't walk in on us."

I glanced automatically at the door to the suite. "Why the secrecy?"

"Do you really think Ian drowned in that hot tub?" she asked.

I still wanted an answer to my question but I answered hers anyway. "No."

She threw back her head and gulped her drink. "I don't, either."

"I think his death had something to do with testifying before your committee," I said.

Her voice was grim. "I'm sure it did."

"Why?"

"Cameron got pressured this morning to cancel the hearing altogether now that we don't have a witness."

"Pressured by whom?"

"Harlan Jennings."

I blew out a breath. Harlan, again. Deeper and deeper. "What did he say?"

She shrugged. "Cameron didn't go into detail, but apparently Jennings said the publicity surrounding Rebecca Natale was already making investors at Thomas Asher Investments so uptight it was affecting the markets. Did we want to be responsible for pushing things closer to the edge—or even over it—based on one person's unsubstantiated allegations?"

"Harlan actually said that?"

"Strongly hinted would be more accurate," she said.

"Or threatened?"

"You say tomato." She shrugged. "He also brought up the hoopla surrounding that antique Asher's ancestor stole from the White House. Another unflattering development. Now the news about Ian. They don't need this on top of everything else."

"Yeah, it wasn't so good for Ian, either."

She made a face. "You know what I meant. Look, our hearing would have probably merited a lousy paragraph somewhere on the federal page or what passes for the business section in the *Trib* or the *Post* these days. Instead we're in the A Section. Asher's supposedly so mad he's talking to the paintings on his boardroom wall. His people are pulling out all the stops to shut down any negative publicity that's out there. Especially a Senate hearing."

She slugged more of her drink.

"And now you've decided to do more digging on your own?"

"CYA, baby, CYA. I want to know what's going on."

Cover your ass. I wonder if she meant hers or her boss's.

"I can't believe Harlan would lean on Senator Vaughn like that," I said.

"Why not? He's probably got Tommy Asher breathing down his neck," she said. "Not something I'd relish. I met Sir Thomas. Once. He intimidated the hell out of me, though I have to admit he's enthralling. A shameless name-dropper. The guy could probably talk God into leaning on Cameron."

"Asher and Harlan go way back," I said. "They met when Harlan's father was the British ambassador and Asher's was an embassy driver."

"Are you serious?" Her eyes narrowed. "How do you know that? Don't tell me you know Harlan Jennings personally?"

"I've known him for ages. He lives in Middleburg. It's a small town. Our parents used to socialize together."

She sat up straight and slid her feet to the floor. "Whoa, there. Hang on. Who are you, anyway? First I meet you with Ian, now I find out you and Harlan Jennings are childhood buddies. Whose side are you on, Lucie?"

"No one's. I could ask you the same thing."

Summer stood up and moved to the window, looking out at the view. "I'm keeping an eye out for Cameron. Until I find out what's what, I want to keep it under the radar."

"Why? Are you worried someone's watching you like they were watching Ian?"

She spun around. The afternoon sunlight shining through the window cast her in shadow, making her seem somehow less substantial.

"Oh, my God," she said. "Someone was watching Ian?"

"He thought so." I half-wished I'd accepted her offer of a drink. Now I needed it.

"What was Rebecca Natale going to tell Ian, Lucie? What did he tell you last night?"

"I have no idea what Rebecca wanted to tell him," I said. "But he thought Thomas Asher Investments is no more than a giant Ponzi scheme."

Summer put her hands in front of her mouth like she was praying. "That would be a financial catastrophe."

"No fooling."

"Rebecca must have known if that was true," she said.

"Apparently she didn't believe Ian at first when he confronted her about it," I said. "But she might have changed her mind."

"And now she's dead and so is he." She paused. "Wow, that's pretty damn scary."

"I know," I said. "And Rebecca is still missing. No one's found her body."

We both heard footfalls in the corridor and a man and a woman talking loudly. Summer went rigid, her eyes fixed on the door. The voices receded.

Our eyes met and she let out a long breath.

"Just because you're paranoid doesn't mean they're not really after you." Her laugh was nervous.

"You said no one knows we're here," I said. "Let's try not to scare ourselves over nothing."

She nodded and finished her drink. "How did you get dragged into the middle of this? You own a vineyard. What's Asher Investments to you?"

"Rebecca is an old friend," I said. "And it's a lot more complicated than you know."

"Meaning what?"

"Nothing I can talk about right now."

Summer glanced at an antique clock on the mantel. "I've been gone too long. No one is going to believe I had my phone turned off all this time."

"Then maybe you should get me out of here," I said.

"We need to talk again. Will you get in touch with me if you find out anything?"

So she could cover her ass?

"Only if you agree to do the same."

"I'll call you in a few days," she said. "Let's see where we are then."

We walked back to the Rotunda in silence and took an elevator to the basement. She led me to a doorway to the portico under the east steps to the Capitol.

"It's less conspicuous than letting you walk down that big marble staircase," she said. "Sorry to deny you your Jimmy Stewart moment."

We swapped my jacket for her lanyard and the papers.

"Watch yourself," she said.

When I turned around she was gone and I was alone in the darkened passageway with only the noise of the wind whipping past me, howling in my ears.

CHAPTER 16

It was just after four thirty when I crossed the visitor center plaza and headed for my car. A dark-suited man with a craggy face and snow-white hair surrounded by aides who enveloped him like a cloud swept past me. It wasn't hard to understand the heady sense of power that pervaded this place and how it could be seductive—even addictive—if one worked here long enough. How difficult would it be not to succumb to feeling invincible or entitled—above the laws made here for everyone else in the country to obey? Is that what had happened to Harlan, strong-arming Cameron Vaughn to cancel that hearing looking into Asher Investments now that Ian was dead?

What I couldn't figure out was why Harlan was playing such a high-stakes game of chicken. Did he know something the police hadn't yet figured out about Rebecca's disappearance and Ian's so-called accidental drowning? Was he covering up for his blood brother Tommy Asher—or himself?

I reached the Mini as a police officer strolling down A Street tucked parking tickets behind the windshield wipers of cars whose owners had violated the two-hour limit for nonresident parking. I pulled out of my space when he was still half a block away, aware that I'd been there more than two hours. I wondered if he'd chalked my tires.

He looked up as I drove away.

★ ★ ★

It took forty-five minutes to drive the twenty-odd blocks down Constitution Avenue and across the Teddy Roosevelt Bridge. The second-worst traffic in the country after L.A. Somewhere I'd read how many days per year Washingtonians wasted sitting in their cars in traffic. Days, not hours. A radio traffic reporter rattled off the daily litany of pileups and jammed roadways clogged with what he called "volume." It would be a long trip home.

Just after seven o'clock I exited onto Route 15 in Leesburg, the traffic now settling into the thinned-out remnants of rush hour. At Gilbert's Corner I put on my headlights as I turned west onto Mosby's Highway, the home stretch. Another car turned off 15 and pulled up behind me. He was still there, too close for comfort, when I slowed for the twenty-five-mile-per-hour speed limit through the village of Aldie. At the Snickersville Turnpike, I sped up. The other car did, too. On this winding two-lane road, with a solid yellow line painted down the middle, I was stuck with him until we reached a stretch that allowed passing.

But even when the road opened up and I dropped below the speed limit hoping he'd take the hint and pass me, he didn't budge. From what I could see in the rearview mirror, the other car was big and dark, like a Navigator or a Suburban. Maybe it was only kids clowning around or someone on a cell phone who wasn't paying attention.

We were back to the no-passing zone so I sped up. The speed limit was fifty, but I pushed it to sixty, then sixty-five. He was like a shadow, right there behind me, just the two of us with no other cars on the road. My heart began rabbiting in my chest. This couldn't be whoever had followed Ian, could it?

Mosby's Highway was a dark ribbon of twists and turns the rest of the way to Middleburg, and that was five more miles on what was now a deserted country lane. Except for the occasional light from a farmhouse window and the wash of moonlight on treetops or the crest of a hill, the only other light came from his headlights. I checked my rearview mirror at the exact moment he flashed his brights. It was like looking into the flash of a camera or directly at the sun. I swerved. These were not kids fooling around.

Thank God I knew every hill and bend in this road. With any luck, whoever was following me wasn't a local. I pushed the Mini to seventy and sped away from the big car. Seconds later he gunned his engine and caught up with me again. Now I'd provoked him. If he wanted to, he could sideswipe me, send me into the ditch, and drive on.

It looked like that was exactly what he had in mind. His head-lights disappeared from my rearview mirror as he shifted left into the lane for oncoming traffic. As he did so, a deer leaped over a low stone wall on his side of the road. For a second the animal stopped on the shoulder, like a lawn ornament frozen in the glare of our headlights. The other car's brakes screeched and the deer darted across Mosby's Highway, disappearing into the brush. Where there's one deer, there are usually two or even three. The second one emerged almost immediately from a pine grove beyond the wall. It was a buck with six, maybe eight points. I swerved once again, this time onto the right shoulder as the other car hit the deer head-on. I heard a crack, followed by a loud thump and breaking glass. Probably his wind-shield. I slalomed back onto the road and prayed there would be no third animal. When I finally dared to look in the mirror, his head-lights were receding in the distance. The buck lay sprawled across his hood, and neither the car nor the animal was going anywhere.

I sped through Middleburg even though I knew the driver could no longer be following me, running the lone traffic light at the intersection of Washington and Madison. Businesses were shuttered for the night and the streets were dark and quiet. For the rest of the trip home, I had the road to myself. This time I'd been lucky. What about next time, or the one after that?

When I finally reached the entrance to the winery and turned onto Sycamore Lane, our private drive, I was thinking more clearly. What if he hadn't been the only one pursuing me? What if a com-panion was waiting here, at my house? At the split by the trunk of the two-hundred-year-old sycamore tree that gave the road its name, I went left instead of right, turning into the cul-de-sac where Quinn's and Antonio's cottages were located. Even though it was only eight o'clock on a Wednesday night, Quinn's place was dark. But lights burned from every one of Antonio's windows.

I parked in his small gravel driveway and banged on the front door. When he finally opened it, his jet-black hair was wet like he'd just showered. He was barefoot and wearing an undershirt and faded jeans. The planes of his face were in shadow, backlit by the cheery lamplight inside, but I could see the alarm in his eyes when he realized who I was.

"Lucie! What are you doing here? You okay? Everything okay in the winery? What is it?"

Antonio was only the third farm manager to work at the vineyard since my parents founded the place, but he reminded me of Hector Cruz, who'd managed the crew and taken care of the equipment for most of the last twenty years. Antonio was a young double for Hector with his strong good looks and even-tempered personality. I'd hired him the day we met. The men liked and respected him; he had good instincts with the vines; and what he didn't know about fixing broken equipment wasn't worth knowing. It hadn't taken long before he became as indispensable in the field as Frankie was in the winery.

"Are you okay?" he asked again. "Something's wrong?"

"Someone was following me on Mosby's Highway. They started back on Fifteen when I got off the Toll Road," I said. "I lost whoever it was when he hit a deer. I'm sorry, Antonio . . . I feel stupid bothering you."

"Don't be silly. Come in." He put a brotherly arm around my shoulder and pulled me inside.

His dining room table had been set for two and the place smelled of onions, garlic, and roasting meat. A man didn't go to all this trouble if a guy was joining him for dinner. Antonio was expecting a woman.

"You have a guest coming."

"It's okay. Can I get you something? Wine? A beer?"

"Just water, please."

He led me to a brown leather sofa with a colorful serape draped across the back. The rest of his living room was simply furnished— coffee table, armchair, and television—but it looked like someone's home, unlike Quinn's place, which reminded me of a combination locker room and monastic cell. Brick-and-board shelves held a collection of music and movies. Two primitive paintings that looked Mexican hung on the wall above the sofa.

He returned with a glass of water. I needed both hands to hold it.

"Tell me what happened," he said.

When I was done he said, "Do you want to stay here tonight? You could have the couch, if you wouldn't mind? I, uh, might have, uh—"

The smell of something burning drifted into the living room.

"Your dinner," I said. "I think you'd better rescue it."

He muttered in Spanish and bolted for the kitchen. I followed and leaned against the doorjamb, watching him stir the contents of an ironstone casserole dish as he checked what was in the oven with the ease of a practiced chef.

"You're welcome to stay and eat with us," he said.

Before the near disaster with his dinner he'd been about to tell me that his guest probably planned to spend the night as well. Antonio kept his personal life to himself and I'd never pried, but I was glad to learn he had a girlfriend. As for me staying, three was a crowd.

"I nearly ruined your meal. I'm not about to ruin your evening. Thanks, but I'll be okay. I feel better now, I've calmed down. When I get home I'll lock all the doors and windows."

He gave his casserole another stir. "You need a gun? You can take my hunting rifle."

I'd never shot a weapon in my life, even though Leland had a gun cabinet that could outfit a small militia.

"I've got plenty of guns, thanks."

"I will go with you to make sure you're all right, check around the house and make sure everything is good. But if anything happens—you hear something or you get worried—I want you to call me right away. *¿Entiendes?*"

"*Sí, entiendo.* I understand."

"I can be there like that." He snapped his fingers. "And if you change your mind, you come back here, okay?"

"Thanks, Antonio."

"Give me a minute."

He pulled his phone out of his pocket and punched a button. She was on speed dial. He left the kitchen as she answered. I heard his staccato Spanish, probably telling her to make herself at home if he wasn't here. When he returned, he had pulled on a hooded fleece with the vineyard logo on it. I saw the bulge underneath on his right hip.

His revolver.

"You don't have to go home if you don't want to, you know?" he said. "Nothing wrong with being scared of the bad guys."

"For how long? I can't let someone stop me living my life. Besides, I'll have one of my father's guns for protection. I'll be okay."

"You know what you're doing with such a gun?" Antonio looked skeptical.

"It won't be target practice. I'll shoot until I hit something. Or someone."

"Guess I won't pay you a surprise visit, then." He flashed a brilliant smile and I grinned back at him.

"Come on, *hija*," he said. "Let's saddle up."

He took Hector's old Superman blue pickup truck and I followed him in the Mini through the velvety black night. Antonio was a crack shot. I'd seen him take down deer and crows. I hoped he wouldn't need to use his gun once we got to my house.

I hoped no one was already there, waiting for me.

CHAPTER 17

⎯⎯⎯⎯⎯⎯⎯⎯⎯⎯

The house was dark and silent as we pulled up in the driveway. Maybe it was time to start locking the doors when I left in the morning. Most days I didn't bother in case a neighbor wanted to drop off a bag of homegrown tomatoes or return a borrowed book or garden tool. Atoka was that kind of town—but maybe not anymore.

Antonio stopped the pickup and I pulled up beside him.

"Stay right there," he said. "I'm going to take a look around. If I don't come back in a few minutes, get out of here and call the sheriff."

I nodded, afraid if I spoke it would betray my nerves.

Within two minutes he was back. "All clear. Let's go inside. Me first."

He turned on lights and checked every room, but I could have told him we wouldn't find anyone. Somehow the house, which had been in my family for more than two hundred years, would have given me a clue that an intruder waited for us. The Montgomery clan motto—*Garde bien,* "watch well"—was carved into the lintel above the front door. For two centuries, the house had taken care of my ancestors and me. It wasn't going to let me down now.

"Where are those guns?" Antonio asked.

"The library."

It had once been my father's office. I'd had the floor-to-ceiling cherry bookcases on either side of the fireplace rebuilt after a fire a few years ago, though we'd lost most of Leland's vast collection of rare books on Jefferson and early American history. Gradually I'd filled the shelves with my own selection, adding a few small water-colors and bronzes I'd bought at Macdonald's Fine Antiques to fill some of the empty spaces. Besides the bookshelves, the room con-tained my father's antique desk, two wing chairs, a coffee table, and a sofa and love seat upholstered in the Montgomery clan's heathery blue, green, and red tartan—and my father's gun cabinet.

Antonio had never been in this room and I didn't think he had any idea how many weapons Leland had owned. He let out an appreciative whistle as I unlocked the etched-glass doors, revealing what was inside.

"*Madre de Díos.*" He ran a hand down the barrel of an antique shotgun. "That's a Baker Rifle. The Mexicans used it at the Alamo. Look at all these. The only thing you don't have is a cannon."

"Leland wanted one. My mother said over her dead body."

He smiled at the feeble humor. "Let's get you set up, Lucita. Do you really know what you're doing?"

"I watched Leland shoot enough times."

He gave me a skeptical look. I hadn't answered the question.

"Pistols and revolvers in there?" He pointed to a drawer.

I pulled it open. "Yes."

Another low whistle and something under his breath in Spanish.

"How about you take the Colt forty-five?" Antonio lifted his fleece so I could see the gun on his hip. "Like mine."

"Why not the Glock?"

"I got a friend in the marines. He says never trust a gun if you can't divide the caliber by five. If the guy's wearing body armor and all you've got is that nine-millimeter Glock, he might not even go down. Then he gets off a couple rounds and you do."

"Oh."

"So you gonna use the Colt, okay? It's got good stopping power."

I nodded.

"Where's your ammunition?"

I showed him the drawer.

"Want me to load a clip for you?" He eyed Leland's ample stock of magazines and loose rounds.

"Sure. Thanks."

"Before I do that, I wanna be sure you know how to slide the safety off. Use your thumb like this. See?" He showed me. "But keep it on until you need it. We don't want no accidents."

"I know. Believe me, I know."

He showed me the gun. "Okay, this is a semiautomatic, so when you pull the trigger, it shoots once. But it gets easier after you get off the first round, *entiendes*?"

"Yes."

"Don't worry, Lucie. You hit someone with this and it's gonna stop him good. Better, it's gonna go through him and hit whatever's behind him. So aim for the center mass, okay? He probably won't be expecting you to have a gun, but you don't want to give him a chance to fire his. Even if he's hurt."

"Right."

Antonio looked doubtful. "You sure you want to do this? I can stay here with you for a while, or you can come back to my place. The offer's still good."

The offer was still tempting. But how long could I go on hiding and living in fear? It was also possible the tailgater out on Mosby's Highway was in no way involved in Rebecca's disappearance and Ian's death—and that I had an overactive imagination.

I patted his arm gratefully. "Thanks, Antonio, but I'll be okay. Besides, I'll bet that guy has other things on his mind right now, like the damage he did to his car after plowing into that deer."

"Where were you when it happened?" He finished loading the Colt and handed it to me. "Here. Be careful."

"Thanks. On the other side of Middleburg. Just after Mickie Gordon Park."

His cell phone vibrated and his eyes darted to the number. He turned off the phone. "I'll check it out tomorrow."

"Don't you need to get that call?"

He gave me his warm smile. "I call her back later."

"Thank you for doing this, Antonio."

"You gonna lock the doors when I go, okay?" he said. "I'm going to drive around Sycamore Lane one more time and check the front gate by Atoka Road. Want me to call you when I'm done?"

"Sure. Thanks."

We walked to my front door. Antonio peered through one of the sidelights.

"Looks quiet." He pulled his gun anyway and my heart started hammering again.

He waited outside until I locked the door. Then he got into the pickup and I watched until his taillights disappeared.

There was no way I was going to sleep tonight. I found one of my mother's crocheted afghans in an antique carved cedar chest in the back hallway and brought it into the library. Then I locked a door that led from the kitchen through that hallway to a staircase to the second floor. If anyone got into the house, I wanted them to come through the central foyer, not sneak upstairs the back way.

My cell phone rang and I almost dropped my gun. Antonio, reporting that all was quiet. I tried Quinn's number one more time, but it went to voice mail, so I disconnected without leaving a message.

I pulled the curtains shut and settled down on the sofa, positioning myself so I could see through the doorway into the foyer. I sat there with my eyes on the door and my hand inches from my gun, waiting until morning.

The shelf clock chiming in the parlor across the foyer woke me at five. It was still dark and the sun wouldn't be up until six thirty. I had dozed off and on, possibly even slept a little, but the inside of my eyelids felt like they were coated with sandpaper.

I got up and made coffee. One more night like this and I'd be walking around like the living dead. By the time I showered and got dressed, the lacquered pearl sky promised a sweet spring day. Last night's fears receded. I walked into my bedroom and looked at my unslept-in bed. Maybe if I just lay down for a few minutes . . .

The next time I woke up, the telephone on my nightstand was ringing, sunlight was streaming through the windows, and it was nine thirty. I sat up and answered the phone.

It was Frankie. "You okay? I thought you were coming by the villa this morning to go over the events calendar."

"I overslept. Sorry. Can we do it later?"

"Sure." She sounded puzzled. "Is something wrong?"

"I didn't get much sleep last night."

"Did everything go okay in D.C.? Did you see that woman from the Hill? What happened when you talked to the cops?"

How much did I want to share with her, especially after what had happened last night? No point alarming her right now.

"Everything went fine in D.C., I did see the woman on the Hill, and nothing happened when I talked to that detective."

"That's all you've got to say?"

"Pretty much."

Silence on her end. Frankie wasn't used to me shutting her out, but right now it seemed the less she knew, the better. I didn't want to tell her I'd slept with a gun last night, though it probably wouldn't be long before she weaseled that information out of Antonio.

"I've got to go to Middleburg for an errand," I said. "I'll be in later, okay?"

"How about if I order lunch for us here? Just the two of us." She switched to the sweet, persuasive voice she used to bend someone to her will. "I'll get sandwiches from the deli and a couple of cow puddles from the Upper Crust. Your favorite. Then you can tell me what really happened."

"I don't succumb easily to bribes."

"Make an exception. You're a walking zombie lately, Lucie. You can't keep all this stuff bottled up inside."

She waited.

"Okay," I said. "Noon."

"Good," she said. "I'll be all ears."

Quinn called on my way out the front door.

"I just went for a little drive with Antonio." His voice sounded unnaturally calm. "Out on Mosby's Highway near Mickie Gordon Park."

"Oh?" My hand tightened around the phone. "How'd it go?"

"Just fine. Nothing out there to report."

That couldn't be true.

"Are you sure? No dead deer by the roadside, maybe?"

The other car had struck it head-on. I was sure it went through the windshield. If the animal hadn't died instantly, I didn't see how it could have survived the night. Had Animal Control hauled away the carcass so quickly? Usually it took them a few days.

"Just a dead squirrel. That's all." He paused. "So how come you went to Antonio last night and not me?"

"You weren't home and your phone was set to voice mail. The guy who followed me hit a deer, not a squirrel."

"Sorry to disappoint you, but the only roadkill was that squirrel. And I was playing poker with a couple of guys. Got home by ten. There weren't any messages from you."

"I didn't leave any."

"Why not?"

I didn't like his challenging tone. What right did he have to jump all over me? I was the one who'd been chased by some nut driving like he was at a NASCAR rally, not him.

"I don't know why not. Look, everything worked out fine. Antonio got me set up with Leland's forty-five so if anybody had gotten into the house, I would have been able to defend myself."

"You slept with a gun last night? Jesus, Lucie."

"I didn't actually sleep with it. It was beside me on the coffee table."

I heard him mutter something that sounded profane. "You should have told me, left a message, something. Why in the hell didn't you?"

I was tired and irritable, and, since he asked for it, I gave it to him.

"Because in a couple of months or maybe weeks you're not going to be here anymore, that's why. I figured I might as well start getting used to it. I heard you went to look at the Jenningses' land yesterday. Did you buy it?"

There was another long silence on his end and I knew my remark had been the start of drawing the boundaries of how it would be between us once he left.

"No," he said in a quiet voice. "I didn't."

"Why not, if you don't mind my asking?"

"I've got some money stuff to get in order first. But it's a great piece of property. I'd like you to see it."

I felt a small stab through my heart. "Sure. Anytime."

"I'm racking over that bad lot of Viognier this morning," he said. "It's getting worse, so I decided we should at least try that and see if it helps. And I'm thinking about continuing the bench trials. Maybe this afternoon. Work for you?"

His voice was cool and back to all business.

"I'm having lunch with Frankie to go over the events calendar but I can do it after that."

"Okay. See you this afternoon."

"Right."

I drove to Middleburg, feeling battered and bruised. Why had I told him I wanted to get used to life without him when I really wanted him not to leave? Why was it so hard to tell him that I still cared?

I knew why. Because I didn't want to know that he could get used to life without me.

I stopped by Books & Crannies in Middleburg and ordered a copy of *The Poetical Works of Alexander Pope*. The book wouldn't be in for a day or two, but they'd be happy to mail it if I couldn't come by to pick it up. I said thanks and went across the street to the Cuppa Giddyup for the largest coffee they had to go.

I climbed the little staircase back up to Washington Street and thought some more about last night. Hitting that deer must have done some serious damage to the other car—body damage, a cracked or shattered windshield, things that now went clunk under the hood. Had the driver already taken it to a repair shop? Some place around here? How long would it take to find out—and would anyone tell me if I asked?

Mickie Gordon Park was a mile or so down the road. After what Quinn said about finding nothing more than a dead squirrel, I needed to check things out myself. They might have looked in the wrong place. I'd heard brakes so there ought to be skid marks. Surely I'd find blood from the deer, even if the carcass were gone.

I crossed Washington and walked toward my parking place on Jay Street. Through the open door of Macdonald's Fine Antiques, I saw Mac in a heated conversation with Austin Kendall, the retired owner of Kendall Real Estate a few doors down. Austin divided his time between the golf course and checking in on his daughter Erica, who now ran the business. He wore his usual golfing attire, but he was holding a rolled-up copy of *The Wall Street Journal,* which he whacked on a desk as he spoke, punctuating his words. Mac kept shaking his head, as though he couldn't believe what he was hearing. I stopped in the doorway when he brought up Harlan Jennings's name.

Mac had a special radar when it came to potential customers, even if they were not in his direct line of vision. His head swiveled in my direction and he gave me a dispirited wave. Austin was too absorbed in what he was saying to notice me. His voice boomed like a carnival barker's.

". . . find out if this is true or not. I swear, if it is and Harlan's known about it all along, I'll get the tar and you and the boys get the pitchforks."

Any other time I wouldn't have walked into Mac's place holding a cup of coffee since he was death on people eating or drinking around his antiques. But I knew they were talking about the unraveling of the shroud behind which Thomas Asher Investments had conducted its business, and what I'd overheard sounded like Mac wasn't the only Romeo who had invested with Harlan. Mac looked so distraught I probably could have rolled a wine barrel into the store and he wouldn't have noticed.

". . . damn near everything," Mac was saying. "At least I own the building."

"That's more than I can say," Austin said. "When I sold the business to Erica, I parked everything with Harlan, including my 401(k). God, wouldn't that be a kick in the head? Asking my own daughter for a job at my age because the old man's broke."

Mac touched his finger to his lips, silencing Austin and indicating that they had company.

"Can I help you, Lucie?" he asked. "You looking for another of those bronzes for your library?"

"No, thank you. I'm sorry, but I couldn't help overhearing. *Both* of you are clients of Harlan's and Thomas Asher Investments?"

Austin turned around and gave me a how-dare-you look. "I don't believe that's any of your business, young lady."

At the same time Mac said, "Why do you want to know? Did you give him money, too?"

"Of course she didn't." Austin looked annoyed. "Harlan promised us it was going to be just the . . ." He broke off. "Did you, Lucie?"

"Every dime I make goes right back into the vineyard," I said. "You were starting to say something about what Harlan promised?"

Austin had spent his lifetime putting people in the home of their dreams and he was usually pretty smooth and glib. Right now he looked the way he did when the housing bubble burst a few years ago.

"Aw, Austin, what difference does it make if she knows?" Mac said. "The cat's out of the bag, anyway."

Austin gave in, but not gracefully. "Fine. You tell her."

"Harlan manages our money," Mac said. "He did it for the Romeos. A favor."

"He set up something just for us," Austin said. "That's how we kept it. With a small group he could be more nimble, have more freedom. For years we were doing great, especially after he got involved with Asher."

"Why are you asking about this?" Mac asked.

"I'll tell you why," Austin said. "Because of that woman. The one who worked for Asher and drowned in the Potomac. I heard you knew her. What'd she tell you, Lucie? Now it's your turn to talk." He folded his arms across his chest and tapped the rolled-up newspaper.

"She didn't tell me anything," I said.

That, at least, was true. What Ian had told me about the Ponzi scheme was another matter and I didn't want to bring it up with either of them just now—especially without concrete proof. But before this, I'd thought of Tommy Asher's clients as nameless, faceless individuals who got suckered into something that seemed too good to be true. People who were motivated by the old-as-time irresistible urge to get something for nothing, or nearly nothing. I never thought my neighbors, men who were sophisticated and savvy about money, would get swept up in the tide.

"Look," Mac said, "I've had enough stalling. I'm calling Harlan and getting to the bottom of this. I want my money back today. I don't want to lose everything."

There was a moment of ominous silence before every clock in Mac's store, including a tall grandfather clock by the front door, began chiming the hour in a lovely cacophony. Another uneasy glance passed between Mac and Austin as the clocks finished tolling eleven and the phone rang on Mac's desk.

"I'm not answering that," Mac said. "The machine'll get it."

His message echoed in the quiet room followed by the voice of Seth Hannah, president of Blue Ridge Federal Bank. Everyone in Atoka banked with Seth, including me.

"If you're there," Seth said, "you'd better turn on CNN right now. There's something you need to be watching."

Mac picked up the phone and spoke a few terse words before hanging up. Austin found the remote for a small television that sat on a walnut end table. He punched buttons until CNN came on.

I'd almost expected to see Harlan, but it was Tommy Asher, flanked by two sober-faced men in dark suits. He was reading from a piece of paper, half-glasses slipped down the bridge of his nose, more Rock of Gibraltar stolid calm.

". . . is my unfortunate duty to inform the many people who have put their faith and trust in me that I have been the victim—we all have been victims—of a massive fraud perpetuated by an employee of Thomas Asher Investments. In the past twenty-four hours we have uncovered evidence that one of my employees has systematically moved funds into an as-yet-unknown account or accounts. Let me assure each and every one of my clients that your money is as safe today as it has been for the last two decades. What I need now is your cooperation while we take some measures in the process of getting to the bottom of this. I am temporarily freezing withdrawals from all funds until further notice. It is a prudent precaution to ensure the safety of everyone's assets and I thank you for your continued faith in me, which I promise will be justified, as it has always been."

Asher looked up and removed his glasses. He was no longer reading. "On Monday I stood before you, devastated by the loss of one of my most brilliant and talented advisers. Just yesterday I learned that this young woman, Rebecca Natale, is the thief. She is the traitor who betrayed us all."

CHAPTER 18

Rebecca? Tommy Asher had to be delusional or lying—or both.

Or else he was as wily as a fox, which was more likely. Why not blame everything on her? The damage was still done—investments gone up in smoke—but now he, too, had been duped along with everyone else, or so he said. Rebecca wouldn't be the first young rogue trader to take down a financial empire—back in the '90s, Nick Leeson had single-handedly caused the collapse of the personal bank of the queen of England with his unchecked risk taking.

"What did I tell you?" Austin was saying. "Lucie's friend. She's responsible for this. I knew it."

"He's lying," I said. "She didn't do what he said she did."

Mac clicked the remote, turning off the television. "Who the hell cares whose fault it is? Did you hear what he said? He's freezing everything. All my money is with Harlan. Everything. My God, this is a catastrophe."

"Asher said he's good for the money. Let's not panic. Harlan's never let us down before." Austin sounded like he was trying to persuade himself, along with Mac and me.

"Oh, for God's sake, Austin. It's gonna be a goddamn stampede." Mac picked up the phone again. "I'm calling Harlan. I want my money *today*. In cash. Anybody who waits is just plain stupid."

"All right, maybe you're right. But let's be smart about this. Close the store and I'll drive us into D.C. We'll talk to Harlan face-to-face.

Get to the bottom of what's going on." Austin eyed me. "It's also possible Asher was telling the truth about that woman. That the money's parked in an account somewhere and they'll find it."

I felt numb. "Rebecca didn't steal any money."

"How do you know?" Mac's pale blue eyes were icy and the color had drained from his face. "She's gone, isn't she? And no one's found her."

He took his pin-striped charcoal gray suit jacket off a hanger on an antique coatrack and put it on with stiff, angry movements.

"Yes, but I know—" I began, then shut up. What did I know?

I'd told Ian that I believed Rebecca had faked her death after leaving behind information—somewhere—that would expose what was going on at Asher Investments. But to be honest, it was possible she had stolen enough money to set herself up so she could live a comfortable life off the grid. Maybe she hadn't left behind anything for Ian and me to find but an apology . . . or an explanation.

And what about her pregnancy? How did that fit in?

"Go on," Mac said. "You were saying?"

"Nothing," I said. "Except that I can't believe that Rebecca did what Tommy Asher just said she did."

"Well, I'm sure she's grateful for your loyalty." Austin didn't bother to hide his sarcasm. "Wherever she is. Come on, Mac. Let's get out of here and talk to Harlan. Get some straight answers from that boy. Because if Asher is lying about being able to make good on our investments, then all my money—everything I own—just went up in smoke."

I abandoned my plan to check out the stretch of Mosby's Highway by Mickie Gordon Park and drove back to the vineyard instead. Frankie took one look at me when I walked through the door and got a bottle of wine from the refrigerator.

"I think we'll have this with our lunch," she said.

I looked at the wine. Viognier. How many days had it been since the Ashers' gala when Harlan and I shared a laugh over the fact that it meant "road to hell"? Today was Thursday. Five days since last Saturday that seemed like five years.

Frankie handed me the bottle. "Here. You'd better open it now."

The weather had warmed up enough to dine on the terrace. We brought sandwiches, dishes, and the white bakery bag from the Upper Crust to a table next to the railing. Frankie poured the wine as I sat there, numbly staring at the tidy rows of bare vines anchored by the timeless Blue Ridge. Somewhere a tractor motor started up, a comforting, placid thrumming. Probably one of the crew cutting the grass for the first time this year. Spring was definitely on its way.

The seasons would unfold as they always did, beginning with the hopefulness I felt each year at this time when winter was done and gone. In a few short weeks the vines would begin to bud and then they'd be flower-covered and fragrant. Later the grapes would emerge as *véraison,* the ripening process, played out through the wilting heat of summer. Harvest would begin in August and continue into autumn as we spent hectic days and nights turning the grapes into wine.

Life would go on with its rhythm and cycles, except this year would be unlike any other I'd known. Neighbors and friends could possibly lose everything they'd spent a lifetime working for—in some cases, money that had been in families for generations. No matter the wound was self-inflicted; if it happened, it was going to change Atoka for good.

And I was losing Quinn.

"You want to talk about it?" Frankie asked.

"I don't know where to start."

"Try the beginning."

I shrugged. Why keep it all inside anymore?

So I told her, except I left out Rebecca's pregnancy test and my speculation that Harlan was probably the baby's father. The story was lurid enough as it was.

"You think Rebecca did what Sir Thomas said she did?" Frankie asked. "Stole all that money?"

We finished our sandwiches and shared the cow puddles. She picked up the wine bottle and refilled our glasses.

"I think he's blaming her for what he did, and she's not around to defend herself or contradict him," I said.

"You still think she's alive, don't you?" Frankie asked.

"Nothing would surprise me anymore."

"Lucie." Her voice was gentle. "Maybe you just want her to be alive because they haven't found her body."

"That's a pretty good reason, don't you think? Nor has anyone found 'Robin Hood,' the mysterious guy who gave the Madison wine cooler and her jewelry to that homeless man. That's a lot of missing people."

"All right, assuming you're right, then who helped her disappear?"

I drank some wine. "I wish I knew."

"Someone inside Asher Investments? Although they'd probably be in on the scam." Frankie frowned, working out her own logic. "Wouldn't they?"

"Not if it was confined to a very small circle that excluded Rebecca. If what Ian said is true, Rebecca didn't know what was going on under her nose the first time he told her about his suspicions. She told him to go to hell," I said.

"Then changed her mind and decided to help him once she found out he was right?" Frankie asked.

"I think so. Although that's the million-dollar question—or billion-dollar question, in this case. What was it she left for Ian to find?"

And who was Rebecca's ally? Someone I knew? Olivia Tarrant, Sir Thomas's personal assistant? Simon deWolfe, his half brother? Olivia had purposely excluded Rebecca from her definition of who made it into what she called "the Asher family." So I doubted she was the one. But what about Simon? He'd been in the perfect position that evening to meet up with Rebecca down by the river.

"You know," Frankie said, "you might consider the obvious. That Sir Thomas is telling the truth about Rebecca."

"Frankie, Rebecca did *not* steal that money."

"Just because she was your friend—"

"I know she didn't do it."

Frankie held up her hands like a shield. "Okay, okay. I give up."

"Sorry. I didn't mean to snap at you. I know you think I can't be objective, or that I'm just being naïve—but I'm not."

"It seems to me," she said in her calm, reasoning way, "that

Rebecca left quite a lot at your doorstep. Counted on your loyalty and your integrity to do something she wouldn't do herself."

The tractor motor cut off. I let her words sink in as a soft breeze rustled the tree branches and the birds twittered cheerfully. Was she right?

"Unless," I said at last, "there was some reason Rebecca couldn't do it herself."

"What reason would that be? Aside from the possibility that she is, in fact, dead."

I finished my wine. "I don't know. But something must have changed. Maybe Rebecca and her partner made a plan, then something went wrong."

"You don't have to pick up the pieces, Lucie."

She stood, lips pursed in disapproval, as she gathered our dishes and the other lunch debris. I grabbed the empty wine bottle and the two glasses as we cleaned up in silence.

In the kitchen she began stacking plates in the dishwasher. "What are you going to do now?"

"See if I can figure out what Rebecca left for Ian. She wanted me to know or she wouldn't have set it up for the two of us to get together."

"Lucie!" Frankie crushed the lunch wrappers into a tight ball. "Don't do this! You don't have to get involved. Do you want to end up like Ian?"

"I already am involved," I said. "Whether I want to be or not, someone thinks I know more than I do."

"Let the police handle it."

"I tried. That detective . . . Horne . . . thinks I'm nuts. Anyway, there's something else."

"What?" She threw the papers into the trash.

"If it's true that Asher Investments is nothing but a Ponzi scheme, people we care about could lose a lot of money."

"No one held a gun to their heads and made them give their life savings to Harlan Jennings."

"The Romeos, Frankie. Retired guys who worked in the community and still volunteer around here. They trusted Harlan—and why wouldn't they? His father was a Romeo, too. One of them."

She picked up the coffeepot and turned on the tap full force. Water splattered all over the sink. "I wonder if Harlan managed to get his money out in time. If he knew what was going on, then he's as guilty as Asher is. If he was in the dark, you've got to wonder what was going through his head that no warning bells ever went off."

"I don't know," I said. "Either way, he loses."

She filled the pot and wiped the sink. "Walk away before it's too late."

I didn't say anything. Too late was a long time ago. And now there was no one else to find what Rebecca had left behind except me.

Unfortunately my only clue lay buried in the poetry of a man who had been dead for two centuries.

CHAPTER 19

When I showed up in the barrel room later that afternoon for the Viognier bench trials, Quinn was sitting on a stool in the lab, twirling a pencil between his fingers. His mouth moved soundlessly as he stared into space and ignored the lab book, which sat open on the workbench in front of him.

"You're talking to yourself," I said.

"I'm doing mental calculations." He squinted at me and slapped the book shut. "You look like you can hardly keep your eyes open. When's the last time you got any sleep?"

"Last night."

"You are one lousy liar." He threw down the pencil. "Sure you want to work on the blend?"

I sighed. "Honestly, no. You got a better idea?"

"Why don't we go somewhere, get lost for a while? Don't tell the boss. She's a slave driver."

"That's not what I heard. She's hardworking, benevolent, and not appreciated nearly enough for what she does around here. She also, I might add, pays your salary."

He grinned and stood up. "Let's vamoose."

He'd left the red Mule, one of our ATVs, on the crush pad. We owned two of them—red and green like Christmas. I put my cane on the backseat and climbed in beside him.

"Are you going to tell me what's wrong?" I asked.

"Nothing is wrong."

"No offense, but you weren't doing mental calculations. When you run out of fingers, you take off your socks. You were talking to yourself when I walked in."

He started the motor. "Take off my socks. Aren't you funny."

"Still avoiding the question."

He shifted into gear and hit the gas. The Mule lurched forward and I grabbed the dashboard.

"I might have trouble financing the land I want to buy." He kept his gaze fixed straight ahead.

I watched his profile and saw a muscle tighten in his jaw. Money woes. Him, too? Had one or several of his investors gotten sucked into the miasma of Asher Investments?

"Might or are?" I asked.

"I'm still working on that."

"Have you talked to Seth? Maybe the bank—"

"It's more complicated than that, believe me. Seth's the first one I went to."

"Want to talk about it?"

"Nope. To be honest, I'd just as soon forget the whole thing for now."

I knew him well enough to hear the clank of a drawbridge coming up, closing off that fortress of privacy he erected around himself. He had just shut me out.

We drove along the outer edge of the south vineyard, passing some of the first vines my parents had planted more than twenty years ago. Quinn seemed to have a destination in mind since he didn't detour down the rows of Riesling or Chardonnay to check on things like we normally did when we were in the field together.

"Have you seen your mother's trees lately?" he asked.

At this time of year, I knew exactly which trees he meant. Shortly before she died, my mother had planted a spectacular allée of flowering cherry trees just off the south service road near the larger of our two apple orchards. They reminded her of the trees that lined the drive at the entrance to my grandparents' summer home in Provence.

"I haven't been by in the last few days," I said.

He turned the corner at the end of the Chardonnay block and the trees came into view in a blizzard of lacy pink flowers. Quinn parked the Mule and we got out.

"I love this place," he said.

"So do I," I said. "It's so peaceful here. Nothing like the Tidal Basin. When I was there the other day you could hardly move. Beautiful as it is, it was like being in a packed Metro car."

"I'll take your word for it. That's why they make postcards. I hate being jammed someplace like a sardine, especially when it's outdoors."

"Oh, come on. You have to see those trees for yourself at least once in your life. That's like visiting Napa without stopping at a vineyard."

He looked at me like I'd stabbed him through the heart. Before he moved to Virginia he'd been a winemaker in Napa.

"Next year we'll go together," I told him. "It's too late this season. They're past their peak."

Quinn flung himself onto the wooden bench my brother and sister and I had put here under the trees last year on our mother's birthday.

"Next year is a long way off. Who knows what I'll be doing then?" He leaned back with his hands clasped behind his head and crossed one work boot over the other.

"What are you talking about?"

"I might not even be here."

"Don't be ridiculous. Of course you will."

I sat down next to him and ran a finger over the engraving on the brass plaque attached to the bench. A quote from Thomas Jefferson, whose *Garden Book* had been among my mother's favorite reading: "No occupation is so delightful to me as the culture of the earth, and no culture comparable to that of the garden."

"I mean it," he said. "I might not."

He sounded serious. He wasn't kidding around.

"Don't say that." My voice wavered. "You can't leave."

He reached over and brushed the sleeve of my jacket with the back of his hand.

"After what I found out last night, I may not have a choice."

"I thought you were playing poker last night."

"I was. Harlan and Ali Jennings's stable manager got up the game for a bunch of guys. He's got an apartment above one of the barns. Ali came back from riding with Tommy Asher's brother while we were playing. You could hear 'em a mile away. Guess they didn't realize the windows were open and we were there."

"Simon deWolfe went riding with Alison Jennings?"

"They hunt together. Simon rides with the Goose Creek Hunt now, along with Ali and Mick Dunne."

"What were they talking about?"

"What else? Harlan and Tommy Asher." Quinn shrugged. "Ali was completely flipped out about the money that's gone. Simon was trying to calm her down. He told her she needs to keep her head, stay calm. Same with Harlan. Panicking is just going to make things worse for everybody."

"What did Ali say when she heard that?"

"She sure didn't calm down, I can tell you that. They parked their money with Asher, too. She sounded hysterical. Blames your friend Rebecca for everything."

"I don't think Ali can be—" I began.

"Can be what?"

"Nothing."

A sudden gust of wind showered blossoms around us like we were inside a snow globe. I didn't want to get into Harlan and Rebecca's affair with Quinn.

He picked up a flower and held it between his fingers. "Can't be objective about the woman her husband was screwing?"

My cheeks turned red. "That's vulgar."

"Aha. Then it is true?"

I looked away.

"Lucie," he said, "I'm a guy. Sorry I'm not all touchy-feely, but I've heard the rumors about Harlan. Your friend was one good-looking babe who happened to be working for someone Harlan does business with. You didn't tell me anything I wouldn't have found out in a day or two over coffee at the General Store."

"I didn't tell you anything at all."

"Aw, come on. Lighten up." He put his arm around me and

pulled me to him. "You know me. I don't mean to be crude, but the fact that they were, uh, having an affair just makes it worse. People trusted Harlan. Now they don't—or won't until they get their money back."

I leaned my head against his shoulder and breathed in his clean, outdoors smell and a hint of whatever detergent he used to wash his clothes.

"What if they don't get it back?" I asked.

"I watched that press conference. Asher says he's good for it."

"Uh-huh."

He pulled away from me. "What's 'uh-huh' supposed to mean? You were Rebecca's friend. You got insider information?"

"Nothing I know for sure."

"Join the club. Nobody seems to know anything for sure. What do you think you don't know?"

"I don't think Rebecca stole the money Tommy Asher says she did. She's a convenient scapegoat because she's not around anymore."

"Then who did steal it?" He watched me.

"Maybe there wasn't any to steal."

Quinn smashed the blossom he'd been holding between his fingers. "If that's true, then you're telling me it was all smoke and mirrors?"

"I don't know for sure," I repeated. "But I think that's one possibility."

"Jesus H. Christ, Lucie. Then nobody's gonna get anything back."

"Maybe not."

We sat in silence.

"Come on, let's get out of here. I've had all the bad news I can take for one day."

On the drive back to the winery he said, "I think your theory's way off base about there not being any money. I told you what Simon told Ali last night. All everyone has to do is keep their head and it'll work out. Simon ought to know what's going on inside his brother's firm. He would have told Ali the truth."

"Quinn—"

"No offense, Lucie, but you said yourself you were just speculating. I'm not so naïve I don't believe people are going to lose money by the time this shakes out. But hell, the market giveth and the market taketh away. Tommy Asher's not God, though people have been acting like he was. Now he's just human."

"I don't think—"

"Can we drop this, please?"

I saw the unmistakable message in his eyes. Go no further. I nodded and we finished the rest of the drive without speaking. How many people I cared about were going to lose money because they trusted Harlan and Tommy Asher?

It seemed to me the body count was still climbing.

Kit called when I got home just after five o'clock. I peeled off my sweatshirt and threw it on the toile-covered Queen Anne chair in the foyer. Across the room, Leland's bust of Thomas Jefferson looked out from a lighted alcove. Jefferson knew what it was like to be broke. It was part of the reason he sold his personal library to the Library of Congress. He'd needed the money.

"The only thing harder than tracking you down," Kit said, "is figuring out who's lying and whose telling the truth at Asher Investments. Didn't you owe me a phone call after you talked to the cops yesterday?"

I rubbed my forehead where it had begun to ache between my eyes.

"Yesterday got a little complicated."

"I heard. David Wildman talked to your new friend Summer Lowe. You remember David? My Podland cubicle mate?"

A small shiver ran down my spine. Summer made it clear she didn't want anyone to know we'd spoken together in the Capitol. How had a reporter from the *Trib* found out about our off-the-radar meeting?

"What's he doing? Following me around?" I didn't mean to snap at her.

"Not on purpose, he isn't." Kit sounded surprised at the rebuke. "But every time he finds a new piece of the puzzle, the seat's still warm because you were just there. In fact, you seem to be the connecting link to all of it."

"Is that so?"

"Apparently it is."

"Has David had any luck putting the pieces together?"

"Ask him yourself. He's dying to meet you."

"You could choose another expression."

"What? Oh . . . sorry." She paused. "He's up in New York talking to people all day tomorrow. How about the three of us get together on Saturday? I'll drag him out to Atoka and bring him by the vineyard. Maybe first thing in the morning?"

"Uh . . ."

"What?"

"It might be better if we didn't meet here," I said.

"Sure." She sounded puzzled. "Why?"

"I think someone besides David might be following me. Why make it easy for them?"

"Good God, are you serious?"

"'Fraid so." I told her about last night's car chase after I left the Hill but left out the part about sleeping with a gun.

"Lucie, you'd better watch your back."

"I'm trying to. That's why I'd like to meet somewhere out of the way."

"Any preferences?"

"How about our old hangout?"

"Ah." I could hear her smile through the phone. "A reconvening of what your brother referred to as the Semi-Irregular Meeting of Juvenile Boozers Anonymous."

I grinned. When Kit and I were growing up, I used to filch unlabeled bottles of wine from the barrel room and bring them over to the old Goose Creek Bridge where we'd hang out at twilight and drink. It had been the site of a Civil War battle—the place where Colonel J. E. B. Stuart tried to delay Union troops in order to give Robert E. Lee more time to advance toward Pennsylvania. Ten days later, the two armies met at Gettysburg. Now the garden club looked after the bridge, which was out of the way and generally deserted. We'd probably have it all to ourselves.

"But I'm not up for polishing off a bottle of wine first thing in the morning anymore," I said.

"How about coffee and doughnuts instead?" she said. "David and I'll spring for it. Meet you there, say around ten?"

"Fine. Ten o'clock."

"Before you hang up," she said, "what are you wearing Saturday night? The invitation says black tie but I never know whether to wear short or long."

"What are you talking about?"

"The Library of Congress. The reception and a private dinner afterward for the Asher Collection. I got the press packet and your name's on the guest list. I figured Harlan and Alison Jennings invited you."

I thought for a moment. "No, not them. Rebecca told me about it. She put my name on that list. My God, I completely forgot. She really wanted me to be there."

"So are you going?" Kit asked.

Every player in this unfolding drama would be there. Including, perhaps, my stalker.

"Yes," I said. "I'm going."

CHAPTER 20

After I hung up with Kit I poured myself a large glass of wine from an open bottle of Cabernet Sauvignon on the dining room sideboard. I took it into the library, along with Leland's .45, and set them both on the coffee table next to the sofa. The next thing I knew someone was pounding on my front door.

I picked up the gun next to my untouched glass of wine and walked slowly into the foyer.

"Lucie! Open up in there. Are you okay? Answer the door, and for God's sake, don't shoot me if you've got that damn gun!"

Quinn. I lowered my arm, dizzy with relief, and flung open the door.

"What are you doing here? You scared the wits out of me!"

He was holding a couple of white bags. The appealing aroma of Chinese food filled the air. He'd gone to the new place in Leesburg.

"How come you didn't answer my calls? Next time pick up, will you? And you could have told me you started locking your front door."

"What calls?" I let him in. The food smelled wonderful. "And I'm fine."

He pointed to the gun. "Yeah, I can see everything's just great. You forgot to charge your phone again, didn't you? Bet you didn't eat yet, either. Your face has funny creases on it. I woke you up."

I brushed my fingers across my cheeks and felt for creases. "Who

are you, my mother? And my phone is"—I felt in my pocket—
"somewhere."

"Where somewhere? Carry it with you, okay? That's what it's
for."

It drove him nuts when I forgot my phone, which I often did,
but the level of anxiety in his voice made me uneasy. He was right.
It was dumb not to have the phone with me at all times, under the
circumstances.

"It's probably in my car. And I think it needs to be charged," I
said, as he looked exasperated. "What's in the bags?"

"Shrimp with snow peas for you." He handed it to me and I
peered inside. "Kung Pao chicken for me. Bon appétit."

"Wait. You're not leaving, are you?"

"I was gonna check things in the barrel room."

"And eat by yourself?"

"You, uh, want to eat together?"

Why are men so dense about these things?

"We could make a fire in the parlor. I think there's a really good
Saint-Estèphe in Leland's wine cellar."

Quinn handed me his bag. "I'll be back."

"Where are you going?"

"To the carriage house to get some firewood," he said. "Where'd
you think?"

He was gone a long time, longer than it took to get a few logs.
Our dinner was growing cold and my heart started up like war
drums.

He met me at the front door, arms full of firewood, his eyes traveling to the .45, which I again held in my hand.

"Put that thing away before you shoot somebody," he said.

"That's the general idea of guns."

"And your phone was in your car. Dead as a doornail. Plug it in
and charge it, okay?"

I attached the phone to the charger and put the gun in the cabinet. When I walked into the parlor, he was on his knees in front of
the fireplace, sticking fatwood and newspaper between the logs on
the grate.

"Do you have any idea how to shoot that gun?" he asked. "I

mean, so you hit what you're aiming at? What made you get it just now? That fox crying? Jeez, Lucie, you're jumpier than a june bug."

I sat on the floor next to him and, out of habit, tucked my bad foot underneath me where he wouldn't see it. "I didn't hear the fox. You were gone a long time just to get an armful of firewood."

He got the fire starter from the mantel and lit the newspaper. Without looking at me he said, "I figured I'd check around the house. Antonio's patrolling the grounds."

"He is?"

"Yeah." He hesitated. "We've got a couple of guys babysitting the entrance to the vineyard. They're armed. We're gonna rotate people on security duty. Days and nights. Figured you'd okay the overtime pay."

Security guards at the gate? No one had said a word to me.

I swallowed. "Sure. Thanks."

"How about if I get that bottle of Saint-Estèphe and decant it? And yes, I'm going to check the door in your basement, too. Make sure the dead bolt's in place."

When he came back he said, "I forgot what a fabulous wine cellar your old man had. You sure you want to drink this with takeout? Maybe you should save it for a special occasion, you know? Something to celebrate."

How could I tell him I thought dinner with him was something to celebrate?

"I'm sure."

He looked at me for a long moment and I held my breath.

"You know, it's going to take that wine awhile to decant," he said. "We could stay right here in your nice parlor and enjoy the fire while we wait. Or we could do something else."

We did something else.

It had been months since the last time, but I no longer cared if he realized how much I'd missed his lovemaking. We began kissing and undressing each other right there in the parlor, dropping our clothes one by one on the grand spiral staircase like a couple of giddy kids. By the time we reached my bedroom we were panting and out of breath. He threw me on the bed and bit my shoulder as he climbed on top of me. I tangled my fingers through his hair and pulled him close. Usually he was tender, but tonight whatever fierce demon possessed him caught fire with me and we weren't gentle. Tomorrow we'd both be sore and bruised.

I lost track of how many times we made love, except that the ache that gnawed inside me grew deeper each time, a melancholy void that threatened to swallow me up. Why couldn't we continue what we had before he left for California? Why did things have to change?

After months of abstinence I'd given in without hesitating, thrown away any pride or pretense, like the recovering alcoholic who believes one little drink won't hurt. But as some poet said, one crowded hour of glorious life is worth an age without a name. I'd had my crowded hour. If I had to lose him, at least we'd had this one last night together.

Later he went downstairs to get the Saint-Estèphe, but it again seemed like a long time before he came back to bed with the decanter and two wineglasses. He'd found his clothes and gotten dressed, but he'd brought only a few of my things—which didn't include my underwear.

"Everything all right?" I sat up and hugged my knees to my chest as he sat next to me and poured our wine. I touched my hand to his face. "You're cold. How come you got dressed?"

"Just went outside for a little night air."

I knew then why he was here. "You're babysitting me, aren't you? You and Antonio worked this out. Tonight your turn, tomorrow his. You were checking around the house again."

"If I catch Antonio in bed with you . . ." He grinned.

"Don't."

He handed me a glass and kissed me. "It's not what you think."

"It is what I think. You're here as my bodyguard, aren't you?" I set my wine on the nightstand. "That's the only reason you showed up tonight."

He took my face in his hands and kissed me for a long time. "I wouldn't be here if I didn't want to be."

"I don't know if I believe you."

"Let me prove it," he said, laying me back on the pillows, "so you won't have any doubts."

★ ★ ★

Afterward we lay next to each other in the dark.

"I've missed you," I said.

"I've missed you, too." He rolled over and sat up, turning on the light and reaching for our wineglasses. "Interested in some very cold Chinese food? I'm starved."

Had he not wanted to continue that conversation, or had sex really made him ravenous?

"Sure."

We drank in silence, and it was as though I could feel the filaments of the web we had woven together these last few years slowly begin to tear apart.

"What would it take for you to stay on here?" I said.

He stared into his wineglass.

"A partnership? Think about it. Please? I don't want to lose you, Quinn."

His smile was full of sadness and regret, but he still didn't look at me. "This isn't about you, Lucie. It never was. It's about me, facing some things from my past that have finally come home to roost. I've got to work them out—"

"Work them out here!"

"I can't."

"But—"

He laid a finger across my lips. "Not tonight. Please."

I nodded and he brushed a tear from under my eye.

"About that dinner," he said.

Later he came back to bed with me, but this time we lay in each other's arms.

"Get some sleep," he said into my hair. "You look exhausted."

I didn't want to close my eyes. I wanted to remember everything that we did and said to each other and what it felt like to be in his arms again in bed. But wine and lack of sleep the night before and physical exhaustion from our lovemaking finally caught up with me.

I fell asleep and dreamed I was dropping into the abyss.

When I woke up the next morning, I was alone. I could still see the impression of Quinn's head on my pillow and his body on the sheets, but his clothes were gone. The smell of coffee floated up the staircase. He always made coffee when we spent the night together. I sat up and pulled the wedding ring quilt I used as a bedspread around me.

He appeared in the doorway, holding two mugs. "Morning, sleepyhead. You all right? You look like you've seen a ghost."

"I thought you'd left." I took the coffee from him. "Then I heard someone on the stairs."

"Don't worry," he said. "I already talked to Antonio. All quiet last night."

I nodded. Already our torrid night in bed seemed like it had happened to other people. And Quinn looked ill at ease, a warning sign that maybe he had regrets about what we'd done. I could take anything but his remorse.

"Speaking of talking to people, your cell was ringing when I came downstairs. I brought it with me." He pulled it out of his jeans pocket. "I wasn't trying to pry, but you've got a missed call from Mick and a message. Kind of early to be calling, so I thought it might be important." He said it without emotion.

"I have no idea why he's calling at this hour."

"Call him back and find out."

"I'm sure it's business. Probably something about his vines." I set the phone on the bedside table and sipped my coffee. As usual he'd made sludge that tasted like rocket fuel. "Good coffee."

"I didn't want to make it too strong since I know you prefer that dishwater you drink."

"It's not dishwater!"

My phone rang and we both glanced at it at the same time. Mick, calling again. Did he have radar or a hidden camera so he knew to call only when Quinn was around? Quinn picked up the phone and gave it to me.

"Don't keep the man waiting."

For the past few months I'd lived a life of total celibacy—not by choice. All of a sudden, one ex-lover spends the night in my bed and the other calls on the phone while he's there. What are the odds?

"Do you mind?" I hoped Quinn would take the hint and leave.

He had the unfair advantage of being fully dressed while I was naked underneath the quilt. Last night it was erotic. This morning it felt awkward. I was stuck where I was unless I wanted to drag my quilt and my dignity elsewhere.

He crossed his legs. "Not at all. Go right ahead."

I glared at him, answering the phone in my most brisk, business-like vineyard owner manner.

"Morning, Mick. You're calling awfully early. What's up?"

"Wanted to hear your voice, love. I know you're an early riser."

Quinn grinned and I shoved him with my foot. He didn't budge.

"It's seven thirty."

"I know. I'm just off to the stables."

"That's nice," I said. "Do you want to tell me what this is about? You didn't really call just to hear my voice."

He laughed and Quinn smirked.

"Lucie." He sounded reproachful. "So suspicious when my intentions are honorable. I found out that you're invited to the opening of the Asher Collection at the Library of Congress tomorrow. I thought we might go together."

Fortunately I hadn't been in the middle of drinking my coffee. He was calling at this hour about a date?

"How did you know I was invited?"

"Is that a yes?"

"Who told you, Mick?" I wasn't kidding around.

"Simon. We were talking about it when he came over for dinner last night and your name came up. He wondered if you planned to attend since you never formally replied. I took the liberty of saying yes." He paused. "Told him I was bringing you."

I felt a chill pass through me. "Why did he specifically ask about me?"

"We were talking about your cousin," he said. "So naturally your name came up. How about if I pick you up at half-five tomorrow?"

"Mick . . ."

"Come on, love. There's something I'd like to talk to you about."

"What?"

"Tell you tomorrow."

"What's wrong with right now? Especially since I'm wide awake."

"I'd rather do it in person." He paused. "So, five thirty okay?"

He wasn't going to give up.

"Sure," I said. "Five thirty."

When Quinn was upset a muscle worked in his jaw like he was chewing something. He got up off the bed and went over to the window, but not before I saw that muscle twitch.

I hung up. "Well, that was strange."

"At least I know you'll be okay Saturday night," he said. "Mick'll take care of you. Maybe even all night."

"Don't," I said. "Don't say that."

"You're right. That was out of line." He ran a hand through his unruly hair. "Guess I'd better get home and shower and change. Boss'll expect me at work as usual, no excuses."

"You could always shower here." I let the quilt drop away. "With me."

He caressed my cheek. "Tempting offer, but no thanks. I gotta talk to Antonio and figure out what we're going to do today."

"You mean about the vineyard?" My cheeks burned as I gathered the quilt around me again.

"I mean about you." He walked to the door and turned around. "See you later."

His work boots clattered on the stairs. The front door opened and closed, followed by the noise of a car starting.

I lay back against my pillows. More filaments in that web were breaking, and soon it would become unmoored from everything we'd built together.

I was losing Quinn. And I had no idea how to stop it from happening.

CHAPTER 21

⟨⟨⟨⟨⟩⟩⟩⟩

Quinn was out in the field when I arrived at the villa an hour later. Frankie gave me one of her all-knowing looks the moment I walked into the kitchen so I realized she'd been clued in about my new bodyguards—though I couldn't tell whether she knew or guessed that Quinn had taken his assignment to a more intimate level.

"Sleep well?" She handed me a cup of coffee.

"Why am I the last person around here to find out everything?" I said. "Were you part of this scheme of Antonio and Quinn's?"

She smiled and raised an eyebrow. "What scheme?"

"So it was your idea, huh?" I said after a moment.

"It was everyone's, Lucie. With you staying by yourself in that big house, no alarm, no nothing for security, it just seemed like a good idea to have the guys keeping an eye on things for a while."

Things. She meant me.

I added sugar and milk to my coffee. "Someone should have told me."

"You would have nixed it if we did." She sipped her coffee. "By the way, Books & Crannies called. The book you ordered is in."

"That was fast. Guess I'll go into town and pick it up. You need anything while I'm there?"

"All set, thanks." She eyed me. "What's wrong?"

"I talked to Quinn. I think he got caught up in the Asher mess. He wouldn't say, but it sounds like his investors might have backed out on him."

"He wouldn't tell me anything, either," she said. "I found him reading the *Trib* when I got in this morning, looking like he was ready to put Sir Thomas through the destemmer. His picture is on the front page, looking like Charlton Heston when he played Moses just before he parted the Red Sea. Calm and in control in the face of looming disaster. You've got to hand it to the man. How does he do it? Yoga? Meditation? He ought to be a mess."

"Self-delusion. Where's that paper?"

"The bar. Calm down, Lucie."

How many times had she said that to me lately?

"I am calm." I set down my mug and sloshed coffee on the counter. Frankie picked up a sponge and wiped up the spill. "Go on. Go and read it. You won't be happy until you do."

I found the paper folded so that Tommy Asher stared back at me. Somebody—Quinn, probably—had childishly given him a devil's horns, a tail, and a pitchfork. But Frankie was right about the photo. Asher looked serene as though he didn't have a care in the world. Where did he get that kind of chutzpah? Maybe it came from telling the same lies for so long that eventually he believed them and so did everybody around him. I wondered what he saw when he looked in the mirror. Maybe he never looked anymore.

I sat down on one of the sofas by the fireplace and skimmed the article. David Wildman's byline. Kit's colleague.

> Investors woke up this morning to a potential tsunami in the financial markets as billionaire investment guru Sir Thomas Asher continued to plead for patience while authorities investigate his allegation that Rebecca Natale, Asher's former star protégée who went missing five days ago and is presumed dead, embezzled millions of dollars from his clients by falsifying trades, creating dummy accounts . . .

I kept reading. Wildman must have worked Summer Lowe over pretty good, because he knew all about Harlan leaning on Senator Vaughn to make Ian's hearing go away now that Ian was dead. By the time I finished reading it was clear David Wildman had Tommy Asher in his journalistic crosshairs. I hoped his life insurance was paid up. People who took on Asher Investments seemed to come to a bad end.

Turned out I was more right than I knew when I called Summer Lowe. Her terse voice mail message was a polite version of "Go to hell."

"You've reached Summer. I'm no longer working at the Senate and I'm not taking any calls at this time. Thanks."

Stunned, I hung up. Harlan and Asher had successfully strong-armed Cameron Vaughn into canceling the hearing—but had they also gone after Summer and made her the scapegoat? Was that supposed to be a lesson to any other Senate or House staffer who decided to probe Thomas Asher Investments? Unless she was also being punished for talking to David Wildman. The information in that article could only have leaked from her. I wondered if she'd talked to him in Vaughn's Capitol hideaway like she had with me.

I had no other number for Summer, no idea where she lived or where she might have gone. I wondered if David Wildman knew. Tomorrow I'd ask him. Maybe he wanted to meet me but, increasingly, I wanted to meet him, too.

With Rebecca and Ian gone and Summer now out of the picture, it seemed there were only two of us left who were still players in whatever great game Rebecca had set up before she disappeared. I liked our odds less and less.

I picked up the book of Alexander Pope's poetry at the bookstore later that morning and stopped by the General Store on my way home. If there was anyone in Atoka who would know everything there was to know about how deeply Tommy Asher and Harlan Jennings had reached into the bank accounts and investment portfolios of friends and neighbors, it was Thelma Johnson.

Just as all roads once led to Rome, all news in Atoka—that is to say, gossip—eventually ended up at the General Store, where it was rinsed and spun through Thelma's quirky worldview before being rereleased as something that belonged in a supermarket tabloid. I figured it was her addiction to soap operas that made her find drama and evidence of at least one—and usually more—of the seven deadly sins in every corner of our sleepy little village.

She was sitting by the space heater in her favorite spindle-back rocking chair reading one of her soap magazines when I arrived. Though seventy was probably in the rearview mirror, Thelma always dressed with the giddy joie de vivre of a teenager whose parents hadn't seen her before she left the house on a date. Too much makeup and not enough fabric. At her age, the effect could be more Halloween scary than vampish flirt. Today she was dressed entirely in lilac—short skirt, plunging V-neck sweater, matching stiletto mules, and a mauve and lilac scarf tied around her carrot-colored mop of curls. Though I expect the effect was meant to be stylishly chic, the ends of the scarf flopping on either side of her head reminded me of Bugs Bunny.

She set her magazine on a small table next to the rocker and adjusted her trifocals, beaming when she realized who I was. I knew that look well enough. Thelma could get a monk who had taken a vow of silence to talk. If she thought I knew something, I wouldn't leave until she knew it, too.

"Why, Lucille, honey! Aren't you a sight for sore eyes?"

She jumped up and scooted around to the vintage enamel-top table where she kept three kinds of coffee brewing in pots labeled "Regular," "Decaf," and "Fancy."

"Looking a mite tired, aren't you, child? How about a nice cup of coffee? I got the usual, but you look like you could use an extra bit of pepping up. Today's special is 'Java Good One.'"

"I'll take your special, thanks," I said. "I could use a good one."

Thelma never wasted time beating around the bush. "So what's all this about you being with that young woman who went missing in the Potomac River?" She clicked her tongue. "What's this world coming to, anyway, finding everything but her skivvies in that rowboat?"

I opened my mouth to answer, but she motored on as she handed me a large cup.

"Here you go. Fixed just the way you like it. One sugar, a little cream. Pull up that rocking chair, will you, child, and set a spell." She gave me a significant look over the top of her glasses as I obeyed. "Rebecca, that's her name, wasn't it? Now that Asher fellow is saying she stole folks' money. And then there's that other hanky-panky I heard about. That affair."

The Inquisition had commenced. Next would come the questions. Had Thelma found out about Connor, or was she referring to Harlan?

I drank some coffee, feeling my cheeks grow warm. "Wow, you've really ferreted out a lot of information, Thelma. Plus you have such an amazing memory for details."

She smiled, looking pleased with herself. "Well, I tend to put things under a sharper microscope than most folks, Lucille."

I kept a straight face. "I know that."

"So, tell me." She crossed one leg over the other and leaned forward as though we were coconspirators. "What kind of person was she? I know you know the truth about her. I promise, what you say won't leave this room."

Of course it wouldn't. It didn't need to go anywhere since everyone in Atoka would drop by the General Store and hear it right here from Thelma. I gave her the answer I'd given everyone from Detective Horne to Ian to Summer Lowe, knowing full well she wouldn't be satisfied with it.

"I hadn't seen her in twelve years and she didn't confide any details about her personal life to me in the hour or so we spent together," I said. "But I don't believe she stole that money the way Tommy Asher said she did."

Thelma nodded. I could tell I hadn't convinced her, either, but she moved right along to the next subject.

"Well, then, what about the affair? You may as well come clean, Lucille."

"Rebecca didn't say anything to me about her love life." Technically, she hadn't. Everything I knew I'd learned from other people.

Thelma let one of her mules dangle flirtatiously off her foot. "Aren't you the sly one? I can't believe you don't know about it."

"About what?"

Her eyes searched my face through her thick lenses. Thelma knew better than anyone when I was holding back. "You know, you're like me, child. We share that same psychotic ability when it comes to figuring out other people. We can sense the truth about what's going on. Your sainted mother was like that, too. You know perfectly well that your friend was carrying on with Harlan Jennings, don't you?"

I gave in. "I knew, but Rebecca didn't tell me. How did you find out?"

"Oh, I've known for a while Harlan was having an affair. I just didn't know it was your friend until the other day."

"But how . . . ?" I said, surprised.

She took off her glasses and rubbed them absently against her head scarf. "Why, because of Ali, of course. She'd come in here after driving back from Washington and teaching all day. She seemed so . . . melancholy, I guess. The boys were away at school and I know what buying dinner for one looks like." She pressed her lips together. "You want to say something when you know someone's heart is aching, but she's got her pride—and a person's got to respect that."

"Oh, Thelma, how sad."

I'd seen Ali's outrage. Thelma saw through to her loneliness and hurt. Maybe she did have those psychotic sensibilities she talked about.

"What I don't understand is how someone so book smart could be that blind to what's going on right in front of her nose," she said. "Him moving into town and setting up his little love nest. Why in the world did she put up with that?"

"Because she adores him," I said. "And the boys."

"Well, she'd certainly do anything to protect him, wouldn't she?"

It hung in the air as Thelma waited for my reaction. Sure, Alison hated Rebecca. And I'd had my suspicions about just how far she would go to get rid of Rebecca and save her husband's reputation. But I didn't want to believe Ali would actually commit murder, nor did I want to admit any of this to Thelma.

"Define 'anything.' "

"Whether Ali was involved in your friend's disappearance." Thelma put her glasses back on and watched me.

"I just can't believe . . . she wouldn't."

"I don't believe it, either, Lucille. It'd be a turrible waste of a good person. Just turrible. I mean Ali, not Harlan. I won't say murder's not on folks' minds, but Harlan's the one everyone wants to skin alive. The Romeos are madder 'n hornets they took up with him and let him pass all their money on to Tommy Asher."

"I heard Harlan invested his own money with Asher Investments," I said. "So he lost out, too."

Thelma rapped her knuckles on the wooden arm of her rocker. "That boy's a mile wide and an inch deep. I remember when he was growing up. Always had a taste for the good life, that one."

"Thelma, he grew up with money."

"Money, good looks, and that kind of easy aw-shucks charm that suckers folks in. He knows how to use it, too. Only thing he isn't blessed with is a conscience."

"That's pretty harsh," I said. "Do you really believe that?"

"Somewhere along the way he sold his soul, Lucille. Gave in to greed and temptation and now everybody who threw their lot in with him is paying the price. It's a damn shame." Her eyes glittered and I heard bitterness mixed in with the blame.

I got it now.

"Thelma, don't tell me you invested with him, too? You're one of the people who lost money?"

Thelma seemed to look through me for a long while, her head bobbing slightly. I couldn't tell whether it was a tremor of age or an acknowledgment that I was right. Her smile was tinged with regret.

"I thought I did a pretty good job of keeping that information off people's periscopes. Making out I was smarter 'n everyone else and keeping my hands in my pockets. That I wasn't tempted by easy money. How'd you guess, Lucille? No, don't tell me, I know. It's that extrasensible perception you got going on."

"I hope you didn't lose much. I'm so sorry."

"No one to blame but myself. It was like joining an exclusive club and I couldn't wait to get in. I'd heard the whispering going around about this surefire opportunity to make steady money. Only an upside, no down. So I went to Harlan and asked him. He said he'd see what he could do because normally the minimum investment was a hundred thousand." Her cackle echoed in the small store. "Good Lord. I had my mouth open wider 'n a big-mouth bass.

He didn't even have to work to reel me in. Told me he made an exception for me but said I had to be very circumcised about it. You know, keep quiet because it was all hush-hush."

I had been about to take a sip of coffee. Instead I coughed. "He said that?"

"Yes, indeedy. He threatened to give back my money if I uttered one peep. Now I know he was just trying to keep me from talking to everybody else he made an 'exception' for."

Amazingly, she'd kept her word.

"You weren't the only one, Thelma. Don't be so hard on yourself."

"Oh, phooey. I was just as big and dumb as the rest of the sheep."

"You have every right to be angry."

"What good would that do me, on top of everything else?" She shrugged. "I still got some of my little nest egg put away, plus I own this place. So it's not like I lost everything the way I suspect some folks did. I know a few of the Romeos who are just fumigating they're so mad."

"Well, Tommy Asher's still saying he's got everything under control."

"They said that about the *Titanic*." She leaned back and started rocking.

"There's still the dedication ceremony for the Asher Collection tomorrow at the Library of Congress. Maybe he's trying to hold things together until then," I said.

"He can do what he likes. It's all over but the crying, anyway." Thelma kept rocking. "You know, plenty of people made money from Harlan and Asher. They always paid with promptitude so you'd just keep on thinking the checks would come in. But lately the economy got so bad folks started needing some of their money to pay bills." She shrugged. "That's when Harlan started trolling for little fish like me. People who got in the end, 'cause they needed our cash. Now we're the ones going to lose the most."

"I know, I know. It's horrible."

"Especially considering one of 'em was Quinn. You must feel awful about that."

I sat up straight. "Pardon?"

"Your winemaker, child. Rumors goin' round he invested all that money he got from his mother's estate with Harlan. Did it right before everything started to fall apart. It'd be a shame about him losing the cash he planned to use to buy his own place, wouldn't it?"

"Are you sure about this?"

"You'd know better than I would."

"I, uh . . ."

"Well, look at me shootin' off my mouth. I just assumed you knew." She stopped rocking. "Quinn didn't tell you. Did he?"

My voice was faint. "I assumed he had investors who lost money because of Harlan and they backed out on him. It never occurred to me that it was his own money."

"I'm sorry, Lucille. You know, I could be wrong."

I nodded. She could be. But she wasn't.

And it explained everything.

CHAPTER 22

For the rest of the day I avoided Quinn. Now I knew why he'd been so evasive about his financial situation. He'd risked all his money just as the ship was sinking.

Like Thelma and the Romeos, he'd been swept along with the tide. Everyone else was making money in Tommy Asher's exclusive club, so why shouldn't he? Asher promised modest gains and steady returns, not wild profits. A sensible way to build wealth. Then there was Sir Thomas himself: a title conferring aristocracy; a man who was urbane, intelligent, and generous, donating millions to charity and supporting worthwhile causes through his philanthropy.

What was not to trust? Who would question someone with his credentials and his long-term track record? His clients were wild about him—until they started losing money.

I ate a solitary dinner in the kitchen, though I brought *The Poetical Works of Alexander Pope* for company and pored over the Epistle to Richard Boyle, highlighting the two passages Rebecca had marked.

I studied the first: *Oft have you hinted to your brother peer, / A certain truth, which many buy too dear.*

Simon deWolfe was Sir Thomas's half brother—but did that make him an equal, a peer? Was Rebecca implying Simon knew what was really going on inside Asher Investments? As for "a certain truth, which many buy too dear"—the "many" could be Asher's clients who were now paying the price for what he'd done. Was

Simon—my cousin's new beau and the muscle for his brother—in on the whole Ponzi scheme, too?

If he was, how deeply was he involved? Enough to commit murder—like drowning a drunk Ian Philips in his hot tub? What about Rebecca? I'd always suspected Simon had been with her on the day she disappeared. Now I knew that he hunted with Mick, who was an excellent marksman. I'd bet money Simon was no slouch, either.

Dominique had seen only one side of Simon, the charming Englishman who'd swept her off her feet. Kit said David Wildman knew his dark, violent side from firsthand experience. How long before my cousin found out about it, too? I knew her well enough to know she'd laugh off my worries. She might even be annoyed or angry with me for saying anything negative about the man she was in love with—enough to go to Simon and tell him what her cousin said so that he could deny it and put her mind at rest.

Then what? For the time being I needed to keep my mouth shut and find what Rebecca had left for Ian. Then maybe I could talk to Dominique.

I went back to the poem and reread the second passage Rebecca had marked.

No artful wildness to perplex the scene;
Grove nods at grove, each alley has a brother,
And half the platform just reflects the other.
The suff'ring eye inverted Nature sees,
Trees cut to statues, statues thick as trees;
With here a fountain, never to be play'd;
And there a summerhouse, that knows no shade.

A park? Somewhere with trees and paths. Manicured trees and statues, a defunct fountain, and a summerhouse "that knows no shade." A formal garden in someone's home? It had to be in Washington because she'd meant Ian to find it; I was her backup.

Tomorrow I'd show this passage to David Wildman and Kit. Maybe among us, we could figure it out—hopefully soon.

Somehow it felt like I was running out of time.

★ ★ ★

Even though Antonio told me a couple of men would patrol the property as usual, I still slept poorly. Quinn and Rebecca haunted my dreams. When I woke on Saturday morning, the sun was already streaming through my bedroom window.

I showered and dressed, stopping by the villa to check in with Frankie on my way to the Goose Creek Bridge. She was outside on the terrace, straightening chair cushions and wiping down picnic tables.

"Looks like it's going to be a beautiful day," she said. "Maybe we'll have a good crowd. You off somewhere?"

"Meeting Kit for breakfast." I left out where and that there would be three of us.

"In town?"

"One of our old haunts." I pulled a chair into place around one of the tables. "Did you know Quinn invested his inheritance money with Thomas Asher Investments?"

Her eyes grew big and she nodded. "He told me yesterday. Said if this goes down the way it looks like it's going, he'll lose everything. The poor man."

That hurt. He trusted Frankie but not me.

"I found out from Thelma."

She set down her spray bottle of glass cleaner. "It's different with you, Lucie. Believe me, he's kicking himself from here to California for being so gullible. He's probably too ashamed to tell you what happened."

"He won't be the only one to lose his shirt."

"Tell him that."

"Any idea where he is now?"

"No, but last night I think he planned to meet up with some friends and get drunk. He might be home sleeping it off."

I'd never known Quinn to go out with the deliberate intention of getting drunk. He was careful; he knew his limits and what could happen to winemakers who liked their own tipple too much and too often.

I pressed my lips together and shook my head. Down the slippery slope . . .

Frankie held up her hand. "Give him some space, Lucie. He's got to deal with this, and you know how much pride he has. It's tearing him up."

If I gave him any more space, we'd inhabit different planets.

"I offered him a partnership the other day," I said. "I wonder if he'll reconsider now."

"Well, it's an ill wind that doesn't blow somebody some good, I guess." Frankie put her hand over her mouth. "Oh, my God, I'm sorry. That came out horribly wrong."

"Or maybe it didn't." I shoved another chair into place. "You know as well as I do that if I bring it up again he'll just think I'm doing it out of pity."

She picked up the spray bottle. "He's proud and you're stubborn. You two are a pair, you know that? How much longer are you going to go on like this? It's wearing me out."

"Like what? You just cleaned that table, you know."

"Oh, go on and meet Kit for breakfast already."

"Thanks. See you." I started to leave.

"Lucie?"

"What?"

"If you're free tonight, a group of us are going to the Hidden Horse for drinks and dinner. Why don't you come along and maybe afterward you could spend the night at my place? Tom's away on business. I'd love some company."

When Tom was away Frankie busied herself with imaginary chores like vacuuming the basement of her immaculate house or straightening the garage. She didn't need company, but if I spent the night with her, my security guards wouldn't have to babysit me.

"Thanks for the invite, but I've already got plans for the evening. Anyway, I think we can call off the nightly patrols, don't you? Antonio and the guys need their beauty sleep and, for all I know, what happened on Mosby's Highway was just a random case of road rage. It's been like a tomb around here ever since."

"You sure about that?"

"Positive."

"What are you doing tonight, if you don't mind me asking?"

"Going to the opening of the Asher Collection at the Library of Congress."

Her eyes widened. "Don't you think you ought to steer clear of the Ashers?"

"On the contrary. Keep your friends close and your enemies closer."

"Lucie . . ."

"Relax, Frankie. I'll be fine. Mick's taking me. Nothing's going to happen. There'll be a million cameras and reporters, and everyone will be on their best behavior."

She wasn't mollified.

"Sometimes," she said, "I just don't understand you."

Kit's Jeep and a silver Toyota Camry were parked at the end of the dirt road next to the gate by the old Goose Creek Bridge when I got there just after ten o'clock. In summer the heady scent of wild honeysuckle would be everywhere, but now the heavily wooded landscape was only beginning to show hints of green. Kit and someone I assumed was David Wildman sat on the parapet overlooking Goose Creek, their legs dangling over the water. Behind them through the screen of bare trees and brush, I could make out rolling hills and the dark parallel lines of a post-and-board fence that ran along the perimeter of a field where armies once had fought.

Kit, in a scarlet jacket, gold scarf, and lime green pants, stood out like a traffic light in the otherwise subdued landscape. As I walked down the gravel path she waved.

"Come and get it! Your coffee's getting cold!"

She and David stood, hands around their coffee cups like they were praying. Another cup sat on the wall next to a rectangular white box. David Wildman picked it up and walked over to me.

"The woman I've been chasing for a week." He handed me the coffee. "Nice to finally meet you, Lucie. David Wildman."

He was younger than I'd expected, short, fit, and bullishly built. I guessed him to be a few years older than I was, probably in his midthirties in spite of the bald head, which I figured he shaved. His skin was the color of burnished mahogany and he wore horn-rimmed glasses and a tiny gold hoop in one ear. He carried himself with an easy confidence that showed in the tilt of his head as he studied me. His smile could have lit up a dark cathedral.

"Nice to meet you, too." I smiled back. He was charming. No wonder Summer had talked to him. "Kit told me a lot about you."

He grinned some more. "Make you a deal. You believe half of what she told you about me and I'll believe half of what she told me about you."

I glanced at Kit, who rolled her eyes.

"Make it seventy-five percent and you're on."

He laughed. "Sounds like we should just start over."

"How nice you two already bonded, thanks to me." Kit gave us a baleful look as she held out the box. "Doughnut, anyone? I bought a dozen."

I took an old-fashioned, David picked a jelly-filled, and Kit helped herself to a Boston cream.

"Shall we sit down and do this?" David said. "I've got a lot of questions."

We moved back to the parapet where he'd left his rucksack. Kit and I faced the creek while David straddled the low wall so he could see the gate and the dead-end road. I wondered if it was deliberate. We ate our doughnuts and drank our coffee.

"It's pretty out here. I grew up in a city, so places like this seem like a foreign country. Does it get many visitors?" David licked jelly off his thumb.

His tone was conversational, but I could tell it wasn't just idle banter. I wondered if he now thought he needed to watch his back after yesterday's article in the *Trib*.

"Occasionally you find someone following the Civil War trail out here," I said. "You probably saw the marker on Mosby's Highway. There's more of a crowd during the spring garden tour when local historians give lectures on the battle. Most of the time, though, it's deserted."

He nodded and pulled a reporter's notebook and pen out of the rucksack.

"Anybody ready for another doughnut?" Kit opened the box.

"One's my limit," I said.

David regarded the choices and eyed Kit. "You want the chocolate-covered one with the sprinkles, don't you?"

"I'll take anything. Take that one if you want it."

He picked up a glazed donut. "I can't. Your initials are written in the sprinkles."

"Where?" She studied the box and looked up. "Oh, for God's sake. Why do I believe you anymore?"

He bit into his doughnut and winked at me. "She finds me irresistible."

"Yeah, well, I'm working on resisting him," Kit said. "I'm nearly there."

David set his doughnut on a napkin. "I thought you should know that Ian Philips mailed me copies of his notes as sort of a backup. He was worried about the threats he'd been receiving."

I stared down at the creek, which flowed peacefully beneath us. Rebecca wanted Ian and me to be her backups—and she was gone. Now Ian had gone to David Wildman before he died.

"When did you get them?" I asked.

"They were postmarked Tuesday. The day he died. He sent them to the newsroom. I didn't get 'em until yesterday. They were sitting on another reporter's desk by accident and he was out sick. Caught me completely by surprise."

Me, too. At least now I knew Ian trusted David.

"Who knows you have them?"

"Besides Kit and my editor, only you."

"What are you going to do?" I asked as a chill went through me.

"Right now I'm still reading them. A lot of dense economics—numbers, formulas, terminology—that I'm trying to wade through. It's slowing me down. I really don't want to ask our business reporter for help since I'd like to keep it on the down low that I've got this stuff." He eyed me. "There is one glaring omission."

"Ian had no proof of any falsified trades or how the money got moved around," I said. "You need what Rebecca left him."

Kit licked sprinkles off her doughnut. "If she left anything. What if Tommy Asher's right and she's dirty, too?" She caught me glaring at her. "Sorry. You know how I feel about her. I did meet her, you remember."

"I remember."

"Look," she said, "be honest. Rebecca would either have to be incredibly dumb or incredibly blind not to know what was going

on, especially if she was one of Asher's trusted advisers. His protégée."

"Okay, okay. Let's say you're right and Rebecca did take the
money," I said. "What if she only took enough to get lost, change
her identity, and set herself up somewhere she wouldn't be found?
Rebecca was fundamentally a casuist. At least she was when we were
in school."

"English, please?" Kit said.

"A person who uses reasoning to solve a moral problem," I said.
"Casuists decide what to do based on ethics—except they consider
the circumstances of each situation before they make their decision.
So stealing may be wrong, but taking enough money to live on
because you need to disappear after turning in your boss for bigger
stealing is okay because that's the greater good."

"Phooey. Two wrongs don't make a right," Kit said.

"I'm not justifying it," I said. "Just explaining it."

Kit wiped her fingers on a napkin and looked cross. "Why didn't
she just give you the damn papers or external drive or whatever it
is? Why have this cloak-and-dagger scavenger hunt? It's ridiculous."

"Because she needed to make sure she could pull off her disappearing act first. Otherwise, she'd be hanging a noose around her
own neck," I said.

David had leaned back with his arms folded across his chest as
he followed our back-and-forth discussion like he was watching a
tennis match.

"Feel free to jump in at any time," I said to him. "With your two
cents."

"I grew up with five sisters," he said. "I know when to keep my
mouth shut."

"He waits to weigh in until after all the blood is spilled," Kit said.
"Less messy."

David flashed a brilliant knowing smile as she reached for
another doughnut.

"Eating comforts me in times of stress." She made a face at him.
To me she said, "What I don't understand is why they haven't found
her body yet."

"I still believe Rebecca's plan was to disappear," I said. "What I don't know anymore is whether someone got to her and she really is dead."

"I heard she might have been pregnant." David spoke up finally.

"Are you serious? I didn't know—" Kit turned to me. "Luce? *You* knew?"

"Her mother told me."

Kit exploded. "Pregnant! That changes everything. Who's the father?"

"It might be Harlan Jennings," I said. "They were having an affair."

Kit snorted. "Harlan and Rebecca. Oh, my God, poor Ali. Though our Senate reporter always said he had a roving eye. But a baby—wow. You never know about some people, do you?"

The Pope book was in my carryall. I got it out.

"Rebecca left me this. Well, not this book exactly. The D.C. police have the copy she gave me." I opened it to the epistle to Richard Boyle. "I got a chance to look at her copy when I talked to Detective Horne. She marked a couple of passages."

David took the book and Kit moved closer so she could read over his shoulder.

"What's this supposed to be?" she asked after a few minutes. "A clue?"

"I guess so. If it isn't, we're really lost."

David rubbed his chin. "If it's a place, it sounds like she's referring to a formal garden. You think she left something there?"

"Wherever it is, it has to be in D.C.," I said.

"Dumbarton Oaks? Hillwood? The Botanic Gardens? There're a bunch of gardens in this city," he said.

"I'd been thinking it was around one of the monuments. But Dumbarton Oaks is in Georgetown," I said. "Rebecca disappeared for a few hours after she left me at the Vietnam Wall to pick up the Madison wine cooler in Georgetown. She spent some time at Harlan's place and left."

"Where's Harlan's place?" Kit asked.

David consulted his notes. "Thirty-second Street, a few houses down from the intersection of Reservoir Road. I parked near Dumbarton Oaks when I went to check it out."

"So she could have walked there," I said. "It would have only taken her ten, maybe fifteen minutes to drop something off."

David sounded eager. "The timing would be right, wouldn't it?"

I nodded. "My mother took me to those gardens when I was little. There are several fountains, I think."

"Any of them defunct?" Kit asked. " 'With here a fountain, never to be play'd.' "

"There's only one way to find out," I said. "I'm sure the gardens are open today."

"Whoa!" David held up a hand. "It's cherry blossom season and those grounds are going to be overrun with visitors. I've got a friend who works at the museum there. Let me call her and see if we can get in when it's closed to the public. We need to keep this off the radar, especially if all three of us show up looking like a posse."

He made a call and left a message.

"Well," he said, "we'll have to wait and see what she says."

I finished my coffee. "So which of you is covering the opening of the Asher Collection tonight?"

Kit and David exchanged glances.

"Neither of us," she said. "Change of plans. It's now closed to the press and it's being billed as a private event."

"When did that happen?"

"Yesterday," David said. "If it turns out that collection was acquired with dirty money, it's only a matter of time before the library announces it's no longer accepting the Ashers' donation. They're already backing away. In the meantime Tommy Asher paid to use the Great Hall. They can't pull the plug on that."

"You're going, right, Luce?"

I nodded. "With Mick Dunne."

"I'd give anything to be a fly on the wall," Kit said. "It's going to be a hell of a party now. Asher better have food tasters on hand. I'm sure there are a lot of people who are ready to do him in. Take notes, will you?"

Someone's phone rang.

"Mine," David said and answered. "Yo, man. What's up?"

He flipped to a clean page in his notebook and began scribbling.

"Right. Thanks. I'll be there. I owe you, man." He hung up.

"They just pulled a body out of the Potomac. Not sure if it's male or female."

I reached for my coffee cup on the parapet and knocked it over. It was empty and I caught it just before it fell off the bridge into the creek.

David leaned over and squeezed my shoulder. "I didn't mean to upset you. I'm sorry."

"It's okay."

"I'll let you know as soon as I find out anything. Maybe it's not her."

Or maybe it was.

CHAPTER 23

⊶⊷⊷

From the moment Mick and I walked up the sweeping granite stair-case of the Library of Congress's Thomas Jefferson Building, I knew this evening was going to be about money and not philanthropy. Last Saturday at the Pension Building gala the Ashers had been honored like royalty. Tonight the beautiful Italian Renaissance–style library, with its paintings, mosaics, and statuary depicting mythology, legend, and flesh-and-blood icons of poetry and literature, could not have been a more ironic setting to mark the beginning of Tommy Asher's fall from grace.

As the saying goes, success has a thousand fathers but failure is a motherless child. Mick and I joined the queue to pass through security and enter the Great Hall as the streetlights came on for the evening and, on the other side of First Street, the floodlit Capitol dome looked timeless and serene. While we waited on the stairs I overheard snatches of conversation that made it clear many of tonight's guests were clients of Thomas Asher Investments—those who desperately needed reassurance that all was well and everyone else who knew the game was up and wanted their money back.

I'd learned which camp Mick was in an hour earlier on the drive from Atoka to Washington. He still believed in Tommy Asher. I also found out why: The alternative was too terrible to contemplate. In the cocoon of his sleek black Mercedes listening to Miles Davis and John Coltrane on the satellite radio, I discovered the real reason

Mick had asked me to be his date tonight, why he'd been so persistent—the early morning phone call the other day. He needed me as a business partner. Would I buy the grapes from the ten acres he'd planted and bottle the wine under a new label? The price, he promised me, would be a steal.

"Why?" I'd asked. "This fall would be your first harvest. After all you've been through for the past three years, why not make your own wine?"

"I don't have the head for it. Takes too much of my time and energy. I need to choose between horses or grapes."

Even I knew that was a Hobson's choice for Mick. Riding, hunting, polo, and raising horses were in his blood. Growing grapes and making wine had been part of the romantic fantasy he harbored of becoming a gentleman farmer, until he found out how much work it was, how tedious the chores—and, unlike horses, that it wasn't terribly glamorous or exciting.

"Does this have anything to do with investing with Tommy Asher? How much have you lost, Mick?"

He kept his eyes focused on the road. "More than I'd care to say. Simon tells me it's going to be okay if I sit tight. Not to be like the folks who panicked after the NASDAQ bubble burst in 2000 or Black Monday back in '87. Wait it out and ride it up again. He says in six months it'll all be tickety-boo and everyone who bailed will be holding an empty bag."

I doubted that. Boo-hoo was more like it. "And you believe him?"

"Yes." He still didn't look at me. "I do."

I wondered whom he was trying to kid—himself or me?

"What about the grapes, Lucie? It'd make sense for you to do this, especially since the land sits on our common boundary."

I couldn't think straight.

"I need to talk to Quinn," I said.

"Can you give me an answer soon? If you turn me down, I'll go elsewhere, love. Not a threat, but I just need to know."

He must need the cash urgently or he wouldn't press me so hard. Maybe he was in danger of losing the horses, too.

I could have told him the last thing I wanted was to expand since we had our own new varietals, like the Viognier, that we were just beginning to introduce. But maybe I could use Mick's proposal to tempt Quinn to stay on. He'd know I couldn't handle something this big on my own. Like Frankie said, it was an ill wind that didn't blow somebody some good.

Mick and I spoke no more about this or about Tommy Asher for the rest of the drive into D.C., but when the music slid into Billie Holiday crooning "Stormy Weather" in her haunting, raspy voice, he reached over and savagely punched the button, turning off the radio.

He parked behind the library on one of the residential streets and we walked to the Jefferson Building. On Wednesday, when I'd met Summer Lowe at the Capitol, I'd entered through the basement carriage entrance. Now the enormous bronze doors at the top of the main staircase, which were usually closed for security reasons, had been thrown open in honor of the evening's event. Light from the two large outdoor candelabra at the head of the staircase and a golden shaft of light spilling onto the plaza from inside the building gilded the long line of guests in tuxedos and evening dresses as though we were one of the carved marble friezes gracing the exterior of the building.

"I need a drink," Mick said after we shed our coats in the vestibule where, from every corner, statues of the Roman goddess Minerva, patroness of knowledge and protector of civilization, watched us. More irony. I wondered if Tommy Asher would share any new information tonight or if he'd continue to stonewall his clients. The only person he was protecting now was himself.

We walked through a marble archway into the Great Hall. I'd been here before, but I gathered Mick had not because he stopped, openmouthed, in the middle of the room and stared. A docent tried to hand him a glossy brochure with a black-and-white broadside cartoon depicting the burning of Washington and "The Asher Collection at the Library of Congress" written in swirling calligraphy on the cover. I took the brochure and thanked her.

"First time here, huh?" I said. "It's pretty spectacular."

"Reminds me of the opera house in Paris. The Palais Garnier. Have you ever been?"

"I've only seen it from the outside when I used to visit my grandparents."

"It looks like this on the inside."

A waiter with a tray of glasses offered us drinks. Mick took two champagne flutes and handed one to me. I took a sip. It wasn't Krug.

"Shall we look around?" I said. "The library owns a copy of the Gutenberg Bible. And we ought to go upstairs to see the Asher Collection."

Mick nodded. "Crikey. Look at everyone, will you? Every woman is dressed in black, except you. All the men in tuxes. I feel like I'm at a bloody funeral."

My gown was the color of spring sunshine. He was right. Everyone else was wearing black.

I slipped my arm through his. "Let's not get into metaphors, shall we? You brought me here. Now at least go see the exhibit with me."

Two marble staircases on either side of the Great Hall swept up to the second-floor galleries. At the foot of one of them a small knot of people had gathered in a semicircle.

"What do you bet Tommy's at the center of that scrum? I wonder where Simon is?" Mick said.

"He's there," I said. "On the stairs by the statue."

Simon deWolfe stood next to a bronze statue of a slender-armed woman gracing the newel post at the base of the staircase around which the crowd had gathered. The globe of the torch she held glowed like a small moon above his head as he signaled for everyone's attention.

"Ladies and gentlemen, though this evening you have been invited to the premier of the fabulous Asher Collection that Sir Thomas and Lady Asher have so generously donated to the Library of Congress, it is apparent that recent events in the press weigh on the minds of many of you. At this time, Sir Thomas would like to make a few remarks." His stilted speech echoed in the now silent gallery. I wondered if he had rehearsed it or if perhaps Sir Thomas had written it for him.

Voices bubbled up from the group as Tommy Asher and his wife climbed the steps, stopping on a landing decorated with a marble frieze of children at play. Simon and Miranda Asher stepped back as Sir Thomas, ravenlike in his tux, began to speak. Behind him the brilliant Mediterranean hues and rich gilding on the vaulted ceilings and walls of the second-floor gallery glowed like the inside of a Fabergé egg.

"We're here this evening in this magnificent place—once called the book palace of the American people—for the unveiling of an astonishing collection of maps, paintings, architectural drawings, and documents pertaining to the early history of our nation's capital, a city built by men who, though they revered classical architecture for its timelessness and beauty, were some of the most visionary and forward-thinking individuals of their time," Asher said.

For someone who grew up as the working-class son of a driver to the American ambassador to Great Britain, I noticed for the first time that he'd somehow acquired the cut-glass accent of aristocracy. How much of the man was real and how much was fabricated?

"Long ago when many parts of the world were unexplored, cartographers wrote 'Beyond This Point There Be Dragons' when they didn't know what lay at the edge of their maps," Asher continued. "But explorers, men like Columbus and Magellan, were not afraid to venture beyond what was safe and known. They were daring, courageous—bold. Some of you have been with me for years—decades—trusting me in uncharted waters to steer a prudent course for you and your financial future. I ask that you please continue to give me the trust and confidence I have earned many times over as we work through a difficult time where some now fear dragons. Thank you and I hope you enjoy the evening and the exhibit."

There was a smattering of applause, barely enough to be polite. Asher looked grim as he surveyed the crowd. Perhaps it was my dress, a splash of sunny yellow in a sea of black, but it seemed to me that Tommy Asher's gaze lingered on us as we stood apart, next to a bronze bust of George Washington, longer than on anyone else in the room. He leaned over and said something to Simon, who glanced our way as well. Then Asher took his wife's arm and descended the stairs. I lost sight of him when he plunged into the crowd and it closed around him again.

"Tommy's absolutely right," Mick was saying. "You can't let a few people running scared turn this into a stampede that will take everyone down with them. If we just hang tough we'll get through this."

I finished my champagne and thought of Ian and his theories and David Wildman who was now poring over Ian's notes. Who was Mick kidding? Did he really believe Tommy Asher could bluff his way through this firestorm and stanch the outflow of money so his firm wouldn't go under?

"You promised me we'd see the Asher Collection," I said. "How about it?"

"Sure." He gave me a quizzical look. I hadn't been subtle in changing the subject. "Why not?"

We had just started up the stairs when Simon called Mick's name.

"Do we have to?" I said under my breath.

"His brother is our host."

Mick led me down to where Simon waited for us.

"Tommy spotted you in the crowd, Mick. And your lovely lady. Good evening, Lucie. Don't you look stunning? I seem to have lost your cousin somewhere in the Great Hall, but she and I would like the two of you to sit at our table for dinner."

Simon smiled and kissed my hand as his eyes locked on mine. I felt like a butterfly pinned to a museum display.

"We'd love it," Mick said.

"Excellent." Simon clapped Mick on the back. "I think Tommy did a lot to calm the waters just now, don't you? I know you're going to stay the course, old man. You'll be glad you did. Tommy'd like a word with you, by the way. You come, too, Lucie."

My cell phone rang from the depths of my sequined evening purse. I'd turned off the ringer before Mick picked me up but kept the phone on in case David Wildman called. It must have caught on something in my purse and switched back on. Mick looked pained and a flash of irritation crossed Simon's face.

"I'm so sorry," I said. "I'm sure I silenced the ringer before I put it in my purse."

"Turn it off, darling," Mick said.

"It's caught on something."

I tugged and the phone flew out of my grasp, clattering on the marble floor. Simon picked it up, his eyes flitting to the display before he handed it back to me.

"Afraid the call's gone to voice mail," he said. "Hope it wasn't important."

I tucked it back in my purse. "Thank you."

"Don't you want to silence that phone, Lucie?" Mick asked.

What I really wanted was to see who called.

"Of course," I said. "Would you both please excuse me? I need to use the ladies' room. I'll turn it off there. And Mick, I'll meet you upstairs at the exhibit in a few minutes after you men have your talk."

I started toward the Minerva foyer, but Simon caught my arm.

"Wrong way, love," he said. "The ladies' is in the east corridor by the Giant Bible of Mainz. Behind the staircases next to the elevator. We're walking that way. I'll show you."

Mick looked at me like I'd lost my mind as we entered the east corridor through an archway with LIBRARY OF CONGRESS carved in gold above it. Was he right? Already this evening seemed off-kilter, weirdly disconnected from reality after that little pep talk about dragons and cartographers and trust. Then there was Tommy Asher himself now walking purposefully over to the three of us. Who was he, really? A Svengali? The Pied Piper?

He took my hand and held it between both of his.

"Michael," he said to Mick. "You're a lucky man. Who is this beautiful creature? Have I met you before, my dear?"

"Lucie Montgomery—" Mick began.

"We met last week at the Pension Building, Sir Thomas," I said. "Harlan Jennings introduced us."

Something flickered behind his eyes, which strayed to my cane. I didn't have it with me last week at the gala and that lightning glance told me he remembered. Had this been a spurious question and I'd taken the bait? Tommy Asher knew exactly who I was.

"Of course." He turned the full wattage of his smile and charm on me. "How could I forget?"

I felt a draft across my bare shoulders and neck. My evening shawl had slipped down my back and I hiked it up. Rebecca's spirit suddenly seemed to hang in the air as if I'd conjured her.

Harlan hadn't linked Rebecca and me when he'd introduced me to Asher, but there were plenty of people in his entourage who knew I'd been her guest. Olivia Tarrant, for example. So far I hadn't seen her this evening, but I had no doubt she was around somewhere. Had she or anyone else in the Asher inner circle figured out that Rebecca was the one who'd added my name to tonight's list of invitees? Maybe no one had noticed since I was now here as Mick's guest—and he was clearly a favored son.

"If you'll excuse me," I said, "I was just on my way to the ladies' room."

This time no one stopped me. I checked the phone message in the old-fashioned bathroom, which I had to myself. The exchange was one of the *Trib*'s numbers. Not Kit's, so probably David's, meaning he was still at work on a Saturday night. I punched in the access code and listened.

"Hey, Lucie, David here. You're probably swilling champagne from a glass slipper at the library but I wanted to tell you the ME hasn't ID'd the body yet." He sounded tired and I heard him slurp a drink. Probably something caffeinated. "It's female but the decomp is pretty bad. What he did say is that it's been there too long to be Rebecca. Also, we're on for tomorrow at Dumbarton Oaks. Five o'clock, as soon as the place closes. Give me a call if you need to. I'll be here late."

There was a pause and I thought he was finished, but then he added in an ominous voice, "Asher ought to be passing the hat to get everyone to pick up the tab for his little soiree. He sure can't afford it. Hope you brought your checkbook. Heh-heh-heh."

I disconnected as Alison Jennings pushed open the bathroom door, a large glass of red wine in one hand. Her face, ghostlike against her black-and-ivory gown, was drawn and she looked like she was about to pass out. I shoved the phone in my purse.

"Lucie," she said, "I didn't expect to see you here tonight." Her voice was hazed with pain.

"What's wrong?" I took her wine, afraid she'd drop the glass on the marble floor. "Ali, are you all right? You look like you ought to sit down."

She clenched her teeth and put her fingers to her temples, but at least she let me guide her to a wooden chair in the bay of a large window. I set her wineglass on the counter.

"I've got the beginning of a migraine," she said. "I hope I make it through dinner because I've got to give that talk."

"Can I do anything?" I nearly dumped her wine in the sink so I could fill the glass with tap water until I saw the nonpotable sign. "Shall I try to find you a glass of water somewhere?"

"That's okay. I've got something but I hate to take it. Makes me woozy. I never should have had that wine."

"Shall I get Harlan? I haven't seen him this evening but—"

"He's somewhere," she said. "I think he's wandering around the exhibit."

"I'm on my way upstairs to see it. Why don't I find him and let him know you're here?"

"It's okay. I'll be all right in a minute." Ali closed her eyes. "Still having Harlan's party on Tuesday, y'know. Did you forget? I've got no wine."

Her Viognier.

"Oh, gosh, I'm sorry. I've been so distracted I forgot to tell Frankie, but it's no excuse. I promise I'll take care of it myself first thing tomorrow. You mind a Sunday delivery?"

"Nope." Her eyes were still closed.

"Are you sure you're going to be all right?"

She opened her eyes and looked at me. "Harlan says we'll get through this. I wonder."

I wondered what "this" she was talking about.

"Did you hear Sir Thomas's speech?" I asked.

Her laugh sounded like glass shards. "Tommy can woo an audience like no one you've ever met, get you to believe he can walk on water. Amazing, isn't he?"

"What do you mean?"

"Oh, Lucie, come on." She waved a tired hand, dismissing me, Tommy Asher, everybody. "He's hemorrhaging so badly it would take a miracle to salvage that sinking ship. Not that he isn't expecting one. Neither he nor Harlan wants to admit it. I don't know how much longer they can hold off their clients, refusing to allow them to make withdrawals from their accounts. The worst of it is—well, for me—that Tommy's going to have to sell this whole damn collection. He can't afford to donate it and I've already heard from a friend in the librarian's office that they no longer plan to accept it anyway. It'll be a temporary exhibit."

"What does Harlan say?"

Her eyes were bright with tears. "He doesn't want to talk about it. This isn't his fault, y'know? Harlan's a good man, Lucie."

"Ali—"

"Please. If you could just give me a few minutes alone to pull myself together."

She fled into one of the stalls, banging the door shut. I heard her hiccupy breaths and thought about waiting until she was ready to come out. But she wouldn't, not as long as I was still in the room.

"I'll find Harlan," I said, but I didn't think she heard me. The bathroom door creaked on its hinges as I left.

I took the elevator around the corner from the Giant Bible of Mainz to the second floor. The Asher Collection's glossy brochure contained a map showing the chronological time line by which the exhibit was laid out in the four loggia galleries that overlooked the Great Hall. It began in the north corridor, which ran along the front of the building closest to the Capitol. The elevator let me out in the east corridor, which was three-quarters of the way through the collection, dedicated to the War of 1812 and the rebuilding of the Capitol and the Library of Congress after the fire. A glass étagère striped with red and gold paint depicting flames held the newspaper cartoon that had been on the cover of the brochure. More paintings, watercolors, lithographs, and newspapers showed the city of Washington ablaze on the night of August 24, 1814.

"Nobody but the English would do such a thing."

I whirled around. My cousin Dominique, regal in a smoke-colored sequin-spattered chiffon gown that perfectly set off her auburn hair, stood on the stairs to the Visitors' Gallery that overlooked the Main Reading Room. She moved and the sequins glittered like dark diamonds. Behind her was an enormous mosaic of Minerva, her spear in one hand and a long scroll in the other.

The animosity between the French and the British was legendary, dating back to Joan of Arc. Even though Dominique was now an American citizen, my cousin held up her end of the grudge on behalf of the French. She descended the last few stairs, swaying slightly. I wondered if she'd been drinking.

"Do you know why they burned Washington?"

"As a matter of fact, I do. The British were furious at the Americans for attacking their navy and burning the city of York in Canada. The plan was to destroy Washington, not capture it. That way they would humiliate the Americans."

I took her arm and smelled her breath. She'd been drinking, all right.

"It was a vendetta," she said. "Revenge on their former colonies. A blood feud that began with the Revolution. That's *les rosbifs* for you."

The Roastbeefs. The French nickname for the British. The British reciprocated with "Frogs."

"I hope you didn't use that term around Simon," I said. "Since he's English."

"He's not really English. His father was French and his mother was Dutch. He just happened to be raised in England while his mother was married to Tommy's father."

That laid to rest one mystery why she was seeing him—he wasn't really British.

"How well do you know him?" I asked.

Dominique hesitated. "I need to tell you something. In private. There's no one upstairs in the Visitors' Gallery. We can talk there."

"Are you okay?" I asked. "How much have you had to drink?"

"Not enough," she said.

"Or maybe a little too much? Maybe you should knock it off."

"Come on," she said.

We climbed the three flights of stairs, the marble treds worn so uneven I needed to hold on to the brass railing. I followed her into the glassed-in corridor that overlooked the immense octagonal Reading Room with its soaring coffered dome. Eight massive arched stained-glass windows with the seal of the United States and the seals of the states gave the room its natural light during the day. Now at night they were opaque, with an occasional glimmer of the jeweled stained glass winking in the dim light. Flanking each window was a carved figure on a pedestal supported by a dusky red

Corinthian column. Two stories of arcades with views of book-lined alcoves ringed the perimeter of the room. On the balustrade across from us, eight pairs of bronze statues watched over hundreds of desks arranged below in concentric rows.

"Lucie." Dominique shook my arm. "I need to talk to you."

"Sorry, I got distracted. This place is so beautiful."

"I know. *Mon Dieu,* I'm like a tiger at the end of my chair. I wish I could smoke. Do you think I could get away with it if I did it here? No one's around. Just a puff or two?"

"In the Library of Congress? Oh, sure. No problem. There's only miles and miles of books under our feet and some of the rarest books in the world all around us . . . Are you out of your mind?"

I grabbed her cigarettes and stuck them in my purse.

"All right, all right." She sounded peeved. "Well, I need something."

I thought of Ali Jennings, who probably had the something she needed.

"Calm down and tell me what's going on."

"You can't repeat this to anyone, do you understand?" Her voice dropped to a whisper so I had to lean close to hear her. "This has to stay between closed walls."

"Okay."

"Promise?"

"Yes, yes. Between closed walls."

She played with an antique onyx dinner ring that had belonged to our grandmother.

"It's Simon. I overheard him talking to someone on the phone tonight. We were at the Inn and he asked if he could use my office while I finished up some things in the kitchen. When I came back the door was ajar. I almost walked in until I heard him talking about your friend Rebecca. Something about seeing to it that she disappeared for good."

She reached for my hand. Hers felt like ice.

"Lucie, it scared me. I left and went back to the kitchen until he came for me. He doesn't know I heard."

I rubbed her hand, trying to warm it, hoping she didn't notice my rising alarm. "What do you mean, seeing to it that Rebecca disappeared for good?" I asked. "Did he say how?"

"No. I don't know . . . I don't know. Don't talk so loud. Someone might hear us. All I know is that it sounded like he had some idea where she is. I thought a homeless man killed her, or that Robin Hood person."

I stared at the lovely carved figures across from us. Allegorical statues representing all that was good and decent in civilization. Poetry, Philosophy, Art, History, Commerce, Law, Science, Religion. Dominique and I were talking about none of these things.

"Is she alive or dead?" I asked.

"I don't know," she repeated. "Simon's probably looking for me, so I'd better go find him. I've been gone too long thinking about this. I don't want him getting suspicious."

"Don't go back to Atoka with him tonight. You can come home with Mick and me. And for God's sake, don't drink any more. You know what they say, if you have secrets drink no wine."

"I have to leave with him, or he'll wonder what's wrong. But I'm going to break it off after this. Tell him I'm not ready for a relationship . . . that I'm too busy with work. He'll believe it with everything he's got on his mind."

"Dominique, if he finds out you overheard him . . ." I stopped.

What if he already knew? What if he'd seen her shadow on the threshold or heard the floorboards creak in the hall? Before I could speak, she leaned over and kissed me on the cheek.

"Don't worry," she said. "He won't."

"What are you going to do now?"

"Nothing. Just carry on like everything's all right. As for the rest of it, I'll burn that bridge when I come to it. Don't worry," she said again. "I can handle this."

She slipped out of the gallery and left me alone with the silent statues and busts that watched over the Reading Room.

And my fears about what might happen when the two of them were alone together and she burned her bridge.

CHAPTER 24

━━━━◦◦◦◦━━━━

After Dominique left, I stayed in the Visitors' Gallery until I was sure enough time had passed that no one would connect us being together. I had told Mick I'd meet him at the exhibit and I'd promised Ali I'd find Harlan.

I walked downstairs past Minerva and the beautiful double marble columns that reminded me of a temple. While my cousin and I had been sequestered upstairs, the loggia had filled up with people touring the Asher Collection. I scanned the crowd but didn't see Mick, so I pretended to study the contents of a glass cabinet containing a rough-looking cloth bag in case anyone happened to be watching me. I read the display card.

> One of the linen bags sewn together by State Department clerk Stephen Pleasanton to transport documents including the original parchment of the Declaration of Independence, the Constitution, the Articles of Confederation, the correspondence of General Washington, the secret journals of Congress, and all treaties of the United States to Leesburg, Virginia, for safekeeping after fire destroyed much of Washington.

It was a source of pride for Leesburg that for two weeks in August 1814 the town had been the "temporary capital" of the

United States when Washington was considered too unsafe to keep the country's most important documents. I looked at the coarse fabric and tried to imagine our entire heritage being shoved into a couple of sacks, thrown on a wagon, and driven off into the night by a lowly clerk who thought it was a good idea to get our national treasures out of town.

I had nearly reached the end of the exhibit. The last few display cases contained drawings and architectural plans for rebuilding the White House and the Capitol after the fire. The very last case contained a drawing of Frederick Law Olmsted's 1874 plans for landscaping the Capitol grounds.

> Not only were the Capitol grounds designed under Olmsted's direction, he also added the elegant West Front terraces along with a lovely grotto on the Senate side of the grounds where a bubbling spring was to be contained within a sheltered rocky enclosure.

Another fountain, more gardens. But this one was not defunct. Tomorrow we'd look for Rebecca's package—or whatever it was— by the fountains at Dumbarton Oaks. What if she were still alive? Was she somewhere in Washington? Who would know besides Simon and Tommy?

Harlan?

As though he'd heard my thoughts, I looked up as he slipped through a doorway at the end of the south corridor. I couldn't tell if he was hurrying toward someone—or away. The banners hanging from the doorways indicated it was a separate gallery containing two exhibits, one on the creation of the United States and another called "Thomas Jefferson's Library." I followed him, catching a glimpse of Sir Philip Sidney's quote written above the doorway: THEY ARE NEVER ALONE THAT ARE ACCOMPANIED WITH NOBLE THOUGHTS.

I lost Harlan in the softly lit mazelike display of rare documents. Apparently he wasn't here to see Jefferson's handwritten rough draft of the Declaration of Independence or Washington's notes scratched on a copy of the Constitution. I found him in the last gallery, a jewel-like circular room of mosaics and frescoes. He was alone, inside a coiled display of glass-enclosed bookcases filled with Jefferson's original library. The books had been arranged as Jefferson had them at Monticello, into categories called Memory, Reason, and Imagination. In the dim light given off by tiny pinpoint spotlights—to preserve the rare books—it seemed as though we were bathed in the candlelight of Jefferson's days.

"Harlan?"

"Lucie? What are you doing here?" He looked up like a man coming out of a dream.

"Looking for you. Ali's downstairs trying to ward off a migraine. She doesn't want to take her pain medicine because she's afraid she won't make it through her talk tonight. She was in the ladies' room by the Mainz Bible the last time I saw her."

"Ali?" He looked confused, then his face cleared. "Oh, right. What a shame. She gets those real bad headaches. Hell of a time for this one to come on."

"Don't you want to see her?"

"Sure."

"Harlan, what are you doing here? Everyone's downstairs or looking at the Asher Collection."

"Thinking," he said. "About things."

"I know how bad it is. Ali told me."

"You have no idea." He seemed, just now, like someone who had come unmoored from his soul. "It's worse than bad."

All my life growing up I had looked up to him, respected him. Right now I wanted to shake him.

"Are you really surprised?" I said. "Didn't you know what was going on inside Asher Investments? Or at least guess? Didn't you ask questions?"

"What the hell do you think?"

I thought the answer was no, because if he had he never would have invested the money of friends and neighbors in a Ponzi scheme, that's what I thought.

"Tommy told me it was highly sophisticated, too complicated to explain," he said. "Jesus, Lucie. It was like a gift from God. Who was I to say no when everyone was making so goddamn much money?"

"When did you find out it was all gone?"

"It's not *all* gone. Tommy says we'll be okay if we can get through this. It won't be like it was before, but it'll be okay."

"Oh, for God's sake, Harlan! You still believe anything he says?"

His eyes were bleak. "I have no choice."

I'd heard that before.

"What about Rebecca? Did she know what was going on? Surely she told you something since you two were—" I broke off, embarrassed.

"Screwing?" He raised an eyebrow. "Is that the word you were looking for?"

I blushed. "Didn't she say anything to you?"

"Our affair didn't last long. Rebecca was looking to hook a bigger fish."

"What are you talking about?" I said. "She came to see you the day she disappeared. To tell you she was—"

The look in his eyes stopped me. He didn't know.

"She was what?" he said. "Don't tell me she was pregnant. Was she?"

"I thought—"

"What? That it was mine?"

"Yes."

His smile mocked me. "You flatter me, my dear. I fire blanks these days. No little surprises anymore. A vasectomy."

I could feel the color draining from my face. "Then who?"

He shrugged. "Rebecca didn't confide in me about her latest lover—or lovers. She kept that information to herself."

"Do you have any idea where she is now? Did she say anything about leaving or going away that day when she came to see you?"

He held out his hands as if trying to ward me off. "I've been all over this with the police. I don't want to talk about it anymore."

So much for being accompanied by noble thoughts. Harlan was definitely alone here.

"How do you think I got invited tonight?" I gestured at the book-filled room. "Rebecca put my name on the guest list, that's how. She wanted me to come. Look, Harlan, if you know what happened to her, please tell me. Her mother is completely distraught, devastated, not to know—"

"No!" He moved closer to me, no longer friendly and suddenly a menacing stranger. I retreated, my back pressed against the glass. "Let it go, Lucie, will you? I have no idea what happened to her. And now if you'll excuse me I'd better go find Ali."

I listened until I could no longer hear his staccato footfalls. My face was hot with embarrassment and anger. In the middle of the bookshelf in front of me, a tiny book in Latin lay open. We had been standing in the section called Reason. I leaned over to read the card. A copy of Sir Thomas More's *Utopia,* dating from 1555.

Utopia, a perfect world where everything was bliss.

This wasn't it.

Somehow we all managed to get through the rest of the evening, though Dominique's nerves showed when she spilled a glass of red wine during dinner, barely missing the Oriental rug in the exquisite private room normally reserved for functions involving members of Congress. I hoped Simon would chalk it up to jitters and the beautiful setting. Fortunately, Harlan and Ali sat at another table. Her talk seemed flat and dispirited, probably a combination of the migraine and the heartbreak of realizing that the collection she had spent so much time putting together was about to be scattered to the winds. As for Harlan, he never looked my way as I watched him down glass after glass of wine. At the end of the evening he was leaning on his wife's arm and not walking too steadily as everyone moved toward the exit.

Mick, too, had gone quiet, lost in his thoughts on the drive home. I didn't need to do much to hold up my end of the conversation. He turned the radio on as a buffer, I thought, though this time he chose a classic rock station that had a one-hour tribute to Jackson Browne. Tonight, it seemed, I found irony in everything, including the playlist, "Running on Empty" and "Here Come Those Tears Again," as though we'd requested them.

Mick noticed, too, and killed the music. At my front door, his voice was hoarse in my ear. "Why don't I stay tonight? I think we both need it."

Sex to forget all his problems?

"It's not what I need, Mick. I can't do this."

His lips brushed mine and he left. No doubt he'd find what he was looking for in someone else's arms. I went upstairs and threw myself on the bed. As evenings went, this had been one I would rather forget.

The overcast skies Sunday morning only added to my gloom and a sense of foreboding that the other shoe was about to drop. Exactly one week ago Rebecca's clothing had been found in that rowboat on the Potomac.

I made coffee and toasted a piece of baguette with some Brie for breakfast. Then I drove over to the winery. David Wildman's article on Asher Investments had made the front page of the *Washington Tribune*. Frankie was in the middle of reading it when I got there.

"How is it?" I asked.

She slid the paper across the bar. "Bad, if your name is Tommy Asher, or maybe Harlan Jennings. Here, read for yourself while I make us a pot of coffee."

It was bad, all right, but factual and well written, putting together Rebecca's disappearance, Ian's death, and the canceled Senate hearing so the puzzle started to look like a picture of cover-ups and subterfuge at Thomas Asher Investments. David had alluded to Rebecca's frequent visits to Harlan's office and tied Harlan to Tommy as an old childhood friend from their London days, making it seem implausible that Harlan didn't know what was going on or at least have suspicions. He left out the romance and stopped short of using the term "Ponzi scheme," though he did have a couple of investment fund managers from two of the big New York firms on record saying they wondered how Tommy Asher never had a down year, even when the market was in the toilet.

I set the newspaper on the bar. It was the beginning of the end. Or maybe the middle of it.

Frankie came back with our coffee.

"How did last night go?" She set a mug in front of me.

"Like a train wreck where you know you ought to look away but you can't." I sipped my coffee. "Which reminds me, Ali told me that we never delivered the Viognier she ordered for Harlan's birthday party. I said I'd see to it myself first thing this morning."

"I can't believe she wants to hold a party for him after all this," Frankie said. "Anyone else I'd say it was a little tone-deaf, but that's Ali for you. Standing by her man."

"She told me none of this is Harlan's fault. He's a victim, too."

Frankie shrugged. "You're not going to change her mind. As for the delivery, let one of the guys do it. It's their job."

"Not this time."

"At least let someone load the boxes in your car."

"All right." I picked up a corkscrew and studied it. "Seen Quinn?"

"Not today. He told me yesterday he was going out last night with a bunch of guys. Then he thought he'd get lost today."

I spun the worm with my index finger. "Okay."

"Lucie, let it go. You can't go on like this. The two of you are tearing each other apart."

I slapped the corkscrew back on the bar. "Go on like what?"

"Do you act obtuse on purpose, or does it just come naturally? I'm still trying to figure it out."

"Who's being obtuse?"

"I give up. Make your delivery. Don't worry about a thing around here, either. I got it covered. Don't need you. Don't even want you. Go away and do something nice for yourself after you drop that wine at the Jenningses' place."

I blew her a kiss on my way out the door.

But I did not do something nice after I brought the wine to the Jenningses' place.

CHAPTER 25

———— ∞∞∞ ————

Harlan and Alison Jennings lived at Longmeadow, a two-hundred-acre estate off Zulla Road that had been in Harlan's family for generations. A working farm with outbuildings and tenant houses since the time Leven Powell founded Middleburg in 1787, it had a storied and colorful history. On New Year's Eve in 1850, a fire of questionable origin destroyed the modest stone house that had been there since colonial days. In its place, Harlan's great-grandfather, recently married to a tobacco heiress with a taste for lavish entertaining, built a Greek Revival mansion with a columned front porch and a grand pedimented gable that rivaled the James River plantations. Their parties, especially during Prohibition, were legendary.

Harlan's BMW convertible was parked in the circular drive when I pulled up in front of the house. I got out of the Mini and walked up the flagstone path lined with masses of pink and white tulips and daffodils of every shade of yellow, white, and orange. Ivy twined around the two columns flanking the front door. Stone urns were filled with fragrant-smelling Easter lilies. It looked as if someone recently had been sitting outside despite the dull day, leaving a glass and an empty bottle on a wicker table next to a Windsor rocking chair. A jacket—Harlan's by the look of it—hung over the back of the chair.

I rang the doorbell and heard the Westminster chime echo inside. While I waited I stole a look at the bottle. Tequila, nearly empty.

A brand I didn't recognize. Maybe Harlan had read the *Trib* and decided to move directly from breakfast to happy hour.

A pretty Hispanic maid in a gray uniform opened the door. Her face was composed but she looked like she was in some distress.

"May I help you?"

"I'm Lucie Montgomery," I said. "Dr. Jennings ordered a couple of cases of wine from my vineyard for her husband's birthday party. I promised her I'd deliver them this morning. Is she around?"

She shook her head. "The señora went riding. Didn't the senator tell you?"

"Harlan? No—I didn't see him."

She stepped out onto the porch and her eyes fell on the tequila bottle.

"*Díos mío,*" she said. "He drank all that?"

"All what?" I said. "You don't mean he drank a whole bottle of tequila just now, do you?"

Good Lord, it would kill him.

"No, no. It was already open." She gave me a reassuring smile that didn't mask the lie. He'd drunk a lot and she knew it.

I picked up the bottle and held it up. "How much?"

She touched her heart with one hand like she was trying to catch her breath or compose herself. "It's not for me to say anything about what my boss does, you know?"

"Maybe you ought to tell me your name. And it is for you to say if he drank as much as you seem to think he did. You'd better tell me what you know. He could be suffering from alcohol poisoning, meaning he needs medical help."

The girl looked like a guilty child who'd been caught flat out in a lie. "My name is Dulcie. He drank half, maybe two-thirds."

I groaned.

"Well, Dulcie, at least he didn't get behind the wheel of his car," I said. "Any idea where he is now, where he might have gone?"

"He might have gone back inside while I was upstairs," she said.

I didn't like the growing urgency in her voice, which now matched my own escalating anxiety. She still wasn't telling me everything.

"What is it?" I asked. "Come on."

The girl hesitated, too well trained to tell tales about her employers to strangers.

"Please," I said. "I know about what's going on, about the money problems. We need to find Senator Jennings. *Right now.*"

"He and the señora had an argument. They were screaming so loud I covered my ears, but I could still hear. When you came, I was cleaning up in the bedroom."

"Cleaning up?"

"A broken lamp. I think Señora Jennings threw it. Then she left. That's when he must have gotten the tequila. To get *borracho.*"

I knew that word. Drunk.

"You check the house," I said. "I'll look in the garden first. Then I'll drive down to the stables."

"He didn't go to the stables," she said. "That fight was pretty bad. She might . . . leave for a while."

If Ali were contemplating walking out on Harlan, it must have been a fight for the record books.

"Okay," I said, but Dulcie had already vanished.

I bumped into the rocking chair as I turned to leave the porch, knocking Harlan's jacket to the ground. When I picked it up, something rolled out of one of the pockets.

A pill bottle. Alison's prescription, her migraine medicine. At least it wasn't empty. Tequila and pain pills. He wouldn't be feeling a thing.

In fact, he might not even be breathing, wherever he was.

"Oh, God, Harlan," I said. "Please don't have done anything stupid."

He'd be drunk and disoriented. I doubted he'd gotten far. The swimming pool in the backyard. It was heated and they kept it open year-round. One of Middleburg's more eccentric traditions was the Jenningses' annual impromptu pool party in honor of the first snowfall. No one admitted without a bathing suit—and you had to go swimming.

I stuck my head through the front door and yelled to the maid. "Call nine-one-one and tell them to send an ambulance. Tell them to hurry!"

He was facedown at the bottom of the deep end, fully dressed except for his shoes, socks, and a sweater that he'd taken the trouble to leave in a neat pile next to the diving board.

I dropped my cane, stripped off my jacket, and kicked off my own shoes. As I dove in, the image of Rebecca's folded clothes on the dock last week flashed through my mind. Was I trying to rescue the man responsible for her disappearance? The water felt almost tropically warm. Thank God for small blessings. The air temperature was probably in the fifties. In an unheated pool with hypothermia brought on by the consumption of so much alcohol, he'd probably be dead within minutes. I touched the bottom, grabbing one of his arms with two hands and pulling on it. His body floated up enough for me to crook an arm around his neck and drag him with me.

Dulcie was on her knees by the steps in the shallow end when I surfaced with Harlan.

"*Madre de Díos,*" she said. "He's dead."

"We don't know that. Come on, help me pull him out." The contrast between the water and air temperatures felt like a slap across the face. "Hurry!"

We wrestled Harlan up the stairs and hauled him onto the deck of the pool. I rolled him onto his back. His lips and eyelids were blue and his skin looked waxy.

Dulcie started to cry. "What do I do?"

"Stop crying. I'm going to need your help. Go in the house and get some blankets. We have to warm him up."

She rubbed her eyes with her fists like a child. "Okay."

"Where's the ambulance?"

"Coming." She got up and started for the house.

"Run!" I yelled at her.

I tilted Harlan's head back and put my ear against his chest. He wasn't breathing. My hands were shaking too much from the cold to tell if he had a pulse. It had been years since I'd learned CPR and I'd never done it on anything except a dummy.

Dulcie returned with an armful of blankets that looked like they'd been pulled off someone's bed.

"One for you, too," she said. "You are shivering."

She wrapped the blanket around my shoulders and we piled the others on top of Harlan.

"You push on his chest with both hands," I said to her. "Like this. Do it when I tell you. I'm going to blow air into his lungs."

I have no idea how long we worked together, me pinching Harlan's nose and blowing into his mouth as hard as I could while Dulcie pumped his chest. She began murmuring in Spanish and I recognized the Lord's Prayer. In spite of the blanket, I couldn't stop shivering as my hands cramped up and I began losing feeling in my fingers.

It felt like I was losing Harlan, too, his life ebbing away in spite of our efforts. He had wanted to die. I needed him to want to live.

Finally we heard the sirens. Dulcie lifted her head and made the sign of the cross.

"Go around to the front and show them where we are," I said.

This time she ran. I heard shouting and footsteps running toward the swimming pool. Two men in navy fire and rescue uniforms knelt on either side of Harlan. Around me voices swirled and colors flashed. Someone put her hands on my shoulders and gently moved me aside.

"We got him," one of the paramedics said to me as he pulled off Harlan's blankets and began tearing open his shirt. "How long have you been at it?"

"A couple of minutes I think."

"Any idea how long he was in the water?"

"No."

A blond woman in a yellow Loudoun County Fire Department jumpsuit helped me up. "Thanks, hon. Come on over here. Let them take care of your husband."

Dulcie came over and stood next to me. She seemed calmer now, though she still looked pale. The blond showed me Ali's pill bottle as the paramedics hooked Harlan up to a heart monitor and fitted an oxygen mask over his face. It took them about thirty seconds.

"I found these out front on the table next to an empty tequila bottle," she said. "What's he got in his stomach?"

I heard the man who had ripped open Harlan's shirt say, "Body temp ninety-three point four. He's got no pulse. Get the pads."

Dulcie moaned and I put my arm around her.

"Half a bottle of tequila," I said to the woman. "I don't know how many pills."

We watched a third paramedic unpack a defibrillator.

"Don't look," I said to Dulcie. She buried her head on my shoulder and I closed my eyes.

I heard the jolt as the machine went off and then someone said, "We got something. He's back, but just barely."

The blond said to me, "You can go to the hospital with him if you want. The battalion chief just showed up. He'll drive you, but you ought to go inside and get out of those wet clothes first."

"It's not my house," I said. "I'm just a friend of the family."

She looked momentarily nonplussed, then turned to Dulcie. "Can you take her inside and get her something dry to wear, please?" To me she added, "Sorry. I thought you were his wife. Where is she?"

"The head groom is trying to find Señora Jennings," Dulcie said.

"Jennings?"

"You don't know whose house this is?" I asked.

"I'm new to the area. Sorry."

"That's Harlan Jennings lying there. Senator Harlan Jennings."

"Oh, God. I read the paper this morning. That article on the front page." She shook her head. "What a waste. Go change, hon. You're shivering."

I followed Dulcie as the two paramedics lifted Harlan, who now wore a cervical collar, onto a backboard. I wondered if they would put him on a suicide watch in the hospital. Would he try again to take his life?

I was changing into some of Ali's clothes in the guest bathroom when I heard her frantic voice in the foyer. I finished dressing and went to find her.

She looked surprised to see me. "Why are you wearing . . . Oh, God! Dulcie told me you found him. I didn't realize . . ."

"Sorry. My clothes were wet." I fingered the buttons of her sweater. "I'll return these later."

"It's okay, don't be silly. Keep them. I'm so glad you were here. He could have died . . ."

"Don't think about it," I said. "He didn't. Go to the hospital with him and everything will be fine."

She laughed a mirthless laugh. "That's so funny. Nothing will be fine. Not now, not ever. It's over. Finished. We've lost everything."

"Mrs. Jennings." The battalion chief opened the front door and stuck his head inside. "We have to go. Would you like to ride in the ambulance or with me?"

"With you." Ali laid a hand on my arm. "Good-bye, Lucie."

I went outside as the ambulance pulled out of the driveway, sirens blaring. A Loudoun County fire engine followed and the battalion chief's cruiser brought up the rear, first circling around the driveway in front of Dulcie and me. Dulcie clutched Harlan's jacket against her chest like a shield. Ali never looked at either of us as the cruiser drove off.

"Thank you for saving his life," Dulcie said.

"It was both of us," I said. "We did it together."

I got in the Mini and thought about Harlan and what Ali had just said before she left for the hospital. The latest—and probably not the last—casualty as the Asher empire continued its downward trajectory of destruction and ruin.

CHAPTER 26

———— ∞∞∞ ————

Something slid around the cargo space behind the Mini's rear seat as I took the turn off Atoka Road onto Sycamore Lane a little too fast. The Viognier. I'd forgotten to deliver it. Maybe I should void the sale and forget about it. Ali wouldn't want the wine now.

It was just after noon when I pulled into my driveway. Quinn's fifteen-year-old Ford Mustang, which seemed to spend more time at the mechanic's than on the road, was parked in front of the house. Frankie said he planned to take today off, so I didn't expect to see him here. I parked next to him and caught my shoe on the hem of Ali's trousers climbing out of the car. I rolled up both hems to make cuffs and did the same to the sleeves of her fuzzy equestrian-themed sweater.

I called Quinn's name, checking the rooms when I got inside. He wasn't here. I knew, then, where to find him, though I didn't know why. The summerhouse in the backyard by the rose garden. When Quinn first came to work for Leland, he'd asked permission to set up his telescope out there since the wide-open view of the Piedmont and the Blue Ridge was perfect for stargazing. Quinn's fascination with the stars, planets, and anything else in the night sky had always intrigued me because it seemed so out of character with his brash, macho personality. But over the years—as I thought about it now—my sweetest and most memorable nights with him had been spent not in his arms in bed but sitting next to him in one of my mother's old Adirondack chairs outside the summerhouse, staring at the velvet silhouette of the mountains and the star-spangled sky over the valley. One of us always brought a bottle of wine and we'd drink it while he recounted the history of one of the constellations or explained why Pluto had been demoted as a planet or told me some piece of astronomical trivia that fascinated him. Then he'd position the telescope—a Starmaster, the Rolls-Royce of telescopes—so all I had to do was look through the eyepiece as the familiar scent of his cigar floated through the air and we listened to the summer night sounds of a hoot owl or a crying fox or the autumn serenade of the tree frogs and cicadas.

This was the first time he'd been out there during the day. I grabbed a jacket from the mudroom and threw it on over Ali's clothes. As expected, he was in his customary chair, smoking a Swisher Sweet cigar and staring at the valley. I knew he must have heard me, though he didn't turn his head.

"Harlan Jennings tried to commit suicide this morning." I sat next to him in my own chair. "He tried to drown himself."

That roused him.

"Oh, my God, you're kidding." He looked at the rolled cuffs of my pants and the horsey sweater. "Whose clothes are those? You own a sweater with saddles and bridles on it? Where have you been?"

"The clothes are Ali's. And I've been in their swimming pool, pulling Harlan off the bottom."

"Jesus, is he alive?"

"He was breathing with the help of a respirator when the ambulance left, but he wasn't conscious."

"I'm really sorry to hear that."

"Me, too."

"Why did he do it?"

"Why do you think? Didn't you read the *Trib* this morning?"

"No," he said. "I figured a news blackout for the next six months or so would do me good until this blows over. Why, what's in the *Trib*? More dirt on Thomas Asher Investments and what a crook he is?"

"In a word, yes."

He knocked the ash off his cigar and watched it drop to the ground. "Suicide is a coward's way out. You leave behind everyone else to clean up your mess. I feel sorry for Ali and the boys."

"Me, too."

"If he recovers, I'd like to punch his lights out."

"Quinn!"

"So sue me. I would." He shifted in his chair and looked me in the eye. "I lost absolutely everything, Lucie. Every cent of my mother's money and all my savings. I'm flat broke."

I reached for his hand with both of mine, but he pulled away.

"We'll start over," I said. "Mick asked me to buy his grapes for the fall harvest. I can't possibly do that without you—"

His laugh was harsh. "Yeah, I heard about that. Mick lost a bundle, too."

"Mick still thinks Humpty Dumpty can be put back together again."

"There isn't enough Crazy Glue in the world. It's over, Lucie. And thanks for your offer, but no, thanks."

"What do you mean, 'no, thanks'?"

"I'm not interested."

What was he talking about? He was still the winemaker here.

I said, "You think it's too much for us to handle? You want to bring on an assistant winemaker?"

"Do whatever you want," he said. "I'm out."

"Out how? You're not quitting?"

"Look, back off, will you? I got enough stuff to deal with right now without you hammering at me."

"I'm *not* hammering at you." I reached for my cane. "All I asked is whether you quit or not?"

His eyes locked on mine and I knew we were on the brink of crossing another of those can't-go-back boundary lines we'd crossed once or twice before in our relationship. A winning combination—as Frankie would say—of bullheaded ego and stubborn pride because he wouldn't back down and I couldn't.

This time, though, it was for all the marbles. If he quit and left, I'd lose him for good. We needed to step back from this ledge before one of us jumped.

"Wait," I said. "Don't answer that. Forget I asked. We're both upset and overwrought. We don't have to do this now."

"Why?" he said. "It isn't going to change anything or get any easier."

"Quinn," I said. "For the love of God, just . . . don't say anything right now, okay? I don't think I could take it."

"This isn't about you, Lucie, so stop acting like it is."

I never should have said what I said next, but I did—and there was no taking it back. An hour ago I was on my knees trying to breathe life into Harlan Jennings who toxed himself up with enough alcohol and drugs to ease the pain of walking off a diving board into nine feet of water. No, it wasn't about me, but I'd been pulled into it, anyway.

"What do you know about it? Rebecca Natale dragged me into the middle of Asher Investment's free fall and she didn't ask my permission. Since then she's gone missing and presumed dead, Ian Philips is dead, and Harlan Jennings just tried to kill himself." I ticked their names off on my fingers as my voice rose. "It's too bad you lost your money but at least you're still around to talk about it, which is more than any of them are. So stop wallowing in self-pity and venting your anger at me. It's not my fault you built your future on a house of cards. I'm only trying to help."

His eyes blazed, and now the point of no return was well in the rearview mirror.

"I'm going inside," I said before he could speak. "Do whatever you have to do or want to do. I need a shower and my own clothes. I'll see you tomorrow for work and we'll figure out where we are then."

I got up and left and didn't look back. He never said a word. I made my way through rosebushes that were just beginning to shake off their winter dormancy, and banged the veranda door shut on my way inside in case he hadn't figured out just how mad I was.

By the time I showered and changed, the Mustang was no longer in the driveway. I walked into the library and threw myself on the sofa, knocking the book of Alexander Pope's poetry, which I'd left on one of the cushions, to the floor. It landed faceup, open to the much-viewed epistle to Richard Boyle. I picked it up and read, for the hundredth time, the long passage Rebecca had marked.

No artful wildness to perplex the scene;
Grove nods at grove, each alley has a brother,
And half the platform just reflects the other.
The suff'ring eye inverted Nature sees,
Trees cut to statues, statues thick as trees;
With here a fountain, never to be play'd;
And there a summerhouse, that knows no shade.

What if I'd been looking for the wrong landmark? What if there was a summerhouse—like mine—somewhere in Washington? I got my laptop off the desk and brought it back to the sofa. The Internet search took me to the U.S. Capitol website in seconds. The Summer House was a small open-air, hexagonal, brick building designed by Frederick Law Olmsted in the late 1800s and set in a secluded grove on the Senate side of the Capitol.

There was a picture of the place with its charming arched entrances, basket-weave brickwork, wrought-iron gates, and Spanish mission tile roof. It looked like a whimsical folly, completely different from the elegant, austere Capitol. I kept reading. Built as a resting place for visitors and their horses to get a cool drink of water on a hot day, Olmsted's original fountain had been replaced by modern drinking fountains. Plans for a southern summerhouse near the House of Representatives had been scuttled by Congress over concerns improprieties could be already taking place on Capitol grounds since the northern building was so secluded and well hidden from public view.

I had read about this last night at the Library of Congress—the last display showing Olmsted's landscaping plans for the Capitol—though only the grotto had been mentioned, not the summerhouse. It meant, at least, that Rebecca must also have known about it. Could this be what Ian and I had been looking for? Each alley has a brother, grove nods at grove—the House and the Senate were mirrors of each other. But what about the fountain never to be played?

After a few more minutes of research I found it. Olmsted planned for a small water-powered carillon to be set in the middle of the rock garden and produce what he'd called "musical murmurings." Unfortunately, the only one that was built—made by

Tiffany & Co.—never worked, so it was removed and sent to a government warehouse and no one had seen it since. Not a fountain, but close enough.

This had to be the place. I studied the photo, growing more excited. Sheltered from the weather and small enough so it shouldn't be too difficult to locate whatever Rebecca had left—even something as small as a portable external drive. Maybe she'd hidden it under one of the twenty-two chairs. Who would have guessed?

I got my phone from the foyer and scrolled through the recent calls until I found David's number from last night. It went straight to voice mail. His office number. He wouldn't be there on Sunday afternoon, especially after working so late yesterday. I left a message. Too bad I didn't have his cell number. Kit knew it and she could reach him. But she didn't answer her phone, either. I tried every number I had for her—D.C. apartment, cell, office—and left messages on all of them.

It would take me at least an hour to get to Washington. By then one or both of them would have checked their voice mail and called back. I shut down the laptop and got my jacket and car keys.

The trip to Washington took only forty-five minutes since I pushed the speed limit as fast as I dared. But I was excited, apprehensive, and dead certain I'd solved the mystery behind Rebecca's two-hundred-year-old clue woven through the poetry of Alexander Pope.

CHAPTER 27

———⊗———

I kept an eye on my rearview mirror as I sped into Washington, but I didn't see anyone following me. The skies grew increasingly darker as I drove east. By the time I crossed the Teddy Roosevelt Bridge, a fine mist of rain coated my windshield. It turned to spit as I continued up Constitution Avenue and soon would become a steady downpour, probably before I reached the Capitol. The weather seemed to have chased away all but the most determined tourists, and they'd come prepared with umbrellas. I reached behind me and felt along the backseat of the car. No umbrella, and my jacket didn't have a hood.

At least it wasn't hailing, which hurt, or a thunderstorm, which was dangerous. And there was one bonus with the awful weather: I was practically guaranteed to have the summerhouse to myself.

I spent twenty minutes circling Madison and Jefferson drives by the museums, searching for a parking place. A Volvo sedan pulled away from the corner of Maryland Avenue and Third Street next to the Botanic Gardens as I turned onto Third. I slipped into the spot and sat in the car calling Kit and David one more time as the rain drummed on my roof. Already it was quarter to three and we were supposed to meet at Dumbarton Oaks across town at five. I tried Kit first. Still no answer.

David picked up right away. "Where are you?"

"The Botanic Gardens," I said.

"What's at the Botanic Gardens?"

"Nothing. Well, plants and flowers are there. Did you know there's a summerhouse at the Capitol?" I rubbed condensation off my car window with the side of my fist. To my left, the stepped sand-colored dome of the American Indian museum had darkened in the rain giving the building an unusual two-toned look.

He said nothing, so I went on.

"I saw a reference to it last night at the Library of Congress when I was looking at some drawings by Frederick Law Olmsted that were part of the Asher Collection. They only referred to a grotto, but I did some research on the Internet. There's a summerhouse on the site as well. It has a working fountain, but the water carillon Olmsted intended to put there wouldn't work so it was never played. Everything else in that passage of Pope's poem fits. The House and the Senate—two halves reflecting each other."

The silence continued on his end.

"Hey," I said after a moment, "are you still there?"

I checked the display. Call lost. Where was he and when had I lost him? How much had he heard? I hit Redial, but he was still out of range because his phone switched over to voice mail.

"Call me," I said.

By now the rain was coming down steadily, the kind of rain my mother used to call "a nice rain" as in something that would soak the ground and be good for her gardens and flowers. I could either wait for David or check out the summerhouse by myself before it turned into a downpour. I didn't even know where he was or how long it would take him to get to me. For all I knew he hadn't heard a word I said after mentioning the Botanic Gardens and assumed I was still going to meet him and Kit in Georgetown. I got out of the car and headed for the Capitol. The only people I saw were a young couple pushing a baby in a plastic-encased stroller toward the entrance to the Botanic Gardens. Otherwise the streets were empty. Across Maryland Avenue gulls flew over the slate-colored Capitol Reflecting Pool, landing in a bedraggled lineup on the ledge by the sidewalk. A few sailed across to the equestrian statue of Ulysses S. Grant and settled there.

The summerhouse—wherever it was—had to be well tucked

away on the west lawn of the Capitol because I could see nothing as I approached the grounds. There were two paths—a red-and-gray harlequin-patterned walk that led directly to the west steps of the Capitol, and a curved walkway lined with blooming magnolias and flowering cherry trees closer to the House of Representatives. Both ended at the west steps. I took the flower-lined walk for the brief shelter from the rain provided by the trees arching overhead like a canopy. Soggy clumps of petals lay crushed underneath my feet, covering the ground like pink snow. In the middle of a lawn the color of AstroTurf, a bed of red, pink, and yellow tulips gleamed brilliantly against the sharp green. To the west, more patches of green bordered by the somber-looking buildings of the Smithsonian museums along the Mall. In the distance, the top of the Washington Monument was shrouded in clouds.

I passed one of the two marble staircases that led to the west plaza of the Capitol. Temporary fences blocked it off and security guards watched me from above. I hated how so many public buildings in Washington like the Capitol and the White House had become fortresses, with their concrete barricades, rows of stanchions, and steel plates rising out of the ground like drawbridges being pulled in. That it had become inevitable was a fact of life, but it was still ugly as sin.

Between the staircases, a terraced semicircular garden with a border of yellow, rust, and dark red pansies and miniature trees set in alcoves surrounded a fountain that splashed water over its rim as the rain beat down harder, now an unrelenting downpour. I pushed my wet hair off my face and wiped my eyes. The guards probably wondered what some nut was doing out in the middle of this. Across the street, the Roosevelt Carillon chimed three o'clock.

I passed an ancient willow oak that shaded the curved walkway, the twin of the path I'd taken on the House side, and that's when I finally saw the summerhouse. Set low into the hillside and surrounded by shrubs and trees, it was built not to intrude on the grand view of the Capitol, which explained why the now mature landscaping nearly completely hid the little building. Clumps of daffodils bloomed in the surrounding rock gardens where barberry, gold dust, *Pieris japonica,* hypericum, and other plants I couldn't identify formed part of the screen around it. I walked down two stone steps to a wrought-iron gate that swung open with a creak when I pushed on it.

Inside—or, rather, outside—the summerhouse was the kind of place Rebecca would find enchanting, with its burbling fountain, decorative brickwork, and stone chairs protected from the elements by shelflike orange tile roofs. I threw myself into one of the seats and tucked my legs under me, glad for a temporary shelter from the rain.

If the reason Olmsted wasn't permitted to build a twin building on the House side was due to congressional concern about "improprieties" in this isolated place, I could see why. That, too, would appeal to Rebecca—an exotic and slightly risky place to meet and engage in just such improprieties with a lover. Say, someone like former senator Harlan Jennings.

Her package, whatever it was, was here somewhere. It had to be. Originally I thought she might have hidden it under one of the chairs, but now I realized that was impossible because the rows of seats were set directly on top of a low brick wall. My other thought was the grotto, visible through the grillwork of one of the oval windows. But when I peered outside it was obvious there was no place to hide anything.

What none of the Internet articles I'd read had mentioned was the opening the size of a small hearth on the inside corner of one of the archways. About two feet high and eighteen inches wide, it could be as much as three feet deep if it extended all the way into the wall. It was the only part of the summerhouse whose function wasn't obvious. Storage, maybe—but for what?

Directly in front of the opening was a deep puddle. I used my cane for balance as I straddled the puddle and bent down to see inside. Nothing but inky darkness. I moved my hand inch by inch over the wet walls and ceiling as far back as I could reach. Except for slime and a few lumps that I didn't want to identify, there was nothing there—unless she'd crawled inside and left it all the way in the back, though that didn't seem like Rebecca, who was bigger and taller than I.

My knees began to cramp. I tried to dig my fingers into the mortar between the bricks to keep my balance and I lost my footing on the slick stone. I landed hard on both hands in about two inches of water and muck. I moved one hand inside the opening and felt along the floor. My fingers brushed against something that gave way when I touched it. I pulled it out. A white plastic grocery bag.

A padded brown legal-sized mailing envelope was inside the bag. The envelope was wrapped in more plastic and secured with strapping tape. No writing, nothing to identify it, but this had to be what I was looking for. I turned it over and felt what was inside. Papers and something hard and rectangular. An external computer drive?

Whatever it was, I didn't want to open it out here in the pouring rain. I moved back to the shelter of the benches and reached in my pocket for my phone to call Kit and David. It was gone. Had I left it in the car? No, I'd made sure to bring it with me. I'd even checked that it was there as I walked across the Capitol grounds.

I found it in the middle of the puddle. It probably fell out of my pocket when I stumbled. I dredged it out with my cane and tried to turn it on. The buttons oozed water.

I shoved it back in my pocket, tucking Rebecca's package under my soaked jacket. The walk from the summerhouse across the west Capitol lawn was miserable. A cold wind blew up off the open expanse of the Reflecting Pool and slanted the hard rain so it was nearly horizontal, pricking my face like tiny needles. When I passed the statue of James Garfield at the top of Maryland Avenue, I changed direction and headed for the Botanic Gardens to wait out the storm.

An elegant-looking white-haired woman sitting behind the front desk looked up from her book as I pulled open one of the large glass-paned doors and stepped into the warm, dry Orangerie. She took off her glasses and studied me like I was a specimen who belonged somewhere in the gardens. For a moment I thought she was going to ask me to leave. There was already a small puddle at my feet as water dripped off my clothes and my hair.

I decided to take the offensive and state the obvious.

"Hi, there," I said. "Thought I'd come in out of the rain. I probably look like a drowned rat."

"A drowned rat," she said, "would look a whole lot better than you do. Is it coming down too hard for an umbrella? What are you doing out in this? It's like a monsoon."

"When I left home it wasn't raining."

"You came from Kansas, maybe?"

I grinned. "Atoka. Just beyond Middleburg."

"You look pretty pitiful," she said, "if you don't mind my saying. Where did you come from just now?"

"The Capitol. I feel pretty pitiful. I dropped my cell phone in a puddle. Took me awhile to find it. I thought I might stay here until this downpour ends."

I could let her think I'd stopped by my office on the Hill to put in some overtime and had gotten soaked searching for the phone.

"You've got the place to yourself," she said. "They'd hate you in the museums, but here if you drip on anything we can skip watering for a day."

I laughed. "What I really need is to dry off."

"Use the high-speed hand dryers in the restroom. They're environmental. We're all green here. You can dry your hair in two shakes. Just don't get too close or it will sound like a jet engine taking off next to your ear."

"I think I'll try that," I said. "Everything squishes."

She took a map out of a display rack and opened it.

"Go to the south lobby on the other side of the conservatory. The ladies' room is at the back of the Jungle, in between medicinal plants and the desert."

I took the map. "Thanks."

"One more thing?"

"Yes?"

"May I see what's in the bag?"

I pulled the plastic-encased mailing envelope out of the grocery sack. "Just some papers."

"Thank you." She shrugged. "Security. You know how it is. I told the guard he could take off early since we didn't expect anyone else to come by, but I still need to ask."

I slid the envelope back in the bag.

"You've got about forty minutes," she said. "I'm closing early, before five tonight."

"Don't worry," I said. "I'll be long gone before then."

I went through another door into the light-filled Garden Court. The air was warm and tropical and the rain beat incessantly on the glass roof of the conservatory. Panpipe music played in the background and fountains burbled in two pools at either end of the gallery. The air smelled of hundreds of Easter lilies massed in pots around the pools, along with orchids, hydrangeas, ferns, lavender, and bushy Easter broom.

I walked through a second door at the back of the Garden Court with a sign above the door that said simply JUNGLE. The enormous room, meant to be the re-creation of a ruined plantation, was dense with lush foliage, groves of palm trees, a banyan tree dripping with Spanish moss, and other dark greenery and twisting vines that rose at least two stories above my head. A catwalk ringed the entire room. The view from up there was probably amazing. Somewhere a tree frog croaked and fans whooshed, circulating the humid air, though neither sound drowned out the ceaseless pelting of rain on the glass roof. The air was heavy with the fetid, damp smell of decaying vegetation. Everywhere I looked, lacy shadows of palm fronds from dozens of tall trees shrouded the rain-darkened room in an eerie gloom.

I walked quickly down a path that ran along a stream with a series of waterfalls until I reached the south lobby. The moment I walked into the ladies' room I stripped off my jacket and began to wring it and my clothes out in the sink. The sweet-faced woman at the front desk wasn't kidding about the hair dryer sounding like a jet taking off as I leaned down to dry my hair. Half-deaf, but drier, I put on my soggy jacket and picked up Rebecca's package.

Whether it was still pouring or not, I was going to make a run for the car and drive over to Dumbarton Oaks. There Kit, David, and I could figure out what to do next. I walked up the path on the opposite side of the stream and back through the Garden Court. As I pushed open the door to the Orangerie, I heard a man speaking to the woman at the front desk.

"I won't be long," he said. "Just thought I'd have a quick look around since I'm only in Washington for the weekend."

Maybe it was the British accent that captivated her or maybe she was flustered because she recognized him from all the press coverage.

"Of course," she said to Tommy Asher. "Enjoy your visit."

CHAPTER 28

In a few seconds he would enter the room where I now stood, though she would ask him to use the door on the opposite side, not the exit where I was now. It was no coincidence that he had come here. He had hunted me down and I'd been stupid enough to let myself be cornered inside the Botanic Gardens with no phone, no security guard, and no one other than a septuagenarian docent whom he'd just utterly charmed. How had I missed seeing him? Where had he been?

I quietly closed the door to the Orangerie and fled across the Garden Court to the Jungle. On this side of the conservatory there was not only a staircase to the second story canopy walk but also a glassed-in elevator. The car, mercifully, was waiting on the first floor. I slipped Rebecca's package underneath a prayer plant and a split-leaf philodendron. Then I stepped in the elevator and smashed the Close Door button and the button for the second floor. Maybe he'd think I left through the south entrance on Independence Avenue. Maybe he'd never look up.

The door slid shut and the elevator hummed. "Go," I said. "Please. Right now."

The car slowly began to rise as the door from the Garden Court on the far side of the Jungle opened. Tommy Asher walked in to the steamy stillness. He wore black jeans, a dark all-weather jacket, and a knitted cap. He looked more like an older version of the tough street-wise kid Harlan had described in London than the world-renowned adventurer and investment guru he claimed to be now. And here we were in a jungle where he was the hunter and I was the prey.

I stepped to the rear of the carriage as though I would become invisible as it rose into the air above the rain forest. Below, a mist hung over the waterfall and vividly colored orchids stood out like colorful birds among the tropical dark green foliage. Tommy Asher heard the elevator whir as it lifted me above him. He looked up and a broad smile creased his face as he reached in his pocket. Did he have a gun?

I saw the flash of a blade, and then he bent over a balustrade enveloped by twining jungle vines. From my vantage point, I couldn't see what he was doing, but I had a sickening feeling he was cutting off a piece of one of the vines. Then he ran up the metal staircase—the man who'd scaled Everest—on the far side of the room as my elevator continued its slow ascent.

I pounded the first-floor button, hoping to reverse direction as he reached the catwalk. He disappeared in the jungle foliage as the elevator stopped at the upper level and the door automatically opened. Before I could close it again, he stepped in front of it, jamming it open with his foot.

"Welcome to the catwalk, Lucie. Lovely view up here."

"No," I said. "Don't do this."

He grabbed my arm and yanked me out of the carriage.

"You have something of mine. I want it."

One of his arms locked around my neck as the other, holding the vine, felt me up, trying to find the package. His grip tightened.

"I don't know what you're talking about. I don't have anything."

"Don't be stupid," he said, "or I'll kill you right here."

"Like you killed Rebecca and Ian? Looking for the proof Rebecca left that you're running a Ponzi scheme?"

"Shut up." He increased the pressure on my throat and looped the vine into a noose. I began to feel light-headed. "Your friend is not so noble, you know. She cared for no one but herself."

"Then why did she try to help Ian Philips?" I tugged on his arm, trying to loosen his grip. He grabbed my arm and pinned it behind my back.

It hurt.

"Stop moving or I'll really hurt you," he said. "As for why she wanted to help that idiot Philips, I have no idea."

"Ian said something changed her mind."

At least now I had his interest. He eased his grip around my neck so I could talk.

"And what would that be?" His mouth was next to my ear. The overpowering scent of his cologne made me feel like throwing up.

"I don't know." Wasn't it nearly five o'clock? Wouldn't the docent be coming in to chase the two of us out soon? How long could I stall? "Unless it was the fact that she found out she was pregnant."

In the long moment of silence that followed, the whistle of an exotic bird cut through the air, a sweet piercing sound. The rain no longer pounded the conservatory roof. Shadows lengthened.

Rebecca had ended her affair with Harlan awhile ago. Ian said she went after rich, older men. Her latest lover had been the richest of them all—or so she thought. Tommy Asher was the father of her baby.

"Did you know she thought she might be pregnant with your child?" I asked. "You know she was caught on camera leaving a pharmacy with a pregnancy test that Saturday afternoon."

"It's none of your business."

"What happened? Did your wife find out?"

"Shut up." He moved the noose closer to my neck. "I never should have trusted that double-crossing little bitch. She played me."

He sounded hurt. The same jilted lover's voice I had heard from Ian. It was the kind of turn-the-tables revenge she had wanted to exact on Connor.

"She tried to blackmail you?"

"Don't be naïve." The rough vine scraped my cheek as he slipped it over my head. "Rebecca wasn't stupid. I gave her access to information she shouldn't have had. She used it to transfer funds to some account God knows where and decided to do a runner. I guess she figured she'd get away with it as long as I went down."

"So you killed her? Who got to her that afternoon before your gala? Who made up the Robin Hood story? You or Simon?"

"What difference does it make? Simon does whatever I tell him."

"In a court of law, it makes a lot of difference who the murderer is."

"Where's the package, Lucie? You've got it somewhere."

"No."

He tightened the cord and the palm fronds seemed to dance as they descended from the ceiling, enveloping me in darkness.

"Let me go and I'll show you."

"Show me now, dammit."

"Down . . . there."

"Where, damn you?"

For a split second he let go of the vine, peering over the railing of the canopy walk. I still held my cane, and now I brought it up and swung hard. It flew out of my hand but I caught one shoulder and the side of his head. He groaned and staggered backward. I shrugged out of his arms and ran for the stairs, using the railing for support, his vine still wound around my neck. I yanked it off and threw it on the catwalk floor. His shoes pounded on the metal behind me. I headed for the stairs and stumbled. He was right behind me, the knife blade gleaming in his hand.

He grabbed me again, just as I reached the stairs. "Where's that package? Tell me or I swear I'll slit your throat."

"Underneath the prayer plant. Down there."

I heard voices in the Garden Court. Coming toward the Jungle. David Wildman and the docent.

"You're too late," I said in a hoarse whisper. "They'll get it first."

He looked over the railing, fury and rage on his face as he hesitated before raising the knife above my head. I wrenched away from him and lost my balance, pulling him with me as I fell toward the staircase. He fell over top of me as I continued to tumble down the stairs. The last thing I heard before I blacked out was Tommy Asher's scream as he plunged over the railing, plummeting into the depths of the jungle forest below.

CHAPTER 29

~~~~~~~~~

Tommy Asher did not recover from the broken neck and the self-inflicted knife wound he sustained from his fall in the Botanic Gardens. I'd cracked two ribs and had some bruises and a minor concussion, but otherwise I was all right.

For the next few days, the stories of Asher's death and Harlan's attempted suicide were all over the news. Miranda Asher was stopped at Kennedy Airport when a TSA attendant spotted her wearing a blond wig and carrying a forged passport as she tried to board a flight to Greece. She pleaded ignorance of her husband's business dealings amid a media frenzy as investors continued to reel from their losses.

David Wildman turned Rebecca's package over to the SEC, though it wasn't like he had a choice. Along with the stories of Harlan and the Ashers, the *Trib* ran his front-page multipart series on Tommy Asher's Ponzi scheme—its victims, its far-flung scope, and all the players involved, including Rebecca. I avoided just about everyone I knew, from Dominique to Thelma and the Romeos, for as long as I could after that news came out. As for Quinn, he spent most of his days out in the vineyard and we hardly saw each other.

Rebecca Natale's body was finally recovered from the Potomac River—ironically, the plastic bag containing her decomposed remains was discovered not far from the Three Sisters. Linh Natale's press conference on television was painful to watch, and though I called her several times, she never picked up the phone or returned any of my messages.

Simon deWolfe pleaded guilty to the murder of Ian Philips and as an accessory to Rebecca's murder. According to Simon, it was Tommy who strangled Rebecca during a violent argument the afternoon of the gala. When his half brother called in a panic, Simon moved her body to a horse stall at his Upperville farm before disposing of it in the river when one of his stable boys complained of a bad smell coming from the barn a week later. After the medical examiner's report confirmed Simon's story, I shuddered to think how close I'd been to dying in the same grim way Tommy Asher had murdered Rebecca.

Between Quinn and me, things remained tense and overly polite. Then one evening, he stopped by my house with a bottle of Château Petrus. He joked that he'd used the last of his money to buy it. When he reached for me, I thought we were going to be all right. We spent a tumultuous night in bed—though it involved some new contortions with my taped ribs.

He made his customary sludgy coffee the next morning, but when he showed up in the bedroom door he was holding only one mug.

"Here," he said, "just the way you like it."

I grinned. "Where's yours? Drank it already?"

His smile faltered and I knew something was wrong.

"What is it?" I said.

He hooked a thumb over his shoulder. "One of the guys is coming to pick me up in a couple of minutes. I need to go back to California for a while, Lucie. You'll be okay. I've talked everything over with Antonio."

"Talked what over with Antonio? What are you saying?"

"I gotta clear my head. I can't do it here anymore. I need to go home."

"Your home is *here*!"

He walked over to the bed and set the mug on my bedside table. Then he kissed me and I tasted good-bye and regret in that kiss.

"When are you coming back?" I held on to his wrists.

"I'm not sure."

"A couple of weeks? A month?"

I saw a muscle twitch in his jaw.

"You are coming back, aren't you?" I said, finally.

"I won't leave you in the lurch, I promise."

"Then don't go. Please."

He cocked his head as a car horn sounded outside. "That's my ride. I can't miss this flight." He gave me a cockeyed smile. "It's nonrefundable."

"Will you call me when you get there?"

"I . . . sure."

The horn tooted impatiently, and he slipped his hands out of my grasp.

"Take care of yourself," he said.

I nodded, feeling numb. His boots clattered on the stairs and then I heard the front door slam a moment later.

He was gone and I was alone.

I met Dominique at the Inn later that morning. We sat on the terrace dunking her homemade croissants into bowl-sized mugs of café au lait. Below us, Goose Creek, still rain swollen, rushed on to the Potomac. Her garden, in sun-dappled sunshine, was a riot of tulips and the last of the daffodils.

"We're a pair, aren't we?" she said, spooning apricot preserves on her croissant. "I can't believe Quinn took off like that."

"Me neither." I still felt numb.

"He probably feels like he's got crow on his face," she said. "That's why he left."

"I suppose it's something like that."

"Are you going to be all right?"

Our eyes met. "Sure. How about you?"

She looked away. "Simon's house is back on the market. Did you know he took me there once? Wanted me to see the place. We skipped touring that barn."

"Oh, God, that's gruesome."

"We'll get through this, the two of us," she said. "We always do. We're tough. That's how our mothers raised us."

"I know."

"What about Easter?" she asked.

"What about it?"

"Why don't we spend it together?"

"Mia called from New York the other day to check on how I was doing. My ribs and all that," I said. "She thought she'd come home for Easter this year. And Eli's been dropping by, too. It looks like he's finally worked out custody arrangements for Hope, thank God. He'll have her for Easter. Brandi's going somewhere with her new boyfriend."

"Well, then we could all be together," she said. "It'd be the first time in ages."

"Let's do something at the vineyard," I said. "We can plan an Easter egg hunt for Hope and then have dinner. The whole family."

I drove home afterward and tried not to think about Quinn and whether he might or might not come back.

Dominique was right, that we'd get through this.

It was spring. New beginning.

Love survives. Family endures.

THE WAR OF 1812 AND THE
BURNING OF WASHINGTON

The War of 1812, called "the second war of independence" and "the war nobody won," was an unpopular conflict between the United States and Great Britain that was urged on the country by a warmongering Congress. Now nearly forgotten, it had its origins in trade disputes, anger at the British navy's practice of impressing American merchantmen into service, and the British military's support of Native American armed resistance to the northwest frontier expansion. Sentiment among congressional War Hawks—who controlled both houses of Congress—that the British ought to be driven from Canada further fueled the push for a military response to American grievances.

The war that inspired the writing of "The Star-Spangled Banner" caught most Americans by surprise and found the young country unprepared to fight. When President James Madison signed the declaration of war on June 18, 1812, the United States had neither sufficient troops nor the money to pay them. Undaunted and hoping for a quick victory, the Americans decided to first launch an assault on Canada, thus gaining control of the Great Lakes waterways. The campaign was a disaster in every possible way; in fact, by the end of 1812 the army's war efforts for the entire year had been described in the press as an unbroken series of disaster, defeat, and disgrace.

Fortunately, the opposite was true at sea, where America won a series of victories over the vaunted British navy. But in 1814, Britain, which had been directing most of its military resources toward a war with France, emerged victorious against Napoleon and now sought revenge for the humiliation of its navy. Britain turned its full fury on its former colonies, blockading the Atlantic coast and sending battle-hardened troops across the ocean to whip the Yankees.

The strategic location of the Chesapeake Bay near the American capital made it a prime target for British troops. Unfortunately, American Secretary of War John Armstrong had been convinced the attack would be on Baltimore, sending troops to that city and leaving Washington almost totally undefended—a decision that would cost him his job. From the beginning, the British plan was never to occupy Washington but to capture and destroy it.

On August 23, 1814, President Madison received a letter from Secretary of State James Monroe warning of the British army's advance and urging him to leave Washington as quickly as possible. By now, Sir George Cockburn, the British naval commander, had sealed off the mouth of the Chesapeake Bay like a cork in a bottle. Particularly keen for revenge for American attacks in Canada, which included the burning of York (present-day Toronto), Cockburn allowed his men to loot and set fire to three Maryland towns in preparation for the big prize of Washington, D.C.

On the morning of August 24, Madison rode on horseback to nearby Bladensburg, Maryland, to join his army—and very nearly led his party directly into enemy lines. The American army disintegrated at Bladensburg as seasoned redcoats led by General Robert Ross attacked. In Washington, panicked citizens fled the city, turning it into a ghost town. Among the last to leave was Dolley Madison, the president's wife. Remaining at the White House until the British were nearly at the city's edge, she loaded up a wagon with valuables that included a copy of the Declaration of Independence. She also had a large Gilbert Stuart portrait of George Washington cut out of its frame and transported to safety.

As she left, the British poured into the deserted city at nightfall, firing on the Capitol and building a bonfire inside the building that set alight both wings and eventually caused the wood-domed roof to crash to the floor. The fire destroyed the Supreme Court and demolished the entire three-thousand-book collection of the Library of Congress. Horrified Washingtonians saw the Capitol ablaze and the Union Jack flying above it.

From there, the British marched to the White House, where they ate and drank their fill of a meal that had been prepared for Madison's cabinet. At the urging of Cockburn and Ross, soldiers looted the place before setting fire to every room of the building. By the time they were finished, nothing was left of the Madison's personal property or the valuable furniture, much of which had been left by Madison's predecessor, Thomas Jefferson. Miraculously, the sandstone walls survived the intense heat; later numerous heavy coats of paint to cover the scorch marks would give the President's House a new name: the White House.

The British destruction of Washington resumed on August 25 as soldiers torched other public buildings, including the Post Office, the State and War departments, and what remained of the Navy Yard, which the Americans had burned preemptively. Later that day a tornado passed through the city, followed by a fierce rainstorm whose rains and powerful winds extinguished the fires. That evening the British departed.

America's complete humiliation at having its capital destroyed did what President Madison had been unable to do: fire up American patriotism and unite most of the country behind the war. After the destruction of Washington, the Americans would never suffer a serious defeat and the enemy would never enjoy a major victory in the War of 1812.

ACKNOWLEDGMENTS

I'm grateful, as always, to everyone who took time to answer my questions, read early drafts of this book, and offer advice and suggestions when I hit the occasional wall. The usual disclaimer: If it's right, they said it; if it's wrong, it's on me.

So, to the following people, my thanks: Cheryl Kosmann, Swedenburg Estate Vineyard, Middleburg, Virginia; John J. Lamb, author and former homicide detective; 2nd Lieutenant Adam Law, USMC; Paula Smith (the "dock lady" of the Potomac); Pam Stewart, Loudoun Museum, Leesburg, Virginia; Rick Tagg, Barrel Oak Winery, Delaplane, Virginia; Peggy Wagner, Library of Congress; and Captain Richard Yuras, Director of EMS Training Programs, Fairfax County Fire & Rescue Department, Fairfax, Virginia.

An enormous debt of thanks to Tom Snyder for early editing help; also to the RLI gang: Donna Andrews, Carla Coupe, Laura Durham, Peggy Hanson, Val Patterson, Noreen Wald Smith, and Sandi Wilson. I'm grateful to André de Nesnera, Catherine Reid, Elizabeth Arrott, Martina Norelli, and Pat Daly for reading and commenting on the manuscript, and for their counsel.

At Scribner, my heartfelt thanks to my terrific editor, Anna deVries, as well as to Christina Mamangakis, Rex Bonomelli, Katie Rizzo, and the many people who make the book you're holding in your hands or reading on your screen look as good as it does. At Pocket, thanks to another wonderful editor, Micki Nuding, as well as to Melissa Gramstad. A special shout-out to Heidi Richter and Maggie Crawford.

Last but not least, to Dominick Abel, who is simply the best.

ABOUT THE AUTHOR

Ellen Crosby is a former freelance reporter for *The Washington Post* and was Moscow correspondent for ABC News Radio. She is the author of *The Riesling Retribution, The Bordeaux Betrayal, The Chardonnay Charade,* and *The Merlot Murders,* as well as *Moscow Nights,* a stand-alone novel published in London. Crosby lives in Virginia with her family. Visit her website at www.ellencrosby.com.